Ladies
in
Waiting

Ladies in Waiting

Laura L. Sullivan

Houghton Mifflin Harcourt

Boston   New York

For my sister, Marla J. Sullivan

All rights reserved. Published in the United States by Graphia, an imprint of
Houghton Mifflin Harcourt Publishing Company. Originally published in
hardcover in the United States by Harcourt Children's Books, an imprint of
Houghton Mifflin Harcourt Publishing Company, 2012.

Graphia and the Graphia logo are trademarks of Houghton Mifflin Harcourt
Publishing Company.

For information about permission to reproduce selections from this book,
write to Permissions, Houghton Mifflin Harcourt Publishing Company,
215 Park Avenue South, New York, New York 10003.

www.hmhbooks.com

The Library of Congress has cataloged the hardcover edition as follows:
Sullivan, Laura L.
Ladies in waiting/by Laura L. Sullivan.
p. cm.
Summary: In the seventeenth-century court of England's King Charles II, three young
ladies-in-waiting discover a palace teeming with love, intrigue, and treachery.
1. Charles I, King of England, 1600–1649—Juvenile fiction. 2. Great Britain—History—
Charles II, 1660–1685—Juvenile fiction. [1. Charles I, King of England, 1600–1649—
Fiction. 2. Great Britain—History—Charles II, 1660–1685—Fiction. 3. Courts and
courtiers—Fiction.] I. Title.
PZ7.S9527Lad 2012
[Fic]—dc23
2011027323

ISBN: 978-0-547-58129-3 hardcover
ISBN: 978-0-544-02220-1 paperback

Manufactured in the United States of America
DOC 10 9 8 7 6 5 4 3 2 1

4500406811

Ladies in Waiting

Chapter 1

The Rich Man's Daughter
England, June 1662

Eliza Parsloe, age fifteen, tickled her chin with her plumed pen and gazed levelly at her latest opponent, Lord Ayelsworth, second Earl of Lambert. To her great displeasure, he took it for flirtation and sidled closer until his foppishly beribboned thigh crushed the delicate moiré of her apricot skirt.

"You slay me with those killing eyes," he sighed.

Those killing eyes rolled, for she knew he was looking not at her decidedly plain brown orbs, but rather at the fortune in emeralds at her throat, or perhaps, to give him credit as a man of flesh as well as avarice, at the swell of bosom lower down.

Why did each and every suitor feel it necessary to harp upon her nonexistent physical charms? If just one had suggested they could use her vast fortune and his court influence to rule the nation, to set the mode, she might have been swayed. But no, they spoke of her languishing eyes, her enchanting hair; compared her neck to a swan's and her skin to pearls, when she knew full well her only beauty lay in the acres of timber, the flotillas of merchant ships, and the masses of gold settled on her as the only child of the fabulously wealthy Jeremiah Parsloe.

She turned away from him and dipped her quill in the ink, dripping a blob, unnoticed, on her buttercup-colored satin under-skirt, and began to scribble.

"What do you write, sweetheart?" Ayelsworth asked, craning his skinny neck to see. "I would pen you a thousand love poems daily, if only you would be mine!"

Eliza dipped the pen again and flicked it as she turned to reply, spattering his multihued ribbons with blue-black. He squealed and leaped up. Eliza instantly kicked up her feet and crossed her ankles, reconquering the lost territory of her chaise.

"It is a play," she said.

"What do you call it, sweet nymph?"

"*Nunquam Satis,*" she said, and though he had no Latin, he knew the vulgar tongue. He wasn't sure whether to laugh or blush.

"My dear, do you know what that means?"

"'Never satisfied,'" she replied evenly.

"Ah, but in the common cant, it means...it means..." He could not tell her what part of a woman's anatomy was, by popular jest, never satisfied. She was from a reputedly Puritan family. Very likely she was not even aware of that particular part of herself.

Ayelsworth, though but twenty, was a habitué of Charles II's court, and accustomed to whores, courtesans, and loose ladies of rank. He was not quite sure what to expect from this provincial heiress. All he knew for certain was that she was the catch of the season, and if he could secure her, his future was assured.

Her father had given him permission to try for her hand, leaving them alone with only a maidservant within, for propriety, and a liveried footman without, in case he should try to claim his prize by force. Now, that was a thought, he mused. It had certainly been done before, though mostly through abduction. Still, if he managed to spoil the goods here on the chaise, she and her father would probably agree to let him buy what remained.

He looked over her big-boned, recumbent form. She was at least a head taller than he, and he didn't think much of his chances in a forcible seduction.

He clung instead to what had worked with other ladies — wit and conversation.

"Pray, what is your play about?"

"An heiress deciding which of her many suitors to accept."

"A tragedy, then, for all but one lucky swain. Will you read me a snippet?"

For the first time she blessed him with a smile — her teeth were good, at any rate, he noted — and blew on her pages to dry the ink before she picked them up to read.

"This bit I just finished is a conversation between Lady Nuncsat and Lord Stormthebreech. He tries to persuade her of the chief benefit of having a husband, and she protests that if husbands are à la mode, another's will suit her just as well:

> *"'Is carnal pleasure prize for married misery I'll reap?*
> *I'll ride the steed — or not — and let another pay his keep.*
> *Who'd buy with precious liberty what she'd get elsewhere*
> *gratis?*
> *I'll keep my heart and hand and wealth,' quoth*
> *Lady Nunquam Satis."*

"Ah . . . ahem. She is a villain, then?"

"Lord Stormthebreech thinks so, and calls her a fishwife and a mettlesome jade who ought to be forced to feel a man's hand on her rein. She replies,

> *"'Touch me and you'll find a fishwife verily, by gods!*
> *One who shucks your oysters and fillets your pretty*
> *cods.'"*

Ayelsworth's hand cupped his own cods protectively, and it was not long before he excused himself with flourishing apology, never to be seen in the Parsloe household again. He would give a great deal to have Eliza's wealth, but not that.

"What did you say to this one?" her father asked sharply when he entered to find her alone.

"Oh, he spoke to me of the theater," she said nonchalantly, placing a book of sermons on top of her manuscript. Her father had no idea she'd read every play on the boards since the theaters reopened with the king's return from exile. Her maid, Hortense, was liberally paid to smuggle them back from her monthly sojourns with the housekeeper to London for supplies that could not be had in the village.

"You cannot allow yourself to become offended because a gentleman speaks to you of plays. Why, I'm told even the most pious go to the theater. I know you've been delicately reared, my dear, but when you are a married woman you might be . . . ahem . . . exposed to things your upbringing didn't prepare you for."

Eliza affected the serene incomprehension of a novice in a nunnery and said, "In any event, sir, I find I cannot love him."

"Love! What nonsense. A pity I promised your mother on her deathbed I'd only give you away with your own consent. A girl can't be expected to know what's good for her."

She bowed her head in seeming acquiescence. Eliza had been there for her mother's final breath a few years ago. "Let Eliza marry for love," she'd pleaded as she fingered the embroidered hem of her sheets weakly. "See what my marriage has been, and let her give her heart and fortune where she pleases."

Jeremiah took it to mean that his was a love union and had worked out well. Eliza, who better knew her mother's secret longings and frustrated passions, read those words otherwise. *I had a chance at love with another man,* her mother said in cipher. *But I threw it all away at my family's behest. I married where they bid me, for money, and had nothing but misery in it all, save for you, my daughter. You have money,* her mother's dying eyes had said so eloquently. *You can afford to wait for affection.*

Eliza clung to that idea, since it so closely matched her own. Though her father was true in the letter to his wife's deathbed wish, he had plans of his own he was not willing to abandon for the sake of feminine sentimentality.

"What am I to do with you, child? Is there no one pious and decent enough to win you? Ayelsworth has a fair reputation among that stew of rakes."

So you believe, sir, Eliza thought. Hortense brought different tidings from gossip gleaned at the Royal Exchange, London's vibrant marketplace. Ayelsworth was known to frequent the most scandalous brothels (Eliza thought she could perhaps forgive an occasional sojourn to London's better brothels) and was deep in debt.

"Also," Hortense had whispered to her before the lord's arrival, "Bab at the Queen's Point Shop told me he takes a bolus regular, no doubt mercury for the pox."

"He's a perfect match," Eliza's father went on. "The highest title to come for you so far."

"Sir," Eliza said, "I know your opinions of the court. Why go to such lengths to ally our family with such a licentious place?"

"I have money enough for Midas," he said, patting her knee kindly. "But His Majesty won't hear a word from me because I'm a commoner. I'm not pleased with his reign thus far. Better to have stuck with Old Noll and his line, though they were far from perfect. But daughter, hear me! I am a man of power, yet powerless. I have more gold than the king himself, yet this nation muddles on without my say-so. A man, however rich, cannot buy much real influence in the court. But if I can link my family to that of some great noble, I will have a voice at last! And my children after me! Your children, I mean, of course, my dear. Marry an earl, and I can catch the king's ear!"

And what do you hope to do, sir? Eliza wondered to herself. *The Lord Chancellor is trying to moderate the king's appetites, to no avail. Then when the king would do good, would bolster the fleet or let people worship as they will, Parliament thwarts him. Do you think because you're father-in-law to some poxy coxcomb who cleans the king's ears each morning you can effect change? The world is what it is, Father. Best to find your place in it, and not try to make the world anew.*

But all she said was "Yes, sir."

Jeremiah sighed. "You must marry, girl. You must marry a nobleman, and you must do it soon, while I can still do some good in that sinful court. I have made a difficult decision."

Eliza's eyes flew open. "You must not force me to marry! You promised Mother!"

"I will not force you . . . not yet. You have one last chance to find a noble you can respect. It pains me to tell you this, for I know what a moral and devout child you are. Eliza, I fear you must go to that den of wickedness, the court of King Charles II. My money cannot buy a place for myself, but I can purchase you a position as one of the new queen's ladies in waiting. They say Catherine of Braganza is convent-bred, and though I don't hold with popery, they do have a knack for keeping their girls pure-minded. She will keep you safe until such time as you find a suitable noble to wed."

Eliza looked at her hands and bit her lip. It was all she could do to keep from screaming with joy.

"Do not fret, my child. A heart as pure as yours is incorruptible. You have nothing to fear from the court."

Her voice trembling with emotion, she said, "I will do as you wish, sir."

Within her breast, her heart exulted.

"Now you may take off that silken frippery I know you despise, and put on your good sober grays again. At court I suppose you must dress like the rest, but here at home you can be your own self."

She ran upstairs and Hortense changed her into her customary charcoal wool. The high neck itched, and she tugged at it in irritation as she told her maid the news.

"No matter, ma'am. Once you get to court he's lost his hold over you. You'll be your own mistress."

Eliza smiled at her somber reflection. *My own, or someone else's,* she thought.

She caught herself up sharply. *No, that's a good line for a play, but not for me. I don't want to be kept in check by anyone — not my father, not a husband, not even a lover. I want to be free.*

Chapter 2

The Queen's Pet

Queen Catherine of Braganza, married a bare two months, sat amid her Portuguese attendants and rubbed each of her fingertips with her thumb in slow succession, counting the prayers of the rosary she was too timid to show in this gaudy, profane aviary that was her husband's court. Bright, winsome creatures moved with a flutter of silks and feathers near the outskirts of the room. It was an honor to be admitted to the queen's presence, but none of them took the trouble to speak with her after the initial ceremonial greeting. At first Catherine excused them, thinking they might be shy. She was almost shy of herself, now that she had transformed from convent girl to this great thing, a queen. She soon realized the ladies and gallants of the court held her not in awe, but in contempt.

Her shoulders ached from holding herself unnaturally straight within the confines of her boned gown. "I'll take a turn," she murmured to her ladies, and as one they rose after her, bobbing their respect and making up a train.

Catherine heard titters and words she only half understood—*fright, monster, olivaster-skinned bat.* She had very little English, but she did not need to speak the language to be aware of the court's disapproval. They mocked her farthingale, the stiffly buttressed hoop skirt that was a Portuguese lady's best defense against the male sex, for no one could approach her within arm's reach. They shook their own tight fair curls in derision at Catherine's soft black waves. They were all so beautiful! She had once been proud of the wardrobe prepared for her union with Charles. This dress was a particular favorite, deep midnight and silver, with yards of black lace. At the convent it had glinted in the firelight as her maids packed it. Now, beside the roses and robin's eggs and spring greens, she felt the way she looked in their eyes—somber, sallow, foreign.

"I think tomorrow I'll wear the blue silk His Majesty gave me," she said with forced calm to her chief Portuguese attendant, the Countess of Penalva. "The one over cloth-of-gold, with seed-pearl slippers."

"Nonsense," Penalva said, like a governess to a child, not a noble attendant to a queen. "You must never succumb to their loose morals and indecent dress. You are their sovereign. It is for you to set an example of modesty and decorum. The farthingale is your national dress. You are still Portuguese. Let them imitate you."

I am English now, she longed to say, but she was a little intimidated by Penalva, and all of the other older, more experienced women sent from her home court. She knew Penalva meant well, but all the same she longed to feel the caress of silk against her legs, to know that every breath revealed a scandalous swell of bosom from a very low neckline.

This is my home now. I should fit in. Charles will like me better for it.

She did not walk long. She could not bear the eyes upon her. *At least when I sit they forget about me,* she thought. *Oh, I wish Charles would return.* He had departed without explanation on an endeavor he said was of vital importance to England, and she'd accepted it. Only later did she think he might be having a liaison. He'd been gone two weeks with no word.

She loved Charles to distraction, first in gratitude for elevating her to the highest feminine seat in the world, and later, when after a year of courtship by proxy they met face to face, she loved him for his handsome, manly courtesy and his convincing show of affection. She thought it was for her alone. Now she understood that he was gracious to every lady, though as queen she was entitled to an even grander show of seemingly sincere gazes and fond caresses. Why, the king doffed his hat to the milkmaids. He was a paragon of masculine respect for the feminine sex.

Still, she thought, *I am his wife, and I will make him love me beyond all others.*

The only weapons in her arsenal were gentle love, enduring courage, and faith. She looked out at the billowing sails of the gaudy ships gliding around her audience hall. They carried a veritable battery of charms — bare skin, paint, bold eyes, and lively tongues.

What do I have to offer His Majesty? Only a dowry, half of which my country has not paid. And maybe, someday, an heir.

Barbara Howard, Countess of Suffolk, parted the tossing fleet of ladies with her own bright galleon and strode languidly toward the queen, her heavy-lidded cat eyes sparkling with mirth or malice, or most likely both.

She made a deep, ballooning bow and handed Catherine a sheet of heavy parchment. "The list of ladies in waiting, Your Majesty. Five ladies of the bedchamber, four dressers of the bedchamber, and as of now, six pretty little maids of honor, though they get married so fast, you'll be picking a new one every month."

Catherine caught some of it, and her translator supplied the rest.

"Thank you," she murmured, one of the few English phrases she was comfortable with, and the one that fit the most occasions.

Suffolk lingered near. "Please sign your approval, Your Majesty, and I will make all the necessary arrangements. If it please Your Majesty, my humble self has been nominated for mistress of the robes."

"Certainly, I quite approve," Catherine said. She couldn't pin Suffolk down. She was unfailingly polite and attentive and smoothed the queen's many flubs of etiquette. At first Catherine was sure she had found a friend. And yet at times she thought Suffolk was like Charles himself, superficially affectionate because she was expected to maintain an act. Still, she was competent and not overtly hostile. Better have her as chief of her ladies than one of the tittering court butterflies who openly despised her.

Catherine scanned the names, with Penalva looking over her shoulder, her stale breath reeking, though Catherine had given her cloves to chew, saying, diplomatically, that they were good for toothache.

"Let's see," Penalva said. "Mary Villiers. A relation of that wicked Buckingham, I presume, though I know no evil of her personally. Katherine Stanhope, hmm . . . she was Princess Mary's governess and dear friend, but there was bad business with some jewels after the princess died. I'll look into the right of it. Jane Granville, a pleasant lady. Oh! Not her! Never her!"

Catherine's eyes lit on the hated name the same instant as Penalva's. She gripped the parchment so hard that it crinkled, and that tiny rustle made the entire room fall still. They had evidently been waiting for the queen's reaction.

Her face burning, her hand trembling, Catherine called out, "Fetch me a pen!"

She dipped at the ink violently and scratched stroke after stroke until the name Barbara Palmer was utterly obliterated.

Catherine knew almost nothing of the court, but she knew the name Barbara Palmer. All England, all Europe, knew the name of the king's reigning mistress.

She handed the document back to Suffolk.

"I have pricked out one name," she said, hardly waiting for her attendant to translate. "I think you know who."

"But Your Majesty, the king himself has approved this list.

Whomsoever he may choose, it is no doubt for the best." Her voice and movements were languorous, but her eyes sharp for the drama that would unfold. As Barbara was Suffolk's niece, she had a vested interest in her success. Would Catherine be a queen or a mouse?

Catherine's nostrils flared as she struggled for composure. "I would rather have the lowest, meanest, poorest, most despised but honest lady at this court wait upon me than the king's . . . the king's . . ." Her lips could not form the word *whore*.

"But, Your Majesty!"

Suddenly resolute (and, Suffolk thought, almost beautiful, for all her yellow skin and ghastly fashion), Catherine stood and said to her audience, "Who is the lowest and poorest among those admitted to the court? Scorned, ridiculed, yet a lady still? I can tell a lady, however low, from a devil, however high. Bring me the worst of your lot, and I warrant she'll be better than Barbara Palmer!"

The translator wisely voiced only about half of the speech, but it was enough. Excited murmurs and titters ran through the ladies and foppish gentlemen, and at last they reached a consensus that apparently amused them. They sent a maid off to fetch someone. Catherine, furious, and frightened at her own temerity, sat down and vigorously fanned herself.

The room grew quiet again, and Catherine wondered how it was that silence could speak so many different things. This was not a reverential hush but the forced, deliberate silence of laughter held in check, a silence that was full of tension, about to erupt at any moment into a cacophony of mockery.

A girl came through the door. For a terrible moment Catherine was sure it was Barbara Palmer, for the newcomer was dressed in the most scandalously low-cut bodice Catherine had ever seen. The pink of her nipples just peeked over the ruffled suggestion of an undersmock, a thing permissible in one of Lely's portraits but not in the flesh. Her skirt was gathered up in front to show trim ankles. Only laboring peasants and professed harlots showed their legs.

She was lovely, too, with an endearing sort of beauty that Catherine, in her limited experience, believed would draw a man better than any other. *If I were a man I would love her,* the queen thought, but because she was a woman she began to hate her instead, at least until she looked more closely.

The girl did not match her lewd clothes. She gave an impression of absolute softness, from the light brown curls twining along her temples with no stiffness of glue or sugar water to hold them in place, to the childish plumpness of her dimpled cheeks, her trembling pillow mouth. Her face was garishly painted: carmine lips, cochineal cheeks, hennaed eyelids, and an etching of blue crayon to deepen the natural veins on her chest. Under all that, though, was something small and timid. She was an alluring creature, but she was no whore; Catherine could see that now. She was nervous, almost terrified. One thing was certain — Catherine would have nothing to fear from this beautiful child. But who was she?

"Come closer, my dear," she said, beckoning so that it didn't have to be translated.

The girl tottered forward, almost tripping on her high-heeled slippers, and the courtiers laughed outright.

"What is your name?"

The girl curtsied a mite too deeply, and her breasts escaped that last crucial half inch. Gasping, she clutched her smock and jerked it up, covering her breasts but exposing several mended rents in the worn fabric. Catherine, peering more closely, saw that the girl's dress, once fine, was worn at the edges, that the metallic braid had lost its luster and the silk was stained with sweat and watermarks.

"Beth, Your Majesty. Oh! I mean Lady Elizabeth Foljambe." She bowed her head and looked as if she would weep.

She wanted to ask Beth more, but Suffolk stepped up and said, "Her mother's Countess of Enfield. The earl, her father, is dead these last several years. The family were staunch Royalists, but he left them here to Cromwell's tender mercies and went to the continent. He claimed he gave His Majesty every penny, but the truth is, he and his friend, that notorious rake Ransley, squandered it on gambling and women. Sold the estate out from under them. One of Old Noll's generals, the new owner, came knocking one day, gave them an hour to pack and leave. For the past two years the old bawd's been trying to pimp the girl's noble blood to regain their fortune, but there've been no takers. She's a pretty creature, but beauty's a hard sell without a dower, particularly when a demon mother comes along."

If there hadn't been a lag of translation Catherine would have stopped Suffolk's cruel words. But by the time it was rendered into Portuguese, the damage was done and two great tears rose, trembled, and spilled from Beth's gentle gray eyes.

Catherine shot Suffolk an angry look, but it could not touch Suffolk's composure. Her place at court was assured, and it would take the wrath of a greater queen than Catherine to shake it.

The queen instead favored Beth with her kindest expression. She felt sorry for the child, but more than that, she liked her — instantly, passionately, protectively. On a more calculating level, she knew it would be good to have someone near her, even a lowly maid of honor, less experienced in the ways of the world. Her timidity would make Catherine feel more queenly.

"Would you like to be one of my maids of honor?" she asked gently.

Beth looked up fearfully.

"Best wait till you meet the other half of the bargain," Suffolk drawled in her sleepy voice. "As every gallant at court knows, you can't have the girl without the mother."

Another hush fell, and Catherine in her newly understood natural history of silence recognized the superstitious fear and awe in this one. A woman limped into the hall . . . at least, it must have been a woman once. Revulsion rose like a live squirming thing in the queen's belly, and she half stood, ready to run.

Another would have tried to hide her condition — not so the Countess of Enfield. Every woman wore gloves, so the queen could not see the lesions on the woman's hands and arms. But she could see the suppurating sores on her throat and chest and could guess what else might be hidden under the blood red of her gown. In that age of infection and pox, sores were commonplace, if generally kept out of the queen's apartments. It was the lady's head that looked most unnatural — a mask, a beast. As Suffolk said, a demon.

The countess's brow was a lumpy, misshapen thing, a bulbous knob the size of a clenched infant's fist rising from her temple, throbbing with her pulse. Smaller tumors scattered through the sparse hair of her skull in such profusion as to confound a physiognomist.

Worse yet, where her nose should have been was a silver hawk's beak, painstakingly polished to a high sheen, strapped across her cheeks and brow with red cord. The great aquiline false nose was a mockery of the court's masked balls, one of which Catherine had presided over, though not participated in, since her arrival. There, stunning women gave their faces animal or angelic beauty, covering one form of loveliness with another. Here, grotesque covered horror, all the worse, to Catherine's susceptible mind, for being unseen. Why would she wear that terrifying raptor's beak if there was not something far more disgusting underneath?

"Syphilis," Suffolk said in her resounding stage whisper. "A gift from her husband. Her nose has crumbled away, alas." She fanned herself lazily.

The horror made a formal curtsy, with that perfect balance that comes of strict early training. She'd been bred in the court, lived a life of luxury until her husband squandered her wealth and ruined her body with the disease he picked up on his extramarital carousing. Her rank allowed her free run of the palace, but her appearance and poverty made her a pariah, her daughter a joke. Still, she persevered, flaunting her daughter's beauty while fiercely guarding her chastity, hoping some man would come along to restore the family fortunes. Her daughter was her widow's portion, the only bounty her wicked husband left her.

"Your Majesty," Enfield said, neither brazen nor timid. "They say you would have my Beth as your maid of honor."

"Yes, better her than another," Catherine said, though now she wanted the girl for her own sake, and to do a kindness to an obviously ill-used old woman. *The poor thing,* Catherine thought. *I will ask Charles to grant her a pension.*

"Well, I suppose she will do as well there as with me. But hear me, Your Majesty, and mark me well. Her chastity is the business of my life, making a good marriage for her my only concern."

"I quite understand," the queen said after the pause of translation.

"I fear you do not," the Countess of Enfield said severely, coming closer, head nodding with the characteristic bob of her disease. "My curse is on her, and on any man who touches her. I will give her freely to the right man, but let any try to steal my beauty, my youth, and I will draw and quarter him with my own hands. Him, or her." She made a motion of twisting and tearing. "And so to you, Your Majesty, if while in your keeping my virgin is debauched." Her hands rent the queen in invisible effigy, and Catherine shrank back. Was the woman mad? She spoke of the girl's beauty and youth as if they were her own.

"You're a Catholic heathen like the last queen, but at least you're not like these others." She jerked her flashing beak at the courtiers, who were torn between mirth and revulsion. "In those

idolatrous nations like Portugal you know men for the evil creatures they are, scourge of women, carriers of filth, great hungry
maws that drain us of all our virtues and leave us as you see me
now. Your husband is such a man. You don't believe me, I see in
your eyes, but those eyes will open soon enough."

Catherine wanted to flee, but the woman was so close now, her
beak thrusting forward, that Catherine could not stand without
almost touching her. Where were the guards?

"Ha!" the countess went on. "I loved my husband once. Now
there's not a man I wouldn't crush beneath my heel if I could." She
turned to a nearby fop holding a nosegay to his powdered cheeks.
"You." She ground her foot into the tile, and turned to a big, virile
golden-wigged man, the notorious Duke of Buckingham. "You,
for certs." She dug her heel in again and looked to the queen. "And
your husband, too, dear. He's a man, like all the others, and will
break you if he can. Make yourself hard, Your Majesty. Deny him
everything and you might survive. Be soft and love him, and you
will end like me."

She broke off in a fit of coughing. "Take her if you will!" she said
between hacks. "Take her, but remember, I'll be watching." She
shuffled off, and the courtiers parted before her, covering their
faces with scented handkerchiefs.

Beth stood through all this with her head bowed, like a dog
well accustomed to the whip. Could this gentle, pretty girl truly
have sprung from the loins of that monster?

Catherine stood abruptly. She would show them what it meant
to be a queen. Perhaps the Countess of Enfield was right about

one thing. She might grant Charles any other request, but she would die before she let his mistress among her most personal attendants.

"Come, child," she said to Beth. "You will begin serving me at once. And my lady Suffolk, please amend this list and return it to me for my consideration."

Beth trailed behind the bouncing farthingale, believing that the little queen was leading her away from the hell she'd endured since she was first brought to court—on the market as her mad mother's only commodity, a world of disease and duty, love and disgust, shame and longing—to a paradise of safety and comfort as one of Catherine's maids of honor.

Chapter 3

THE PECULIAR SPECIMEN

*W*HAT ON EARTH do I do with this?" Zabby Wodewose asked herself as she pulled yard upon yard of rich copper material out of her sea chest. Her father had it sent aboard without letting her see, telling her only to wait until she was ashore in England before wearing it, lest it spoil in the sea air.

"It's the latest fashion from France, so they tell me," her beloved Papa had said to her as she sat with him on the eve of departure, staring into the low hearth, her head resting on his knee. "You will set the Thames on fire, my girl."

"I'm not going to England to impress anyone," Zabby said. "I'm going to learn everything I can—and not about clothes. I can wear any old thing in Godmother Cavendish's library, and I'll certainly wear an apron when I mix compounds and grind lenses."

He kissed her on the top of her very fair head and said, "Ah, my dear, do it for my sake, if not your own. I've kept you like a wild thing here in Barbados, and it would please me to see you in some finery."

"You've had too much Rhenish wine, Papa!" she'd said with a laugh. "Your reasoning is faulty — you won't be seeing me when I'm there."

"All the same, my dear, wear it, and have a few more made up once you've settled. There is nothing in this world so pure as the unruffled, chill beauty of youth. Like rarefied metal, a serene, air-less vacuum. Like a theorem proven."

She laughed and tried to argue, but he only kissed her again and went to his bed. She sailed with the morning tide.

Now, two months later, they struck sounding off Dover, ahead of a storm, and as they eased into port she prepared to wear his gift. She lay the skirt on her bed and unconsciously bent her knees as the ship shifted in the chop of the docks. She was an experi-enced seawoman, and so long as it was not actually raining she could be found strolling along the deck, heedless of the heaving, reading a book as she walked. This was her fourth long ocean voy-age — once from England to Barbados as a child, then to Virginia and back with her father, and now to her natal soil to complete her education with her godmother, Margaret Cavendish, Duchess of Newcastle-upon-Tyne, philosopher and authoress.

She arranged the undergarments and finally pulled out some-thing she knew about but had never worn — a pair of bodies, or a bodice.

She might be an aristocrat, but she was a plantation aristo-crat, who was always looking to the laborers, experimenting with the crops, testing improvements to her fleet of tiny sailboats, and above all, concocting compounds and testing ideas in Papa's elaboratory. She wore breeches most of the time, and since their land stretched hundreds of acres, there was no one except the slaves and indentured servants to stare. If she did wear a dress, for coolness or the occasional social call, it was a loose one-piece tied at the waist and throat with a ribbon, or an unboned jacket and skirt, hemmed above the ankles. She had never laced herself into whalebone, never been in close company of a lady who did. Her father's friends were all men, and she had neither a comrade close to her own age with whom to speculate nor an older woman to guide her. When she looked at the stiff bodice with its spider web laces, she was at a loss.

She puzzled over the luminous copper thing but could see only one way of wearing it, laced in the front. How else was she to fasten it? One of the plumper cooks on the plantation stuffed herself into a front-knotting stomacher; it must be something like that. "Gemini, that's wretched," she said as she wiggled herself into the garment. A stiff board embedded in the material flattened her back from the shoulder blades down, and the neck was so high in the front that it almost choked her. Her bare back felt indecent. "Papa says this is what they're wearing in France," she mumbled as she secured the laces across her chest.

Even loosely tied, the thing made it hard to breathe, and the board at her back prohibited her from bending. *Why are women such fools about fashion?* she wondered. *Imagine, a board at your back!*

"I'll make him happy in absentia this once, though I warrant God-mother Cavendish has more sense than to imprison herself in a cage of silk."

She pulled up the skirt, tied and pinned it into place with much cursing and a few bloody fingertips, then sallied down the gang-plank to the bustling dock. They were two days early thanks to the storm's stiff winds, and she'd have to wait at the inn until her god-mother's carriage arrived for her.

Sailors were already unloading the crates of animals and plants her papa was sending to fill her godmother's hothouses and me-nagerie. Bright jungle birds fluttered nervously in their wicker cages, while an ocelot brought from Spanish territory hissed at the unfamiliar smells. She patted him through the bars — she'd raised him from a kitten, and though he'd rake any servant who disturbed his sleep, he was fairly tolerant of Zabby's affection.

She felt her throat itch as soon as she disembarked. Even with the high wind across the channel the air was rank and heavy with coal soot and a smell of feces, animal and human. Past the orga-nized bustle of the docks she could see the jumble of town: build-ings crowded upon one another, leaning precariously over the muddy roads; the slow-moving trickle of gutters carrying their filth directly into the sea; men and women dressed too heavily for the season, their bodies adding a musky note to the heady medley of stink.

How do they live like this? Zabby wondered as she picked her way along the wharf to the inn suggested by the captain (an agent of her father's) as reputable and clean — the King's Arms. She already felt oppressed by the noise and crowds, and this was only Dover. *Imagine how London must smell, and sound.* She coughed, feeling the grain of coal on her tongue. *And taste!*

Thank heaven she'd be going to her godmother's country estate, not her London home. Zabby didn't think she could bear it after the freedom — and clean air — of her Barbados plantation.

She let herself into the inn, and a dozen faces looked up from their mugs and tankards.

"God's cods!" one cried. "What will the whores think of next? Lacing in the front!"

"Mighty convenient," said another, a young rake who perhaps had more experience with the genuine article. "Keeps the goods locked up till the shilling's paid. That miss can let her udders bounce out at will, and no maid needed to lace 'em up again."

Another argued she'd sell her wares better if her bodice was right way round, giving them an advertisement of what was to come. Yet another claimed all the business was lower down, that only a fool would pay a whore for the top half.

Nurtured by a loving father, surrounded by a virtual city of people beholden to her, Zabby had never felt the sudden rude mortification of being the butt of the crowd's joke. She looked at them angrily, but wasn't quite strong enough to tell them off. Just as well — pertness in a prostitute is an invitation, and the men might well have offered more intimate insult. She stalked to the rear of the public house, a quiet nook where only two men sat in the shadows, and waited for the captain to join her. Once she secured a room she could change out of these ridiculous clothes. It went against reason to lock herself up, backward or forward, in such impractical garb.

"Pick another seat, sweetheart," one of the men said, not unkindly, but she was too deep in her humiliation to hear him, and sat at the next table, staring sulkily at the polished grain of the heavy oak slabs.

The man half rose and, before she could think to stop him, slipped (not without difficulty) something cold down the front, which was really the back, of her bodice. "We've business to discuss, mistress, and would be alone."

She met his eye with a scowl. It was hard to make out his features in the flickering candlelight at the back of the inn, but he seemed almost a gentleman, large and dark, with neat curling mustachios and heavy-lidded black eyes. He was dressed, as far as she could tell, as a merchant, but there was something majestic and confident in his mien. A student of nature wild and domestic, she had spent many hours watching Papa's herd of horses. One male led them all, not always the biggest or strongest, but certainly the most self-assured. Larger, wilder stallions would defer to him, let him have his way with all the mares, though they could easily defeat him in open battle. This man had the same fine carriage, the same haughty eyes, as the herd stallion. He was accustomed to obedience.

Zabby was in no mood to be obedient, particularly when the

only alternative was sitting by the men who thought her a whore, after parading by for their pleasure.

"Sir, I will not move," she said, lifting her chin.

The man's eyes glittered. She saw now that they were blood-shot. A sheen of sweat slicked his ruddy face. Perfect—he was drunk.

"I am newly come to England, but I am told every person is free the moment he steps upon English soil. This is not a land of slaves, sir. There is only one man in this country I would be obliged to obey, and I do not think even he could compel me to change seats at this moment. Leave me be, sir. I'll not trouble you."

She tried to fish for the coin to return it, but it was lodged too deeply down her bodice. It stayed there, cold against her heart.

"Fascinating raiment, mistress," he said wryly.

Zabby glared at him. "I have never worn a bodice before. Papa says that ignorance is no shame, so long as it is corrected. As soon as I can secure a room, my error will be set aright."

She turned away and pretended to be fascinated with the names carved into her table. The men resumed their discussion.

"Blast and hang him," the dark man said to his companion, who looked to Zabby like a baker dressed above his station, plump and comfortable, with soft white hands. His eyes, though . . . small and pale, they looked at her and through her, seeing every vice she'd ever so much as thought of. They sought, and evaluated, but did not condemn. She thought he must see people as Papa saw animals and chemicals, always in their most basic form, stripped of the things they hid behind, things that obscured the truth.

He sighed. "They're sure to be here soon."

"Three days in this pit. I've a good mind to leave."

"That would be disastrous, Your Maj . . . sir. There's none but you who can, ahem, accomplish this." He glanced over at Zabby, whose sharp, bare shoulder blades now faced them. It was a part of a woman men seldom saw in public, and, exposed, it was strangely alluring. "I just saw a ship tie up. His is certain to be close."

Zabby wasn't sure what compelled her to speak. "No more ships will make port for a day at least."

The dark man looked at her with weary amusement.

"Then what, sweetheart? I might as well follow you to your room, or lead you to mine? You're a paragon of your profession, I'm sure. I'll give you another coin if that's what you're after, but I'm too weary to make you work for it."

She raised eyebrows so pale that they were almost white and said, loudly enough to draw guffaws from throughout the tap-room, "I am not a whore, sir!" Her voice fell in embarrassment. "I arrived on that last boat, ahead of a gale, and I know the sea well enough to tell you no vessels will make port until it blows through. A day at least, the seagulls say."

"If she speaks truth, perhaps we should repair to White . . . to home, sir. You look tired, and, if I may presume, unwell."

"A touch of fever, no more."

But Zabby, staring at him now, suddenly knew otherwise. The dark man was not drunk; he was ill, dangerously so.

"Still, perhaps I'll away to bed, just for an hour or so. You'll fetch me, Chiffinch, if they come after all." His breath was labored, and Zabby could see he was trembling. He'd hidden his sickness well, but it was about to best him.

He rose, but as soon as he gained his feet, his knees buckled. Zabby caught him under the armpits and he half fell on top of her. She met Chiffinch's eye. "Plague or smallpox," she said. "Summer ague's not so fierce, nor so quick."

"Plague?" Chiffinch whispered. "No! It cannot be!"

"Here, get him to his room. I'll send the innkeeper for a physician."

"No! You must not!" His eyes darted like frantic mice across the room, scampering over and under all the possibilities. "No one must know."

"Oh," Zabby said, understanding. "They'll throw you out? Papa said folk in England don't understand sickness. Don't worry — plague contagion doesn't spread through the ether. Not unless he's coughing, too, but then there's no hope for him. Take his other arm."

They dragged him upstairs, to a chorus of hoots and howls. "Lusty baggage!" one rake exclaimed. "Two at once!"

"Aye," said another, "but that poor louse is too soused to remember if he got his money's worth."

She didn't even hear them. She'd slipped into that stoic practicality necessary in the sickroom, and their taunts troubled her no more than would a patient's vomit or blood.

They got the man in bed and Zabby gave Chiffinch parting words of advice. "Keep him warm, however he throws off the bedclothes, until his fever is painfully hot under your own hand. Then strip him and cool him with wet cloths and an open window, fanning all the while. Force liquid in him. He'll not keep it down, but you must try. Tea, cooled, or small ale, or if you can, the liquor off boiled vegetables. I see no blackening of his digits, and he's strong, so he'll like as not live, with your care."

She made for the door, but Chiffinch grabbed her arm, his eyes full of panic. "You must not leave me! He must not die!"

Accustomed to frantic relatives, she patted him kindly but said with some warning, "My godmother, the Duchess of Newcastle, will be here for me soon. At least, her men will." Best to let him know she was protected.

"Please, will you wait just a moment? Only a moment, I swear!"

"Very well." She lingered by the door as Chiffinch doffed his hat and fell to his knees at his friend's bedside.

"What am I to do? Send for a doctor?"

The dark man answered weakly. "No. The people must not know. My father was all too mortal. If they hear I am thus, the land will erupt in chaos."

My, Zabby mused, *he certainly thinks well of himself.*

"Do you think it is . . . plague?"

"I know I feel like a dying child, my friend. If that is what plague feels like . . ."

"It is," Zabby said from the door. "But check the pits of his legs and arms to know for sure. Now I'll be off."

She opened the door, but a hushed voice of authority halted her. "I command you to attend me," the dark man said.

She whirled, but bit back her retort. The poor man thought he was dying — and might well be.

"I told you, sir," she said gently, "there is only one man in this realm with the power to command me."

With the last of his failing strength he dug in a leather wallet at his belt and tossed her another gold half crown, which she caught in a deft snap.

"Look at the face on the coin," he said. "I am that man, and I command you to stay with me."

She looked, and saw in profile that same strong jutting nose, the same sensuous curl of lip, the jaw just starting to slack. She gasped, and did not know if she should flee or fall on her face. Instead she did what she'd do for any sick sailor or slave: she tucked up her skirts, pushed up her sleeves, and called for a basin of water. Her lack of courtesy didn't matter, for His Majesty Charles II had passed out.

Chiffinch scurried for spirits and clean cloths, for blankets and basins and knives and anything he thought she might need. After each trip he hovered over her.

"Shouldn't you bleed him?" he asked.

She stared at him. "Whatever for?"

"Oh, yes, of course, how ignorant of me. A clyster then? Or blistering with the cups?"

"Do they really believe that here?" she asked, looking at him as if he were a barbarian suggesting she sacrifice a lamb and read its entrails.

"But his humors must be out of balance."

Zabby sighed. "We do not hold with the theory of humors," she said.

"We?"

"Papa and I. We are the only physicians and chirurgeons for our three hundred slaves and a hundred indentured servants. And for ourselves. We've treated two plague-infected ships."

"And they lived?"

"Of course not. Not all of them, anyway. But a good dozen out of a thirty-man crew on the first, and far more than half of the second. Better than those who put into the main port. They were quarantined and starved as soon as they crawled ashore."

"And you saved them without bleeding?"

"We believe *vis medicatrix naturae*."

"Pardon?"

"The healing of nature." As she spoke she loosed the king's collar and checked his skin for spotting. "My father told me about a great battlefield contest among three famous physicians. Each was brought a man with a sword cut. One physician would bleed his patient and poultice him with moss from an unburied man's skull and salve him with burning cantharides. With the next man, by heaven, the second physician would treat the *sword*—sympathetic medicine, he called it—and not touch the wound. The third would wash his patient's injury with good wine and lay a clean linen cloth atop it, nothing more. The men bled of their angry humors always died. The men with the mystic swords got the creeping blackness up their limbs, yet sometimes lived if the limb was removed. Those who were washed with wine and left to the kindness of nature were likely to heal. The best course is often to do nothing. Failing that, do no more than is necessary."

Chiffinch, who was bled regularly twice a year, looked at the pale, earnest Zabby with some doubt. Maybe he should defy his sovereign and send for a real physician after all.

"Help me strip him," she ordered, and he gave in to her command. Her voice had the same ring of authority as the king's, and he was used to obeying orders.

"No bubos in the arms," she said, palpating her king from his inner arms to their hairy hollows. "Help me strip his breeches."

"But my dear girl—" he began.

"When you thought me a whore, you wouldn't have objected to me handling his privities," Zabby said archly. So the poor man helped denude his king.

"Fetch me some more candles," she told Chiffinch. "I can't see a thing."

He left, and she tried to bend over Charles, but the stiff board at her spine kept her straight. Glancing nervously at the door, she calculated how long it would take Chiffinch to go down and up the stairs, then hastily fumbled at her laces and pins. She had just gotten the contraption off and was about to reverse it when Charles groaned and mumbled something. The bed was wide, and she had to climb on it to lean near his lips.

"You have my thanks," he whispered. "The eternal thanks of a king."

There was a sharp rapping on the door. She ignored it, but the landlord had his own key and let himself in, just in time to see Zabby, bodice off, loose smock dangling, about to climb atop the naked body of the king of England. The landlord had seen him at his restoration two years past, when he rode by in triumph, and knew his monarch by sight.

Chiffinch came up a moment later and paid the man for his silence, but it soon became known throughout England that the king was so fascinated with his new mistress—a pale but enthusiastic young unknown—that he'd locked himself in an inn with her for two solid weeks, enjoying her so much that he never once poked his head out. The queen was in a fury. So was another lady.

When he emerged, they said, he was a wasted shadow of his former self.

He brought Zabby Wodewose to London and informed her that she would be one of the queen's maids of honor, the designation of "maid" being a rich jest to the court. She arrived with an ocelot, a reputation, and the deepest enmity of the king's reigning mistress, Barbara Palmer, Countess of Castlemaine.

Chapter 4

THE KING'S MISTRESS

"YOU DON'T SEEM TO UNDERSTAND, my dear," Margaret said to her goddaughter as they swept their trailing skirts along the corridors of Hampton Court, where His Majesty was making a summer honeymoon jaunt of several weeks' duration. "When a king voices a preference, it is law."

"Unless Parliament naysays him," Zabby quipped.

"You'll not find Parliament interfering with the king's mistresses," Margaret said. Zabby made a choking noise of protest, but Margaret held up her hand. "I know, you need not convince me, child. You've told me the truth of it, and you've virginal eyes if ever I've seen a pair. But the king has a secret, and he feels the best way to keep it is to keep it close. He doesn't want anyone to know he had plague, so we must all bend to his whim — for a time, anyway."

"But I came to England to learn, not to mince around court and fetch the queen's handkerchiefs."

Margaret laughed. "You'll do much more than that. You have an infinity of resources here. His Majesty's menagerie is the finest in the world, learned men are always welcome at his court, and they say his elaboratory has advances I can only dream of. Fetch handkerchiefs? The whole of civilization is made in these halls, child. Every bit of wit and beauty and learning passes like flies through a web, and those living here decide what sticks. A mind like yours, Zabby-heart, can shape society from here. Only get yourself listened to by the right ears, and soon the whole nation will be thinking as you think."

"Then why aren't you here, Godmother?"

"Do you know why I write?" She had already published her autobiography and diverse treatises on philosophy and the physical world. She was at work on a volume titled *Observations Upon Experimental Philosophy*. "I write because I cannot speak. I think highly enough of my own opinions to wish that others might know them, but place me before a crowd and I become mute as a worm."

"You speak well to me."

"My trembling increases exponentially in relation to my audience. I can speak to you, or to my darling husband, but I lack the fortitude to make myself known in the press and rush of court. I was maid of honor to the last queen for a time, you know, though I only stayed for shame of fleeing. Everyone thought me a fool. But you, dear, you're fearless."

"I don't know about that!" Zabby said. "Do you know, although I spent more than two weeks with him, covered in his excretions, his body unclothed before me, I almost fear to see him now, in his natural element."

She feared for more reasons than one. Something had happened to Zabby in those two cloistered weeks, something she herself was hardly prepared to admit.

"He was a tiger in the zoo then, caged and tame," Margaret said. "Now he's a tiger in the Afric wilds."

"Indian wilds, Godmother. There are only lions and leopards in Africa."

"Oh, dear, are you sure? Remind me to amend my manuscript. In any event, he is your king, and it's only natural to hold him in some awe. If you find yourself growing faint, just remember him breechless and purging, and he'll seem no more than an ordinary man."

Zabby had to hold on to the walls so she didn't laugh herself into a puddle. A passing page ran from her as if she were a foreign demon.

That's one thing I can do that the other court ladies can't—*picture Charles naked.* She recalled his reputation. *Or can they?*

She felt suddenly possessive of the man she'd saved, of his body, so hard and handsome even in illness, his fevered skin, the feel of him in her arms when the charcoal braziers weren't enough and she had to warm him with the heat of her own flesh. Her laughter died away as, seized with an unaccountable jealousy, she wondered if she could bear to know that other women had seen that splendid naked body, had lain with it, with *him*.

Stop that at once, she chided herself. *He was a patient then, a king now, and he will never be otherwise. What would he want with you when he has a queenly wife, and if all accounts are true, a bevy of nobly born mistresses?*

And what, her scientific self asked, *would you want with him? You have your studies, your work. What more could you ask for?*

She didn't quite know the answer, but nonetheless thought, perhaps, there might be more, if she dared to ask.

She was still frowning at the thought when they swept into the hall. Generally any newcomer was pounced upon by threescore pairs of eyes, dissected, and devoured, to be regurgitated in gossip for days to come. In the hothouse environment of the court, a new face was that much more manure to till into the fecund soil of scandal.

But now they ignored Zabby. Their gazes were all turned to two more familiar players in the second act of the drama, the prologue of which had been Suffolk's presentation of the bedchamber list. After a necessary intermission caused by the king's surprising absence (an amusing, mysterious subplot), there followed scenes of high melodrama (as Charles tried to persuade the wife he thought was meek and innocent, to comply with his wishes) and of pathos (as the Lord Chancellor was given the unenviable task of forcing the queen to relent to the king's plans). And now, perhaps, came a climax, for Charles was leading Barbara Palmer, known to the world as Lady Castlemaine, up to the chair of the oblivious queen. Catherine still had never seen her rival, for Barbara had just been in what they called an *interesting condition,* resulting in a lad she named Charles Fitzroy, her second acknowledged bastard by the king. Now, full-fleshed and startlingly lovely, she leaned on the king's arm as he brought her to be formally presented to the queen.

Zabby knew none of the actors, except for Charles, who seemed so much more man than king (even her rational mind could not quite yet encompass the idea that he was both) that she hardly knew how to classify him. That small woman with the large, solemn eyes, seated in a position of honor, must be the queen. There were several grand ladies around her in a sort of orbit, as though they had no wish to be any closer but could not quite leave. The only exceptions were two girls about Zabby's own age.

One was a large, dark girl of the coloring she'd heard called black: deep brown hair and eyes; high, vibrant color on her cheeks. She looked the hall over with a wry impassivity, as if she were collecting the most amusing bits to assemble into a collage at her leisure. She stood idly at the queen's side, a silken distaff bodyguard.

The other girl was slim and fair, soft as a dormouse, with huge gray eyes. She sat on a step at the queen's feet, a lapdog too loyal to leave, though she looked a little afraid of getting her paws trodden upon. She seemed such a helpless morsel that Zabby felt an urge to coddle her, and laughed at the thought of having another pet. On Barbados every slave and servant knew to bring her baby birds and raccoons and even snakes, and despite her father's wisdom that sick and orphaned animals were part of the natural order of things, she always interfered and saved them if she could, excusing it as part of her studies. As a result, the plantation was filled with half-tame beasts that would still sneak into the kitchen for handouts, or into her room for a warm, dry bed. She could see instantly that this girl was another such creature, and almost felt her pocket for a tidbit.

But Zabby's gaze was immediately dragged, almost against her will, to the figure in pearl white over cloth-of-silver leaning on Charles's arm. Even from behind, she could see something barbaric in her gait, a predatory prowl that left Zabby glad she was not the prey.

A woman like that doesn't belong on Charles's arm, Zabby thought hotly, but did not let herself think which woman ought to be there in her stead.

The queen's eyes lit up when she saw her husband. She never even noticed the glittering woman with him, only saw the pleasant smile on his face, the fact that he was coming to her voluntarily in public, before all the court. He'd avoided her for days. Her breath caught with hope, and her lips parted in a shy smile that showed one slightly protruding front tooth, a defect she usually tried to hide.

He's so handsome, she thought. *I know he is good at heart. It is only this place that makes him the way he is, and the hardship of his youth. He will love me as I love him. Look how he smiles at me, like he did that first night.*

She heard a low roar of murmurs, but to her it sounded like a heavenly chorus. After miserable days of shunning her, punishing her, Charles was returning to her at last. He bowed before her and presented the lady, some cousin, perhaps, or a minister's wife, like the dozen others she'd received that day. She did not hear and did not care. *He must see now that he cannot favor his mistress over his wife. I'll welcome him with all my affection,* she thought. *He is my lord, my master, my . . .*

"My God!" someone said quite distinctly from the crowd. "Her Majesty has just let Lady Castlemaine kiss her hand!"

The winsome smile froze on the little queen's face. Her eyes widened until they looked fit to pop, while the veins stood in sharp blue relief on the pallor of her neck. Her cheeks mottled red, and a thin trickle of blood dripped from her nose. She sucked in a great breath and held it, as did everyone else in the room. Would she scream? At Barbara or at Charles? Would she stop her breath until she passed out? Until she died? Would Barbara have her marriage to Palmer annulled and become the new queen? Anything might happen!

Zabby knew little of protocol. At times, she was sure, there simply was none. When your king was delirious with plague fever, you wrapped your arms and legs around his naked body to keep him from hurling himself out the window. When your queen looked horror-struck and was plainly about to have a fit, you intervened. Zabby shook off her godmother and insinuated herself between Catherine and the cause of her distress. She cast a quick glance at Charles. It was his business to attend to his wife, and she'd willingly step aside if he meant to sweep her into his arms and carry her back to her chambers. But the king only scowled, as if all this was an overspiced dish or a spatter of mud on his hose, a distasteful inconvenience he'd prefer to dispose of and have done with.

But she's your wife, Zabby thought and half mouthed.

Then she caught Barbara's haughty, mocking eyes, and Zabby thought she understood. Her godmother had idly passed along a rumor that the king was favoring his mistress over his queen, forcing the one to endure the gadfly presence of the other. This must be the notorious Castlemaine. Zabby gave an involuntary gasp. The king's reigning mistress was frighteningly beautiful. No man could resist her, the courtiers said; no man had ever tried. *Why?* Zabby wondered. Was it beauty alone that gave her such a hold on the king?

"Charles," Zabby said, and the intimacy of that Christian name sparked a week's conflagration of gossip. "How could you?" She looked at the man with reproach and turned to Barbara as the thunderclouds began to gather on his brow.

Zabby cocked her head at Barbara and reckoned her up in her scientific fashion — calculating her, vivisecting her — and at last said, blandly, "You oughtn't use ceruse to whiten your complexion, madam. You'll go mad and your flesh will fall off." Spoken so flatly, so surely, with no hint of insult, it sounded like a malediction, and Barbara blanched to the color she had striven for in the first place. She only found her anger a moment later when Zabby turned her back on the pair and curtsied to the queen.

Chiffinch had taught her how to do that, among a few other nice-
ties of court, in their idle hours watching over the king's quiet
sleep in the later days of his illness.

"I am Zabby Wodewose, daughter of Edward Wodewose, Baron
of Nonesuch, lately of Barbados. The king your husband has commanded me to attend you as a maid of honor. May I assist you to
your rooms, Your Majesty?"

Then Catherine screamed. It wasn't the sound Zabby had
been expecting. Hysterics, perhaps, or the high-pitched, desperate shriek of a snared beast when the trapper approaches and it
knows there is nothing more to life but pain. She was not prepared for rage. A ragged roar tore from the tiny queen's throat, a
vibrato that made the beeswax candles in the low-hanging chandeliers tremble. She started forward in her seat, eyes closed, teeth
bared, as if she would spring at her enemy (though which enemy,
Zabby didn't know), but before she escaped the deeply cushioned
seat, her weakness and loneliness conquered her fury, and her
knees buckled.

For an instant she sprawled in unconscious supplication before
her husband. Then two pairs of strong hands scooped her up, Eliza
at her head and Zabby at her feet, and carried her out of the room,
with Beth trailing behind, weeping for all of them.

Barbara looked appalled, but quickly marshaled her aplomb
and gave a tinkling laugh, cut short by a look from Charles. She
sobered, then asked him in mock solemnity, "Whatever could
have affected her like that, Your Majesty? Are my curls in a disarray?" She shook them against Charles's shoulder, loosing a scented

cloud of ambergris and tuberose, and something else no man can resist: the lingering smell of himself, from their recent amours.

Charles's own face was unreadable now. He called for the musicians set discreetly in a corner to strike up his favorite tune, "Cuckolds All Awry," and squired Barbara through the sprightly dance. More than one courtier remarked that it was a shame a woman couldn't sprout a pair of cuckold's horns, and each believed his wit to be original. Charles danced determinedly for an hour, excused himself for a moment, then retired to Barbara's house in King Street, where he and the gayest men and ladies of the court played (and cheated) at cards until past midnight. Barbara's husband was obediently rusticating in their country estate.

Eliza, Zabby, and Beth arranged the queen on her bed of state, a grand furnishing created for the royal consummation, eight thousand pounds' worth of gossamer linen and Flanders point, of carved puttis and canopies, crowned in the cardinal directions with entire ostriches of feathers. On a dressing table with an oval Venetian mirror lay a scattered disarray of beauty tools in beaten gold, the sale of any one of which would have given a clergyman's daughter a dowry handsome enough to catch a baronet.

Catherine, eyes still squeezed tight, thrashed her head back and forth on fat goosedown pillows, clutching the bedsheets in her balled fists. Then, first falling limp, she sat abruptly and said piteously to the wall beyond them, "I didn't know . . . I didn't know. How could I have known?"

"Known what, Your Majesty?" Zabby asked softly in Spanish.

It was not Catherine's natal tongue, but she had learned it in infancy, and it was as familiar to her as the cool stone benches in her convent's garden. Two of the sisters were from Spain.

With some effort the queen focused on Zabby. She was as alien to Catherine as the Portuguese queen was to the court. Catherine had never seen anyone other than a peasant with a deep tan, but Zabby's face was sun-darkened and faintly freckled. Her hair made a startling contrast. At first Catherine thought it was white, and tried to reconcile the unlined face with elderly hair, but soon she decided it was a very pale, silvery blond, pellucid and wispy in an unfashionable straight fringe at the brow and a simple chignon at the nape. Her lashes and high, arched eyebrows were the same uncanny fairy shade, and her face was saved from glacial pallor only by her eyes. *They're cat eyes,* Catherine thought, almost crossing herself—a peculiar amber or bright tawny orange, very large and opened wide. If she'd been a languid painted court brunette, Catherine would never have confided in her, whatever language she spoke, but that familiar speech, combined with Zabby's odd, otherworldly appearance, made the queen forget for a moment that she was in a hostile place.

"What the world is," she said at last. "What a man is."

Zabby had plenty of advice, but she knew it was all theoretical, so she said instead, "But you know yourself, Your Majesty. Begin there."

"Know myself?" Catherine asked incredulously. "Did I know there was such a thing as hatred in my heart until this very moment? No one is what he seems! I am not even a queen."

The others understood none of this, but Eliza said, "Did you see Castlemaine's face, Your Majesty, when this one put her down? Her face will fall off — blast my tripes, but that's rich!"

Zabby looked at her wide-eyed and said, "But it's true. Lead seeps into the skin and —"

"Well, no matter the genius behind it, you've made one enemy today, and found an admirer in me. How do you speak Portugee?"

"That was Spanish," Zabby said. "My father trades with Spanish merchants. Portuguese too, sometimes, but I only speak a little." She turned to the queen. "Your Majesty, what will you do?" No one could loose that howl of rage without following it with action.

Do? Catherine knew how to pray, how to be elegant in her native fashion. She had read philosophy and theology. She could embroider. She could sit or kneel patiently for hours on end. Beyond that she had no skills, knew nothing of the political maneuvering or seduction or blackmail that might sway a husband such as Charles.

"I will go home!" she said at last, and Zabby, finding the waters too deep, began to translate so the others could help.

"Oh, don't go!" Beth said piteously, then wondered if she'd be allowed to accompany the queen. She dreamed of love, but the quiet solitude of convent life sounded tempting. Her mother would never be allowed in a Portuguese convent.

"'Sblood, of course you can't go," Eliza said sharply. "That's just what those painted besoms want, for you to turn tail. Chouse them proper and stay. As for that Castlemaine, why, anyone can see he'll tire of her quick enough."

Zabby translated (though she couldn't recall the Spanish for *besom*) but had her doubts.

"Will he come to me?" Catherine asked.

"Of course," they lied, exchanging looks. "As soon as he can."

He shouldn't have done it to her, Zabby thought. Not in front of that mocking crowd. The man who had lain in bed for two weeks under her care would not have done that. The man whose hand she'd held, who'd talked with her about the herbs of Barbados, about Carib magic, sailing, Hobbes's *Leviathan,* would not treat the woman he pledged himself to thus.

I know him, Zabby thought. *Those days of weakness, of bare skin, of death kept at bay, showed me the real man. He's clever and kind, loyal to what he loves. And he must love Catherine. He will see that he has treated her cruelly, and repent.*

Zabby's only experience with marriage was a dim memory of her mother and father strolling along the shore, hand in hand, exchanging secret kisses, herself a toddler collecting seashells. All she knew of love was Papa. Until recently.

The three girls did their best to perform their duties as maids of honor. Beth silently combed the queen's hair, twining the soft waves around her fingers. The other two kept up a halting, desultory chatter, Eliza teaching Catherine how to say all the parts of her dress and jewels in English, Zabby, in Spanish, telling her all about her godmother's latest work, which together was confusing enough to put the queen into a daze.

If only he'd come, Zabby thought. *I'm sure if they were alone for* a while they'd sort it all out. *He wouldn't make that woman be one of her ladies if he knew how much it meant to her.*

Thinking to comfort her, Zabby said, "When I was with him in Dover he told me about your courtship by proxy, how pleased he was to see you in person. He said . . . "

Catherine jerked away from her handlers, leaving a strand of torn hair in Beth's fingers. "You! That was you with him all these weeks? Penalva told me there was a new one. Another of his whores." She spat on Zabby's chest, and the girl sprang up and backed away.

I can't tell her the truth, she thought. *I promised the king.*

"Did it amuse you to cosset me, lull me with your honeyed kindness, you trull? Did you conspire with that Castlemaine all the while, to laugh together behind my back?"

"Your Majesty, I swear to you——"

"What harlot's tricks do you know that you can keep him locked up with you for two weeks?" She spoke with scorn, but her eyes shifted guiltily to the side. She wished she were brave enough to beg, *Teach them to me.* "Get out! Leave me!" She snatched the gold and tortoiseshell comb from Beth's hands and flung it at Zabby's head. Marksmanship was not among the skills taught in a convent. "By God, if you come near me again I'll . . ." She could not think of a threat horrible enough, and knew in her heart she wouldn't have the power to execute it anyway.

Not knowing what else to do, Zabby opened the door without the mandatory deep curtsy and was about to slip out when a wall of warmth emanating from a large body stopped her before she even knew he was there. She looked up into Charles's dark saturnine face and almost reached a hand to his cheek — to check for fever — before she caught herself.

He was only a breath away, and she stood imprisoned by his proximity. All those days of intimate caress, the tender touch of nurse and patient...Yet now, though the very hairs on her arms rose up and yearned, she could not bring herself to sway forward those scant few inches and touch him again. Behind her, the queen's eyes bored into her back.

Charles looked at Catherine, but it was Zabby's arm he grabbed roughly as he barked, "I am your king!" He glared for a moment, letting the unsaid volumes recite themselves, then shook off Zabby's arm as if it had been clinging to his fingers and not the other way round. He was gone with a clap-tap of heels on the black and white tiled floor.

Chapter 5

THE THREE ELIZABETHS

ZABBY WAS IN BED when Beth and Eliza tumbled in, stripping off their slippers and pulling their busks from their bodices.

"Oh, you're here?" Eliza said archly. "Thought you'd be on the gibbet by now. That or made a duchess, though even Castlemaine's just a countess after all her service to the Crown. Still, even she couldn't keep His Majesty abed for two weeks straight. *Nunquam satis,* indeed!" She scattered pearl-tipped pins on the dressing table and pulled her dark hair out of its topknot, digging her fingers into the sides of her scalp and shaking vigorously.

"I didn't..." Zabby began, but broke off. What was the use of violating her oath to Charles? She was planning to leave in the morning, as soon as she could get word to Godmother Cavendish to fetch her.

Beth sank down on the bed they were to share. "I don't think it's true," she said softly.

"And why not?" Eliza asked. "She's an odd-looking thing, but Gemini, look at Anne Hyde, and she caught herself a royal highness. No offense, sweetheart — you're pretty enough, but you don't look like you belong at court. I can't quite put my thumb on it, but you don't." She snapped her fingers. "I've got it after all! You walk like you've real legs under your skirts."

Zabby laughed. "Don't you have legs under there?"

Eliza lay back beside Beth and crossed one leg over the other so her skirts fell above her knees. "Bless me, there they are. But then, I'm a peasant, and peasants all have legs. Ladies like our little countess here usually act like they float on rarefied air. Till the skirts come off and the legs wrap around someone, that is. On our backs we're all peasants — countess and commoner alike."

Beth blushed scarlet, but stubbornly persisted in her point. "I don't care what they say. I don't think she's the king's lover."

Eliza snorted. "Good for her if she is, I say. He's a handsome devil, and the king, after all. It'll be hot for a while, but Her Majesty will forgive all the king's rannigals in time — just hold out."

Zabby rolled over to Beth. "Why don't you think I'm his mistress?"

Beth answered in a whisper. "I've lived here at court. I've seen . . . my mother has shown me . . . what the mistresses are like. You're no one's mistress — I can see it in your eyes."

"And you know all there is of love and lovers?" Eliza asked archly.

Beth had fed on love, the idea of love, for as long as she could remember. Ever since she was a little girl she'd dreamed of it, and felt it for the first time at age ten, when she became enamored of a gallant neighbor boy, Harry Ransley. Though that budding love had been cruelly crushed, she clung to its memory, and the boy, now long gone, grew to man's estate in her imaginings. She looked for him everywhere. One day, she was certain, Harry would light upon her, reach out his hand, and say, "I have found you, my love." And then her struggle would be over. She would be safe in the shelter of his heart.

"I know what love should be," Beth said. "And my mother has, in one way and another, taught me all that it should not. No, our Zabby is not the king's lover." She paused and examined her new friend more critically. "Or if you are, you're ashamed of it, and I've never yet seen one of the king's mistresses ashamed."

I'm ashamed, Zabby thought, *because with his wife in the room behind me, all I could think about was bathing Charles in his bed.*

"Well, I, for one, don't care," Eliza said. "I'm here to find a husband myself, so my father informs me, as is our Beth, as are you, I suppose, and the king's not going to marry any of us, so who he quiffs is of no importance beyond a jest. Now I think on it, any jest is of the greatest importance. Come, we are all oddments here at court — I can tell that already. Lovely little Beth with her mad mother and noble blood back to Adam; you, whore and not whore from some barbarian land, they say; and me with a lineage of dirt and more money than the king. Let us be friends, shall we?" She shuffled herself until she was between them, then took their hands. "Lord, look at those bruises. His Majesty has a mighty strong grip. No matter, they'll fade, and from what they say he's softest to the women he's wronged, so long as they're soft to him. Now listen, are we friends? I don't want a bedmate who'll stab me in the back and whisper poison over my corpse."

Zabby had never had a female friend, and was pleased—if rather astonished—at Eliza's free, bawdy talk. It had the same flavor as her lively, intellectual conversations with Papa, though the ingredients were vastly different. And she took to Beth immediately, first for her mousekin softness, and also because she'd defended Zabby against gossip. (*Though I could have been his lover,* a small voice whispered. *Why couldn't I have?*)

"Well," Zabby said, "I'll be gone by the morrow, but in the meantime I'm your friend."

"I too, both of you," Beth said, immeasurably relieved. She'd dreaded being teased and put upon by the sophisticated maids of honor, the ones with money and real family to back them, with the confidence to hold their own at court. But these two were different. With them, and the kind queen, she might at least be peaceful, a short jaunt away from happiness. Now she felt like a kitten curled up beside two large and friendly dogs: warm and safe.

"But I don't think friendship can be only for the meantime," Beth went on, gentle and earnest. "If we're friends now, truly friends, we'll stay friends. If we don't, we never were in the first place."

Zabby nodded. "Papa says that certain things, the pure elements, aren't mutable."

"By your reasoning, Beth, sweetheart, we won't know if we were ever friends till we're not friends anymore."

"Proof by contraries," Zabby said.

"I'm no philosopher," Eliza said, "but let us set out our properties now so we don't have to test 'em later. We're the gods of our own beliefs, so if we create a friendship true, then true it will be, and if not, we're blasphemers against ourselves. Say, that would do for the stage. I'll write it down come morning. What do you say to an oath, Beth, and Zabby, was it? What an outlandish name!"

"Elizabeth, really."

"Od's bodikins, three Elizabeths in one bed. A fop's fantasy! Well, that seals it for me. One Elizabeth for all Elizabeths. Stand or fall together, eh?"

Zabby smiled. It was foolishness, all of it, but Eliza's enthusiastic prattle was soothing, and she was sleepy, so she clasped their hands tighter and with them swore a giggling oath of eternal friendship. Released, she rolled to her side, almost asleep. Beth's breathing was like the Barbados breeze, and Eliza's gentle snores like waves grinding on the shore.

The lowliest rose the earliest. Several hours before dawn, scullery maids rubbed the sleep from their eyes, their bodies set like clockwork at the start of their careers by sound beatings meted out for any laziness. They coaxed the banked kitchen hearths into life, then woke the next on the hierarchy, who might get an extra few minutes of sleep, but in exchange had to empty all the servants' chamber pots. This accomplished, they awoke their betters, who in turn awoke theirs, until sometime around daybreak the palace hummed with stirrings of the unseen, unacknowledged underlings who made life pleasant for those above them.

Eventually, the series of human alarms came to wake the genteel servants, ladies' maids and waiting women who were privileged to empty the chamber pots of the nobility. One of these slipped into the bedroom of the three Elizabeths, and opened the shutters just loudly enough to make the bed heave with the simultaneous shifting of a dozen limbs.

"Good morning, ladies," the spry elderly woman said briskly. "Tea, like Her Majesty takes, or good English ale?" Tea was vastly expensive, but a portion of Catherine's dowry had been paid in leaf — when cash was desperately needed — and for the nonce it was plentiful and, despite the queen's lowly position, fashionable.

Eliza demanded ale straight away, while Beth made a polite noise of demur. "Tea, I warrant? It'll put some color into you, dearie, if I may be so bold. I'm Prue. Prudence Honor Goodfellow, and I'll be serving you lasses, or ladies, or whatever you are."

"I've a maid of my own," Eliza said. "She'll be here directly."

"That fumble-fingered bumpkin who calls herself Whoretense? I met her in the kitchen, with her theatrical airs. Rely on her and you'll be poisoned or clapped or pilloried within a fortnight. She don't know the court as I do." She sidled up to the girls and gave them a broad wink. "Treat me right, missies, and I'll see you never come to harm. We servants, we hear all, and tell all too, for a consideration." A swollen-knuckled hand presented itself, and waited.

Finally Eliza reached for an embroidered pocket tossed carelessly on the floor. She pulled out two shining shillings, clinked them together like castanets, and dropped them into Prue's palm. "See you keep your end of the bargain, Mother."

Prue cackled and put a tray of white bread and perfect ivory butter balls on a small table near the window. "Silver always stimulates my memory," she said. "Though gold, they say, is a *sovereign* cure for absentmindedness." The hand snuck out again.

Eliza laughed. "I'll give you a sovereign when you give us something useful, you old gossip. My father's a merchant, and he taught me never to pay before I handle the goods."

"Humph!" Prue said. "Merchants' daughters attending the queen! I never thought I'd live to see the day. Ah, well, two shillings is more than that other lot of maids of honor gave me, so maybe times have changed for the better. Which one of you's the Wodewose girl?"

Zabby untangled her feet from her night shift and presented herself.

"Got a wee bit of a thing for you. You've gone far for your age. There's another maid of honor setting her cap at Buckingham already, but most work their way up through the foppery before they aim for the king. Officially it's from Chiffinch," she added, tapping her nose with one gnarled forefinger. "Ta!"

The three girls crowded together on the bed as if the present were meant for all of them. The wrapping alone was an impressive gift, a rare and costly piece of silk, soft as eiderdown, marked with a swirling pattern of churning sea and a pitifully small boat full of slanting-eyed sailors about to be swamped by a prodigious wave. Something small and dense nestled in the center. Zabby unwrapped it carefully, thinking, *If it is a jewel, I'll return it. I'll pardon him, but forgiveness must be bestowed, not bought.*

It was not a jewel but a seashell, a finger long and three thick, intricately whorled, polished to a high sheen.

"Oh, how pretty!" Beth said, clapping her hands together. "Look at the stripes — they're just the same hue as your eyes."

"And what a shine," Eliza said, claiming it and turning it toward the light. "Some poor underling worked many an hour to bring out that gleam."

"No, I don't think so." Zabby reached out and stroked her own gift in Eliza's hand. "There's a snail in Barbados, the olive, that keeps its mantle wrapped around its shell all its life. The shell never gets marked or scuffed. This shell came from the Pacific, I'm sure, but I warrant it did the same."

"Nature's an odd thing," Eliza said. "Fancy having armor to protect you, then putting your soft, tender parts out to cover it, all for the sake of vanity!"

"I have to give it back," Zabby said, taking it and savoring its cool solidity in her palm for a second before resolutely slipping it, and the silk cloth, under her pillow. "I can't accept presents from the king. What will people think?"

"Just what they think now. It's lovely and rare, and he wants you to have it. Don't give the king offense. Even if he is *Charles* to you."

"Oh! I shouldn't have done that. It just slipped out. After all those days in bed it seemed . . ." She clapped a hand to her mouth and Eliza burst into a guffaw. Even Beth giggled. "I didn't! I swear!"

"Whatever you say, sweetheart!" Eliza said, smiling smugly.

Hortense came in and helped them dress, offering (no doubt with the incentive of a healthy tip from her mistress) her assistance to all three ladies. Zabby blushed as she was laced into her gown, recalling her first attempt at sophisticated dress. As it happened the merchant had deceived Papa — that copper gown was several years out of fashion, and observant Zabby was already — against her will — gaining the keen perception that told her what was à la mode. The court's magnified eye could distinguish subtle differences in the dye of a plume, the height of a heel, the width of point, and summarily condemn or envy the wearer at a glance. It expected conformity but sometimes embraced bold novelty, and had she worn her backwards gown with enough zest, the trend might have been picked up by all the countesses within a week.

Still, Zabby felt ridiculous wearing a garment she needed an assistant to don. She drew the line at her coiffure, waving off Hortense's nimble fingers and twisting her long pale hair into its usual low knot, secured with a coral comb.

"I'll be writing a message to my godmother when I return," she said. "She's in town, so she'll probably be able to send a coach for me before afternoon. If I don't see you again . . ."

"Don't go," Beth said wistfully. After a short time in service she was passionately partisan for the queen, and admired the way Zabby had sprung to her defense, defying the king himself. "We took an oath of friendship."

"Right," Eliza said, "and now we must put it to scientific test. How can we do that in the absence of one of our elemental parts?"

Zabby wavered. "I don't think the queen will let me stay."

"She'll have to, if the king orders it. You and Castlemaine both."

"I wouldn't want to stay if I'm lumped with her."

"Why not ask the king to tell Her Majesty the truth?" Beth suggested.

"Though whatever innocent thing can keep a man closeted with a wench for two weeks and more is beyond my comprehension," said Eliza.

"Mostly we spoke of science and philosophy."

"A clever tongue, then," Eliza replied, nudging Beth, who pretended not to understand. "No matter — we don't want to know, though he ought to tell her, if there's truly no harm in it. Hang me for a liar, though, we do want to know. Tell us, Zabby, or ask Charles if you may."

"Is he Charles to you now, too?"

"Ah, well, my poor simple mind can only parrot what it hears. Go, and do whatever you must to stay. I've not had such a merry time in all my days as I have since you came."

Beth patted Zabby's hand to add her own encouragement, and Zabby, still undecided, put the shell in her pocket and went in search of the king.

Chapter 6

THE ROYAL SEED

H E WAS NOT AN EASY MAN to find. At midday he would have one of his onerous public dinners, where any common man who managed to shove his way into the audience gallery could gawk at his masticating monarch. Mercifully, it was less crowded at Hampton than at the principal royal residence, Whitehall, in the heart of London, where the crowd sometimes got so bumptious that it had to be bribed with whole roast haunches and elaborate spun sugar confections, while Charles made a great show of eating nothing at all, retiring after the exhibition to dine with Castlemaine or in the privacy of his clock closet. It was one of his most unpleasant duties, a tradition he couldn't quite shake.

But now, at his leisure early in the morning, he could be anywhere. A discreet query of a servant lowly enough that she could be guaranteed not to laugh in Zabby's face revealed the king had risen betimes. *Not that I could have gone to his bedroom,* Zabby thought. Now he might be at the tennis courts, or sporting with the spaniels that followed him from palace to palace, or, for all she knew, in Castlemaine's arms. Zabby's jaw felt suddenly sore, and she realized she was gritting her teeth at the notion.

She wandered for a time, all but lost in the hallways, until she came upon a black and tan pup with a petulant face and silken ears trailing the ground, scrabbling at a recessed doorway. Accustomed to indulging animals' whims, she opened the door and peered after the dog as it leaped and frisked toward a tall figure in black with silver braid, hunched over an instrument of some kind.

"I told you not to let the dogs in," Charles said, shoving the fawning creature aside affectionately with his square-toed shoe without turning around. "At least I've no chemicals for him to upset today. Come in, George, come in, and shut the door behind you so we shan't be bothered by any more simpering morts. I can't stand ladies in my elaboratory. Their panting and giggling fogs the lenses."

Zabby edged inside and closed the door, standing where she could see him in profile, his wide, full mouth curved in a smile at whatever he was examining.

Oh, he is handsome, she thought, though he wasn't by the standards of the time, which called for pallor and fair hair, small, neat bodies, gray eyes, and fine lips on men and women both. Charles wasn't like any of the other men she'd seen so far at court. He towered over the tallest, standing six feet, three inches, a physical peculiarity that made escaping capture in the hunted days of his youth especially difficult. His features were large, his long black hair his own, not a periwig, just beginning to gray.

"Come look at this one," he called, beckoning, with his eyes still downward. "I had the devil of a time getting them alive. Not that collecting them wasn't diverting, but a man can only manage so much, and I believe something bad happened to Onan, though I can't recall what. Here, lean in and take my spot. Careful not to singe your hair on the oil lamp. They're still wiggling, though I've found they perish in a very few minutes under the heat of the lens." He shifted his body to the side, creating a space for her. She slid beside him, her hair catching in the stubble of his cheek, and at this near-touch Zabby felt a great void open within her breast, as if her heart had disintegrated.

"Od's fish!" Charles gasped, stumbling back. "I thought you were George." George Villiers, second Duke of Buckingham, had been orphaned near the same time as Charles, and the lads had been reared together. Now, though they were boon companions, George's fractious ways and constant plotting made him a thorn in Charles's side. The court gossips often wondered if the day would come when the king would have no choice but to send his best friend to the Tyburn gallows.

"No," she whispered, staring up at him wide-eyed, suddenly a little afraid. "I'm only me."

He took her arm gently and turned it over, placing his fingers on the livid marks they'd made the night before. "I'm sorry for this," he said. She thought he might say more, but he only let his fingers rest there, as if today's gentleness might heal yesterday's violence. His skin was very warm, and she could feel the beat of his pulse against her inner arm, just out of synchrony with hers. Then the rhythm was broken entirely when her heart raced recklessly away, beating so fast she thought she might faint.

She held his eyes a moment, and felt, for the first time in her life, a strange sort of power, like a sorcerer's in an old tale, as if she need only raise her hand to work a terrible magic and bend him to her will.

Lady Castlemaine must feel this way all the time, she thought, and the distaste of that comparison was so great that she laid the power aside and pulled away from him, allowing the warring tug of science to have a momentary victory over emotion.

"What's that you're observing in your microscope?" she asked. When she'd bent down she'd had a tantalizing glimpse of something wriggling, slightly out of focus.

"It is . . . well . . . ah . . . ahem . . . that is to say . . . what do you think it is?"

Zabby bent over the instrument, adjusting the screw slightly until the creatures came into focus. Most moved listlessly, but occasionally one would give a great thrash of its whiplike tail and propel itself out of sight.

"They resemble tadpoles, though with very odd tails." She withdrew, blinked to freshen her eyes, and glanced at the sample. "But of course no tadpole could be this small." She bent to the microscope again. "Some sort of animalcule? There is motion, so it must be animal life. This is much more powerful than ours at home, though of course we have only a single lens. My godmother would love to see this — whatever it is."

Thinking about his collection method, Charles doubted it.

"What is it, then?"

It was hard to tell with his swarthy complexion, but Zabby believed he was blushing.

"They are . . . that is . . ." He seemed torn between mortification and mirth. "They are homunculi."

A court lady would have giggled, blushed, or made a licentious jest, or more likely not known the word at all. Zabby simply cocked her head and said, "Papa and I looked at pond and sea creatures, and at the beasts that live betwixt the teeth. I had thought to look at homunculi, but couldn't see how to harvest a sample." She looked into the microscope again, and Charles was free to grin.

"Oh, but they're dying, the poor wee things! Can you save them?"

"They always perish quickly."

"Indeed? And this sample, is this all you produced?" With every molecule of her being she willed herself not to dwell on exactly *how* they were produced.

Charles steeled himself not to laugh and said, "A bit more. A dram, perhaps."

"That would mean thousands, many thousands, of homunculi regularly wasted. Do you know, I don't believe what they say about each homunculus being a perfect human in miniature. They certainly don't look it, but beyond that, can you imagine any system, natural or divine, that would sacrifice so many countless creatures? They cannot be complete unto themselves. I don't think they become human until they are in combination with a feminine counterpart. Yet Swammerdam speaks of the ovum as containing homunculi too. Perhaps..."

"Blight me, sweetheart, how you stare!" She was gazing up at him earnestly with her large, too widely spaced, pale-lashed amber eyes. "What a marvel to see the whites of a woman's orbits. D'you know, the ladies here think it a sin to raise their lids above half-mast. They all look like sleepy Chinamen. But you open your eyes like a blind man newly cured. I wonder, do you see more than they?"

She smiled, losing her train of inquiry. "I don't know if I see more, but I'm always looking." She gazed at Charles as though she would devour him. She felt she could look at him forever, the sole object of her studies both physical and philosophical.

"You kept me alive in more ways than one during my confinement," Charles said. "Without your lively mind I should have perished of boredom. Do you always speak so bluntly and fearlessly?"

"What's there to fear from words and ideas?" she asked.

Charles's face suddenly darkened. "Cromwell and a few others had an idea, and it spread like gangrene and sent a king, my father, to the block. Ideas can make action."

"I didn't mean—"

"No matter, sweetheart. Your ideas are pure, from a desire simply to *know*. How could your pretty little delvings into the inner cogs of the universe harm anyone? I don't mean to quell you in the least." He smiled winningly and took her hand with his easy-going familiarity. "In fact, if you ever stop speculating, I'll banish you from my court entirely."

"Oh, Your Majesty, that's what I came to tell you." She pressed her lips together into a fine line, as if she could trap the painful words inside her, then forced them open with a long sigh. "I'm leaving court anyway. And you must take this back." She thrust her hand into her skirt and pulled out the seashell.

"Does it not please you? The traveler I bought it from said they are rare even on their natal shores."

"I've never seen anything more lovely."

"I thought you'd appreciate a curiosity more than a jewel, but if you'd prefer a pretty ring . . ."

"Your Majesty, I cannot accept presents from you. Don't you know what they're saying about me? They all believe I'm your mistress."

"And what of that? Let them gossip. The mistress of a king is as good as the wife of any man."

"But it isn't true!" *It* could *be true,* a demon voice whispered in her ear.

"Better that than let the world know I almost died."

"I don't see that at all. They would think you all the more heroic for having lived."

"No, sweetheart, plague is a pestilence of the poor, a disease of dirt and vermin. I will not allow anyone to know that I contracted it."

"No one would find fault. They know a king is only human."

"If they know that, they must be taught to forget!" he said

harshly. "When I was your age, I was hunted through the countryside like a stag. I lived on the charity of people who scorned me. I, a king, cheated at cards to buy my next meal. Now that I'm back in my rightful place, nothing—nothing, Zabby—will remove me from it by the slightest measure. Not the opinion of the blasted people, not my own wife. I am king, Zabby. That means I rule, without question!" He sighed, his vehemence deflated. "Oh, sweetheart, they come at me from every side. Parliament like carrion crows plucking more of my flesh each day. Catherine defying me before the world."

Zabby hung her head. "And I too, Your Majesty, defying you. Forgive me."

"'Your Majesty'?" he asked. "What of 'Charles'?"

"Please pardon me for that, too. I had no right."

"Well . . . perhaps not in public, or quite so loudly. But it sounds well on your tongue. In private, please call me Charles."

She only nodded, thinking she would almost certainly never see him after this day, unless she joined the gawking crowds at the public dinners. *It's the most I could be to him anyway,* she thought, *I or any other woman. One of many.*

"And you will stay. I order you to stay. Come, help me feel like a king again. Let there be one person who obeys me." He took her chin in his hand.

This is foolishness, she told herself. *What, desire a man not only married but with a stable of mistresses? Love the king?*

She astonished herself at the word, barely whispered inside her. *It is not love,* she told herself plainly. *It is the natural fealty one feels for* one's monarch, coupled, no doubt, with that animal lust which is as evident in humans as in beasts. The bitch in heat claws the door of her kennel from the inside just as fiercely as the dog from the outside. There is nothing odd in a girl of marriageable age admiring a virile man. He is intelligent and charming, looks well enough, understands sciences natural and physical.

He reminded Zabby of her father.

She clung to that. *Yes, I miss my father, and Charles is the closest surrogate. I enjoy his company, no more. I am fond of him,* she told herself. *I do not love him. Love is a question of logic as much as passion, and no equation can ever prove that I love Charles.*

A small, delighted part of her taunted, *If you do not love him, then there's no harm in staying.*

"I cannot stay," she insisted. "I came to England to study with my godmother. I plan to assist her in her natural examination, improve upon the clarity of lenses, increase my alchemical knowledge . . ."

Charles grinned. A gambling man, he always knew when he had won long before his opponents. He understood how to trap her now.

"If you stay, you may have free access to my elaboratory. No one else has that privilege, not even Buckingham. You should see my collection at Whitehall. Lenses much finer than these, blown beakers, every chemical on the sphere, tumors and grotesques preserved in spirits, fresh criminal cadavers to dissect."

How could Zabby resist such an offer? She tried, and failed. *For the elaboratory,* she told herself. And for Beth and Eliza. Certainly not for Charles.

"I'll only stay if you tell the queen the truth. I can't serve her if she believes me to be your mistress. I won't." She stubbornly lifted the chin Charles still held in his hand.

"Very well, if you'll do one little thing for me in return."

"Of course. Anything."

"Swear it first."

"You are my king. I must obey."

He laughed. "Only now you realize it?" He leaned a fraction closer and she drew a breath, half afraid, half eager to know what he might command her. For if indeed it was a kingly command, she'd certainly be justified in yielding.

"Convince my wife to allow Lady Castlemaine to serve as a lady of the bedchamber."

She did her best to refuse. It was a deal with the devil, but when the devil was a charming King Charles, she couldn't resist. Charles in turn agreed to tell Catherine the truth immediately, and even said that Zabby could tell Beth and Eliza what really happened in those weeks in Dover.

"Are you certain you can trust to their discretion? How well do you know them?"

"Not well, though I trust them. We shared a bed for the night."

He chuckled. "Quite well, then. When a woman shares my bed for an hour she rises believing she knows me perfectly.

"And you'll keep this, won't you, sweetheart?" he asked, fumbling in her skirts to slip the seashell back in the pocket that hung against her legs. "Just a little lover's gift." He laughed and strode out before she could throw herself either into his arms or out the window. She thought, wildly, that those were her only two choices. *Love the king, Zabby? You are mad.*

Instead she bent her head and devoted herself to examining his faintly stirring, stymied progeny.

"I forgive you, my child, I forgive you," Catherine murmured to Zabby, who knelt at the queen's bedside. Zabby took a breath to explain that, as she had done no wrong in the first place, there was nothing to forgive, but she was slowly learning that logic had little place at court. If the queen wanted to forgive her for other people's insinuations, she must be indulged.

"Of course you are not the sort of creature to tempt a husband away from his vow, you good child."

Again, it was on the tip of Zabby's tongue to ask, *Why not I as well as another?* She thought of that moment of power, when she knew, even if Charles did not, that she could take advantage of their easy familiarity, of his gratitude, of his natural tendency to fall into any arms that were appealing and convenient, and seduce him, if only for a time. *But I want more than that,* she thought. *I already have more than that from Charles. To love him as Castlemaine and those others love him would be trivial beside the bond we already share. He is friend and fellow scientist, not that lesser thing, a lover.*

She looked into Catherine's relieved face, and was ashamed.

"His Majesty has made a request of me," she said stiffly, "and though I feel it is not my place to speak of this, I must obey any of the king's wishes as if they were decrees from on high." She might as well set the precedent for Catherine to follow.

Zabby came on the heels of the Lord Chancellor, who had also been given the unpleasant task of trying to persuade the queen. Catherine lay in bed, exhausted from another outpouring of rage and tears, and she didn't have the strength left to fight even Zabby's gentle words. Perhaps the fact that they came directly from a woman, one as alien in her own way to court as Catherine was, helped. The Chancellor could not understand a woman's heart, and any sympathy they might have had was further diluted by a translator.

"In my way, Your Majesty, I believe I know your husband better than you. I nursed him, I heard the delirious ravings of his inmost heart. I sat by his side day in, day out. We were as intimate as . . ." The queen bristled. "As master and servant. You know there's no one who knows a person so well as his meanest servant. I emptied his privy pot, Your Majesty. No need to be jealous of that, I promise you!"

To Zabby's relief, Catherine laughed.

"This I know above all things: the king's defining character is loyalty to those who have used him well. He never forgets a kindness, however slight. It would be a sin beyond forgiveness to let someone who has helped him, unselfishly, come to any harm. Do you know, there's an old pig farmer's widow who gave him an apple tart when he was fleeing Cromwell's armies. She didn't know who he was. He hadn't eaten in two days. She has a pension of three hundred pounds a year now. To you, to me, Lady Castlemaine is a strumpet. To the king, she is a woman of whom he took advantage, estranged from her husband, ruined. If he rewards the pig farmer's widow, would you have him cast out a lady he has wronged?"

"Let him pension her, then. I wouldn't have the pigman's widow in my bedroom, and I won't have her!"

"A pigman's widow isn't a lady," Zabby said gently. "The Countess of Castlemaine is cousin to the Duke of Buckingham, and wife of one of the king's staunchest supporters while in exile."

"I don't care who the harlot is related to!" Catherine said, her voice threatening more hysteria. "I am the queen. I won't be treated so."

Zabby changed tactics. "There is one unassailable argument, Your Majesty. He is our king. King by divine right."

Catherine bit her lower lip with her protruding tooth.

"His authority was taken from him by robbery and murder, for fifteen years. Do you know how it feels to him now, to see someone defy that authority, someone who should support him above all others? You took a vow too, Your Majesty."

That bolt struck to Catherine's heart, and Zabby pressed home. "He loves you deeply. Do as he asks."

"He does not love me," Catherine insisted. "He cannot love me if he . . ."

Zabby almost wished the queen would hold her ground. Perhaps she would win, in the end, and Charles would give up Castlemaine and his other more casual mistresses. *If I can't have him* . . . but she had promised Charles, and she too believed in loyalty. She clenched her fist unseen against her skirts, then pulled something from her pocket.

"He does love you, Your Majesty. He gave me this to give you." She fumbled for some convincing falderal as she handed Catherine her precious seashell. "He said that like the shell, you are a natural miracle, a small, fragile object of perfection." She saw the queen's eyes moisten. "He said your . . . soul . . . was like the whorls of the shell." Zabby didn't know what that was supposed to mean, but the queen seemed to like it. "And the creamy whiteness at the lip reminded him of your . . . bosom." They both blushed at this. "He thought you'd appreciate a curiosity more than a jewel," she concluded. When she parroted the king's words she had to dig her nails into her palms so physical pain could beat back the pain in her heart.

Catherine clutched the delicate shell to a breast that heaved with grateful sobs. She longed for a reason to forgive her husband.

I give up his gift, Zabby thought, *and I give up all those childish thoughts of loving him. He belongs to the queen.*

It was a gradual but inexorable thawing. Charles was kind enough to keep Lady Castlemaine out of sight for a few days, and she didn't immediately assume her new duties as lady of the bedchamber. Then, one night, the two women sat on opposite sides of the hall during a court masque, and Catherine didn't have a fit. A few days later Castlemaine drifted nonchalantly into the queen's apartments to seek out her aunt, Lady Suffolk, though she left in a hurry. Before long the king danced openly with his mistress in full sight of Catherine, and the queen merely chatted with her attendants and pretended not to notice.

"Mort dieu," Eliza said one morning while the queen was dressing. (All the fashionable Londoners freely interlarded their conversation with bad French, though they affected to despise French citizens themselves.) "Don't wear that drab black again, Your Majesty. It's as good as sackcloth. Here, why not try this blue? It will brighten your complexion to a nicety." She pulled a lustrous azure confection from the clothes press.

All three girls learned a certain freedom with the young queen in those first few weeks. Because she only understood a fraction of what Eliza and Beth said to her, they grew accustomed to saying whatever they liked. It was a habit that stuck as Catherine's English improved, and she never objected.

Catherine eyed the garment suspiciously but finally put it on. It took only one glance in the mirror, to the accompanying chorus of *ahh*s from all the maids of honor, to make her give up her farthingales forever. When Charles saw her he kissed her before all the court. It was scarcely acceptable to kiss your mistress in public; no one kissed his wife.

That night Zabby dried silent tears on the doomed silken boatmen that had wrapped the seashell, and fell asleep with the scarf twisted so tightly about her hand that her fingers were numb all the next morning.

Chapter 7

THE FORBIDDEN MAN

THE HONEYMOON WAS OVER.

Like a great colony of ants, the court gathered up its effects and on August 23 made the ponderous move from Hampton Court to Whitehall Palace. Catherine's sumptuous bridal bed was left behind. It had not done its sole duty, nor yet had the queen. The three Elizabeths had charge of handing the queen's underthings on to the washerwoman, and knew, as Eliza put it, that Monsieur le Cardinal still visited the queen monthly. Lady Castlemaine laughingly told all who would listen that Charles had not yet mustered up the courage to bed the sallow bat — or had not found her scrubbed clean enough — and boldly hinted that her own sons might one day sit on the throne.

After that spontaneous public kiss, Charles and Catherine subsided to mere civility. He was polite to her before an audience, and regularly performed his marital duties. (The girls soon learned from the more sophisticated ladies to spot the telltale signs of lovemaking as the sheets were daily whisked away. Though they had no desire to probe, that knowledge, once gleaned, was inescapable, and they noted their queen's nocturnal activities as casually as they might notice she left a capon wing uneaten or had a rent in a stocking.)

"Poor Catherine," Beth said as they assembled their own clothing and trinkets for the short jaunt to Whitehall. "She doesn't speak of it, but I know she's terribly distressed not to be with child yet."

"Our Friesian mare was covered for three years before she foaled, but then she dropped one every spring thereafter," Zabby said. "The queen's been trying only for three months. Why is everyone in a pother already?"

"Don't you know?" Eliza asked. "If there's not a Protestant son of Charles, the Catholic brother takes the throne. James isn't a popular man. All the world knows he's Catholic, however he dissembles. If she doesn't give Charles a son, the succession may not stand. We'll have another civil war."

"She would be patient, for herself," Beth said, folding the whatnots she'd acquired since becoming a maid of honor: dogskin gloves and ribbons and handkerchiefs, gifts from the queen or things lent by Eliza that she later swore she couldn't stomach and Beth might as well keep. "But now that she can understand English a mite better she hears the gossip. Oh, the cruel things!

Lady Castlemaine said in her hearing that a barren woman is really a witch who eats her own children inside her womb. Don't they care how they hurt her?"

"No," Eliza said bluntly. "Not so long as they think she can't hurt *them*. And she can't, until Charles elevates her to her proper place, or she seizes it for herself. She's hardly a queen yet."

"She would never hurt anyone," Beth said.

"Even Castlemaine?" Eliza asked.

"I think she feels sorry for her."

"Trust the papists to send us a saint. I'd like to slit Castlemaine's nose. Don't look so shocked, Beth! You should hear what she says of you, and your mother. Prue told me she told Lady Shrewsbury . . . No, don't get snively, pet. Your revenge is being a thousand times more lovely than Castlemaine, the decayed hag. I'm surprised she hasn't tried to pimp you to Charles yet. They do say she plays at flats."

Neither girl understood this.

"Dallies with the maidens. Dances in the figgery of Lesbos. Strictly on an amateur level, of course. Then she throws her tidbits to Charles to whet his appetite for the main course—her! What dish would you say she is, Zabby? Pickled sturgeon? I warrant she'll proposition you soon, too."

"No, she hates me too much for that," Zabby said.

A few days before, when Zabby was leaving the elaboratory after having been closeted with Charles an hour or more, Lady Castlemaine waylaid her outside the door. Before Zabby could stop her, she threw up Zabby's skirts and gave a mighty sniff. "Nothing!" She glared down at her pale competitor, eyes flashing, as Zabby furiously adjusted her clothes. "What do you do for him in there all these hours, eh? Something too filthy for me, I warrant, and that must be a trick indeed. Have a care, fish-eyes. You think you serve the queen, but all England knows who the true queen is. I bore his son. I have his ear. He's not yours, nor yet that preposterous short-legged Portuguese cow's. The king is mine, and I rule beside him. He may swive wherever he pleases. I know men's ways, which your silly queen does not, the jealous trull. Let him sample a bit of coney when he hungers. He'll always return to my arms, and my legs, and my . . ."

At this point Zabby had walked off. "Don't cross me, miss!" Castlemaine hissed behind her.

They were to proceed by barge from Hampton Court to Whitehall. Charles loved boats, and though he preferred a swift, sleek yacht on the channel, he wouldn't turn up his nose at a stately barge ride along the sluggish Thames. It allowed the court to show a great deal of pomp, to be fully on display, without being within touching distance of the populace. "Support me, but not with thine own dirty hands" was the credo of most of the nobles, and though a few rakes enjoyed slumming, most had nothing but contempt for anyone below a baron. Still, they all thrived on admiration, and Charles knew the most important role for a king is symbolic. The people love a figurehead on parade.

Today they got their monarchs twice over, the false and the true. First came a grand pageant, two gilded barges with enameled swan wings, each bearing a royal tableau. On one, the king's champion sat enthroned, in a paste crown with a mock orb and scepter, an overblown caricature of kingliness, with purple wool robes and tufts of fleece dipped in ink, making, from a distance, a convincing show of royal velvet and ermine. Around him stood faux courtiers in exaggeratedly heroic poses. At the four corners were men holding symbols of Charles's reign — a brandished sword for military might, an oversize sextant for overseas trade, a pair of scales for justice (properly ironic, for they tilted crazily with each oar stroke, and never balanced). At the last corner stood a seasick man — the symbol of commerce — tossing coins into the crowd. So great was his misery that hardly any money made it to shore. The scavenging mudlarks — children who lived by salvaging the scraps of coal and rope that fell into the Thames — would reap the benefits come low tide.

The queen had her own proxy. Perched on a filigreed throne was a lady more likely than the true queen to please the populace with her looks, though at least they chose a girl with dark hair. She was the daughter of one of the king's privateers, those quasi pirates with a royal charter to pillage England's enemies on the high seas, to burn and rape and rob, so long as they turned over a percentage of their plunder to the Crown.

The maids of honor watched the panoply from an upper window — it would be another hour at least before the real queen progressed, with a fraction of the fanfare.

"They do say he'll bed the mock queen tonight," said Simona Cary, a luscious brunette who had so far managed to safeguard her reputation by sacrificing that of others.

Winifred Wells made an unladylike noise. She was said to have the carriage of a goddess and the countenance of a drowsy sheep; without possessing beauty, she held herself as if she did, and thus convinced everyone but females near her own age. She made it no secret that Charles had summoned her several times since his marriage. Like many ladies of the court, she did not believe that a bout with the king would sully her name.

"What do you say to that, Zabby?" Simona persisted. "Do you mind sharing his affections? Or if not his affections, at least his pillicock."

"Here, Simona, you have a bow coming loose in the back," Beth said, and jabbed the unsuspecting girl with a pin as she pretended to adjust it.

"We all serve the king," Eliza said blandly as Simona, squealing, whirled to look for blood and finally ran away to make herself perfect before being on display.

Winifred leaned her elbows on the sill and watched the mock king float slowly away to roaring cheers. "My father was loyal to the first Charles, and did his best to die for this one in the war." She shrugged. "To deny him anything would be treason." She smiled at Zabby, no more jealous than a soldier is of another soldier when fighting for his king. She raised her large body rather ponderously and nodded farewell, leaving the three Elizabeths together.

"I didn't know you had it in you, Beth!" Eliza said. "Serves that cat Simona right. Hope you got her kidney."

"I should never have done that," Beth said, hanging her head.

"Yes, you should. We swore an oath. D'you see how Simona and Anne squabble all the time, concoct little bedevilments for each other? Even the dressers, Lady Mary and that Scroope, do nothing but foul each other's name. And none cares a farthing for the queen. We three, we stand by each other, and we stand by Catherine. That way we'll all get what we're here for. By the bye, Beth, any rich young fops catch your eye today?"

Beth blushed. She was always talking about falling in love, though she never so much as raised her gray eyes to any of the admiring gallants. Love, she firmly believed, was not a quest — it was an epiphany. She had no desire to flirt and lure, because she was certain, with all her heart, that there was, somewhere, the man she was destined for. She would not mock love by playing at it with fops, batting her eyes and letting them touch her hand. When true love found her, there would be no need for such rituals of courtship.

"Lord Halifax tried to speak with me last night."

"And?" Eliza asked excitedly. "He's prime prey. How did you answer him?"

"I didn't."

"Not a syllable? Darling, you have to talk to them to make them propose, even if all you say is *yes* before they ask. Why are you so pitifully shy, with all the charms you have to offer?"

"My mother doesn't like me to be pert," Beth answered, avoiding their eyes. "She . . . she's always watching."

Beth trembled, but Eliza didn't notice. "Now, me, I couldn't catch a man save I lured him on with a trail of guineas laid behind me, then snatched him in my snare. But you — why, with that face you could have any man you chose!"

"Not in marriage," Beth said miserably. "For a night, for a month, but not for good. Not without money."

"Poor child," Eliza said, taking her in her arms. "It's a thousand pities *we* can't marry, eh? You need a fortune; I need a grand title. Tell you what: when I find a proper doddering old impoverished duke for myself, I'll stipulate in the contract that you come with me."

"You're an angel, Eliza," Beth said, dabbing her tears. "But kind as you are, I know you'd never take my mother too."

"Ah . . . no. Not even in play. I'm sorry."

"I know how everyone feels about her. Sometimes I hate her. She's such a bitter, cruel, heartless thing now. But she was soft and good once. I remember. My father made her what she is. For so many years, she's struggled to keep us alive, to keep us on the fringes of respectability. Whatever else I do, I must take care of her. I'll marry whomever I can, so long as he'll give her a good home. But I know no one will take me, with her." She gave a sardonic smile. "Even you. Besides, I couldn't let you support me, with or without Mother."

"What good is money if you can't spend it on whom you like?" Eliza said. "But it's not really mine, though I spend freely enough. I'll see none of it if I don't marry with my father's blessing. Precious little, anyway — two hundred pounds a year in my own control, left me independently by an aunt. God's mercy! I spend that much on gloves in a month! Come, let us join the barges. You can tell us your philosophies of panoply, Zabby, and you, Beth, can give us the gossip. For so chaste a maid, you're certainly well versed in scandal."

"I've been watching it for years," Beth said.

"And I'll compose couplets on them all, and turn their sins to song." Eliza took her friends' arms, and they made a formidable fluttering phalanx as they marched through the palace to the waterfront.

Like actors in the wings, they waited out of sight for their cue, then gathered up their skirts to trip down the freshly scrubbed jetty and step onto the royal barge.

Beth looked better than she had in the years when her mother had her dressed like a freshly slaughtered kid for the marriage market. Gone were the garish paint, the false high color, the breasts hoisted to their most globular protuberance. Her face was its own clean white and pink, with a single crescent-shaped black patch perched piquantly high on her cheek. Upon entering her service, Catherine had promptly ordered Beth's shoddily provocative gowns burned (Beth actually smuggled them out to her mother, who sold them to secondhand dealers for two months' rent) and had a half-dozen new ones made up for her, simple and luxurious and lovely. Beth, in her weak way, had tried to refuse, but in truth she was so happy to be rid of her harlot's costumes that she accepted the charity.

That day she wore a draped and tucked gown in sprightly apple green and cream, the low-set sleeves gathered four times in alternating colors to her mid forearm. Beth was hardly aware of her own appearance — she was too happy to see her queen riding in triumph with the king at her side. In public, he treated her as if he were very much in love. Only those close by would notice the pained anxiety in Catherine's face, her pathetic eagerness to please, her knowledge that she wasn't enough for him.

"What a fresh little bud you are," Catherine said to Beth as she passed before her attendants.

Flustered by the praise, Beth stumbled and caught herself just before her knee touched the ground. A collective gasp rose from the crowd, followed by a myriad-breathed sigh of relief when she recovered. Beth looked up and saw a thousand eyes on her.

She'd never been bashful in crowds before. On the contrary, they had always been her best protection, for who, she thought, would ever notice her when there was anyone else to look at? It was only in intimate interviews that she quailed.

Suddenly, she knew what it was to be singled out. It didn't matter that male voices now praised her well-turned ankle (exposed briefly in the mishap) or asked who the pretty little jilt in green might be. The mere fact that she was noticed, even positively, by so many people, oppressed her so that she trembled. Zabby had to take her hand and help her aboard, where she crouched at the queen's feet, shaking, afraid to look up.

Mother will be out there, somewhere, watching, Beth thought. *She'll think I'm being wanton, and beat me.*

The only bad part about returning to Whitehall was that her mother would be there too. Out of their minuscule income she had taken lodgings nearby, and as a countess she had right of entry nearly everywhere in the palace — except the queen's own chambers. At Hampton Court, Beth had been left to her own devices, for her mother couldn't afford the hackney ride, but once they returned to Whitehall she would resume her Janus-faced persecution, pushing Beth at men while ferociously guarding her virginity, so that rather than risk her formidable wrath, Beth (and the men too) chose to do nothing at all.

She felt the rocking, heard the dip and splash of oars as they got under way, but still wouldn't look up. *She's there . . . but he could be too,* she thought. *What if this is my chance? What if I miss him?*

The more her mother schemed to concoct a marriage for her, the more Beth's dreams were filled with Harry Ransley, the boy grown, a shadowy figure with laughing eyes, strong enough to lend her his strength. When she slept, he took her away from her mother to a remote castle. When she daydreamed, and guilt invaded her happy fancy, he took her mother too, and the woman spent her declining years embroidering before a fireplace, peaceful and content.

Beth had never seen his grown-up face, even in her dreams — not fully. But she knew he existed, as she knew heaven existed, through faith. He must exist, or what point would there be to living? Someday he would find her, then all would be well, forever.

"S'wounds!" Eliza said. "I never knew there were so many boats in all England. Look at those warships moored there, bound in by wherries and skiffs. If you had your wits about you, Beth, you'd have made your fortune by telling the Dutch to attack today. Half the fleet's anchored here on display, trapped till this lot clears out." She shielded her eyes as the sun broke between light, fitful clouds. "Lord, what a glare! What is it?"

"Tinsel and brass leaf and mirrors," Zabby said, "handed out to everyone with a rowboat. Charles spent five hundred pounds to make it look like Parliament spent half a million. They wouldn't allocate the funds he needed, so we concocted a scheme ourselves." How blissful it had been, poring over the plans together in his elaboratory. "From shore, it looks like every boat and barge is decorated with gold and silver, but really only the royal ones are."

"Why the deception?" Eliza asked.

"The people don't know what they need a king for," she said, echoing what Charles had explained to her during their procession plans. "He's the voice against the mob, and even when the people think they *are* the mob, they need protection from their worse selves. But they don't know that. What they think they need, even if they can't put it into words, is a glittering show. Like the Roman circuses. They kept the public quiet for generations. The king's like an actor: if he doesn't give them a spectacle, they'll hiss him off the stage."

"You make the public sound mighty shallow," Eliza said.

Zabby shrugged. "They are."

"And is all the public one person?"

"In all ways that matter." She looked at Charles, head held high, smiling at grocers' wives waving their handkerchiefs and tossing roses into the Thames. He looked so sure of himself, but she knew how he feared the crowd. No, not feared. Hated. They had allowed his father to be killed. They might love him now, but to him they were traitors to a man, groveling curs that might turn to bite their master's hand.

Their progress was agonizingly slow. No water could be seen between the boats. Oars snarled and hulls ground together. Once a daring thief snatched a watch on one bank, then hopped from boat to boat across the river and disappeared on the far bank. Another man claimed a reluctant bride in a similar fashion — she said she wouldn't have him until he walked across the Thames dryshod, and so lost her liberty that day. Many boats carried musicians, but there was no concord, and a dozen clashing melodies skipped across the water.

"There's that daggle-tailed slut Castlemaine," Eliza said, boldly gesturing to a raised walkway attached to the palace. "And isn't that her husband nearby, poor Palmer? Look, he doffs his hat to her, pleasant as you please, then turns as if they are strangers. Ah, well, he can wear a pair of cuckold's horns as well as any other man in England. Your Charles should make him a duke for his tolerance."

She hardly made an effort to keep her voice low. Her father had recently paid for a new warship, the *Catherine*. Her place was secure.

"I knew she had a scheme when she didn't press to be on the royal barge. Look at her up there at the corner, with her paps almost out and her hair tossing in the wind. Here, she'd be lost in the rest of us. There, she looks like a queen herself, waiting to meet her king on the battlements. She holds their son, too. Oh! She blew Charles a kiss, the hussy. What's that, now?"

There was some commotion below. Spectators had climbed up a piece of scaffolding erected to carry banners, and it collapsed under their weight. There was a cry that a child was hurt, and suddenly Lady Castlemaine was running down the stairs, her scarlet and gold skirt lifted above her knees and puffing like a mushroom with the speed of her descent. In a moment she was among the rabble and had the child—a little boy, grubby, as little boys of all classes generally are—half on her lap as she felt him for any hurt and, finding none, ruffled his hair and tied a crimson ribbon from her curls around his collar as a keepsake. The crowd roared its approval. No other great lady had even deigned to notice the near tragedy of the lower order. For a moment at least, she was their darling.

"It was staged," Eliza said in wonder, a little awed at Castlemaine's cleverness. "It had to be."

"I don't know," Zabby said. "Perhaps she's not as bad as we think. Or perhaps her sins are limited to lust and greed. Even Caligula was kind to animals and children."

In any event, the crowd forgot the queen and cheered the royal mistress. Every eye was on Castlemaine, and she put on a pretty show of nonchalance as she arranged herself on the stairway, isolated from the crowd and on full display.

"Now, who's that handsome devil come to talk with my lady

Castlemaine?" Eliza nudged Beth, who had yet to look up from her hands curled in her lap. "You know everyone at court. Who's that fellow she's throwing her charms at?"

Beth reluctantly looked up, and saw him. *Him!* It must be, for why else would he, a stranger, look so familiar, if he had not been in her dreams? When she looked on his face she felt like a child again, before the troubles came. Who could make her feel like that but the one she had been waiting for? As if on cue, like trumpeting angels, the great cannons on the far side of Whitehall Bridge went off with earth-shaking booms, proclaiming her love to the world.

Castlemaine and the man were just above her now, as the royal barge struck the jetty with a gentle thud. He wore high riding boots and spurs, and a low-crowned cavalier hat with a dipping white plume, and his golden periwig was a bit disheveled, as if he had just come from a hard ride. His sun-browned, youthful face was marked with mirth, crinkling eyes and curling smile lines, but even at this distance Beth could see two deep furrows between his eyebrows, as if some weighty concern never quite left him, even when he was talking to the most desirable woman in the kingdom.

"Well, who is he?" Eliza asked again, but Beth didn't hear her.

Look at me, she willed. *Meet my eyes only for an instant. It will be enough. I will die content.*

Then he did look, and she knew it would never be enough.

His eyes didn't even flicker over the other women in the golden barge. There was no evaluation, no choice, no comparison. He did not pick her out of the other beauties in the boat — he picked her out of all the world, instantly, unequivocally. His eyes settled on hers like a striking goshawk, heavy and fatal, sinking talons into her heart that would never loosen their hold.

"Are ye having a fit? Who is he?"

"I don't know," Beth said, but she did. "My true love."

Eliza thought it a good joke and turned to tell Zabby. Just then, Castlemaine noticed that a man she'd given her full attention wasn't returning the favor in kind, and a scowl marred the perfection of her face as she sought out her competition. Her relief when she saw Beth below was evident. *Oh, that pretty chit!* her now relaxed features clearly said. *And here I thought it might be real competition!*

Beth felt the full weight of her inexperience and poverty crash down on her, and looked away. *If he can interest Lady Castlemaine, what would he want with me?*

She couldn't help it — she looked up at him again. Castlemaine had commanded his attention, laughing and holding up a hand to shield herself from the rising wind. Her hair was dressed à la negligence, with long lovelocks trailing down her breast. Now it whipped around her face as if she was tossing her head in passion, and though it gave her a wild, barbaric beauty, in a moment she would simply look bedraggled. She appeared to make a request, and the man swept off his hat with an accompanying bow, and handed it over to Lady Castlemaine.

With that gesture, Beth knew him. At once she was back on the Enfield estate in its heyday, a half-grown girl braving the gardener's wrath to pluck new-blown rose blossoms from the avenue of thorny shrubs. It was her last summer of childhood, before propriety forced her into long skirts and poverty into first rags, then tart's clothes. The Ransley sisters had been to call, with their brother, too big for games, tagging along. He'd teased his sisters without mercy, but when Beth got her tumbling hair caught in rose briars, he doffed his own hat and tucked her silky locks up underneath it. They walked together that afternoon, rode together the next day . . . and by the following week Harry Ransley's father had ruined both their families. She hadn't known him at first, so much older, his brown hair beneath the golden periwig, but it could be no other. Here was her dream of love made flesh at last — a dream that was also a nightmare, because of all the men in the world, Harry Ransley was the one forbidden to her.

Lady Castlemaine took the proffered hat, and with a little pretext of embarrassment, she settled it over her deep auburn waves and cocked the brim to a raffish angle, turning slightly to make sure the staring throngs got the full effect. They responded with hoots and whistles, tossing flowers meant for the queen at Castlemaine's feet. Within a week, every woman of fashion and half the whores would be wearing men's hats.

Harry did not look at Beth again.

The people have forgotten Catherine, Beth thought miserably, *and Harry has forgotten me. I was wrong to let myself think Harry was the paladin who would rescue me. He's my family's enemy — I could never marry him. I must take whoever will have me, and then let him desert me and ruin me, as Father did Mother.*

She couldn't help herself—she glanced quickly up at the stair-way, but Harry was gone. She made herself forget him, as he had no doubt already forgotten her.

She scrambled out of the barge, nearly upsetting Simona, who snarled at her before recalling she was on display. While making herself useful to the queen, Beth did her best to disappear.

Chapter 8

THE RAPE OF LOVE

THAT EVENING there was a dance in the Banqueting House. Charles and Catherine sat on chairs slightly less grand than thrones at one end, while the court displayed itself before them in stately, intricate movements that were more like elaborate strolls than dances. The three Elizabeths stood in attendance on the queen, though Winifred danced with Buckingham, and Simona, looking smug, with teenage James Crofts, the king's bastard by the deceased Lucy Walter.

Beth searched the room eagerly, but he wasn't there. At least her mother wasn't there either. That was some small relief. She could look around without fear of being accused of inviting liberties.

She felt like she was in a pagan temple, for the high, open room was lined with classical columns and the ceiling, by Rubens, featured fleshy naked cherubs and lush, bare-breasted women (though she'd been told it was really an allegory of Charles I's own birth). It was windowed all around, and in daytime light poured in, but now it was lit only by low-hanging three-tiered chandeliers. A pair of lads with saucers affixed to rods dodged among the dancers, to catch stray wax before it dripped.

There was a gallery around the second floor where those not quite important enough to attend the fete but moneyed enough to be clean and presentable and not offend noble eyes and noses could mill about and observe their betters, and tell all their friends they too had been to the royal celebration. The separation was emphatic — no stairs led from the gallery to the interior hall.

Absently, Beth enumerated those strolling above. There was Mr. Pepys and his wife, another Elizabeth. He did something with the navy, she knew, and though he was reputed to be a man of parts, learned in a wide array of fields, he looked chronically ill at ease and slightly artificial, like a monkey carefully aping the manner of a man. He had an eye like Zabby, always questing and analyzing, though everything he saw seemed to confine rather than expand him, squeeze him more snugly into some ideal mold of his own imagining. Then there was Verney, whose son had made such a disastrous marriage to a madwoman. Idling among them was Lupa, a notorious courtesan, and a few other harlots of the highest order, plying their trade or angling for bigger fish below.

She knew him at once this time, for he looked like the gallant boy she remembered. The gold periwig was gone and he was even more handsome in his own short-cropped chestnut hair. In place of puffed breeches he wore a suit of sober black, the sort that was just coming into fashion, with coat and vest falling to the knee, and closed, tight breeches. But she would know him if he were covered in smallpox or clad in fur. Seeing him was like a promise kept, and though she knew it was not possible, she felt that old childish love creeping back, tempered now by the bitter knowledge that it would never be, and was thus somehow all the more precious.

Love — she would call it love, for it could hurt none but her — gave her courage. She stared her fill at Harry, and at last he found her too and smiled a slow, creeping grin. He made a subtle gesture no one else in the Banqueting House could have noticed, but she interpreted it right away. *Slip out and meet me,* he said. Before she could respond (or even decide if she should), he darted out of sight.

Heart thudding in her chest like echoes of cannon, Beth looked around for her mother. She didn't bother to search for her face. It was easier to look for any gap in the crowd, any revolted clearing that would indicate the Countess of Enfield stood at the center. But no, all she saw was merriment and dancing, gossip and flirting and backbiting.

I dare not go to him, she said to herself, even as she told Catherine, "You look chilled, Your Majesty. Allow me to fetch you a wrap." She was gone on little green slippers before Catherine could protest that she was actually quite warm.

Gasping at her own temerity, she ran until she was alone, then leaned against the cool, rough wall, plaster painted with a solution of cobalt and crushed glass.

She did not let herself think of what her mother would do if she found her with Harry Ransley. She'd likely murder the man on the spot. But what if he had made amends for his father's perfidy? What if he'd grown rich?

She remembered the touch of Harry's fingers on her cheek those many years ago, gentle as the flutter of moth wings as he tucked up her hair. She felt dizzy, confused, intoxicated.

I won't search for him, she decided. *I'll just stay here.* With all the excitement inside, the hallway was deserted, but the Banqueting House had a straightforward, simple layout, and she'd be easy to find, if he was looking for her.

And if he finds me, I'll speak with him. But I certainly won't allow him any liberties.

Thinking of those liberties, she closed her eyes and let her bright brown hair rest against the wall. She had little practical idea what lay beyond kissing, but knew it must be something that transcended Eliza's bawdy jests and the courtiers' mysterious whispered innuendos. While imagining a mystical (and highly inaccurate) union, bare knuckles slipped under her gloved palm and lifted her hand to something insistent but yielding, warm even through the kidskin. She opened her eyes to find him kissing her hand, passion disguised as chivalry.

"Do you know me?" Harry asked her.

She couldn't bear to pull her hand away, yet she knew that if she confessed she recognized him, family honor would compel her to slap him, or scream, or faint. So she said breathlessly, "I don't know you, sir."

"Indeed? But I've known you all my life."

"All my life . . ." she echoed.

"You've grown, little Beth, but you still smell of late-summer roses. Do you know me now?"

If she said yes the dream would end. She shook her head.

"Swear you will not hate me when you know," he said.

"I do not want to know!" she pleaded in desperation.

He smiled. "Then I will tell you everything but the one fact that will damn me. I have come for your hand, Beth. I have no fortune, but when I do — and I will, one day soon — even if you should hate me, a part of what I have will be yours. And if you should love me, tolerate me, even, my hand will join my gold."

His lips brushed the curve of her cheek. She felt like a mouse in a vacuum chamber, one of Zabby's experiments.

"You can't," she protested weakly.

"Yet I did."

"You mustn't."

"I never will again until you ask me."

"Please!" But she didn't know what she begged of him. Her body felt liquid.

"I found I had to take that liberty, for when you know who I am you will likely claw my eyes out." He chuckled softly, and those eyes, amused and sincere, crinkled. "Ah, out with it, you coward! It was easy when I thought you might have grown up plain." He sighed, smiled, and said, "I am the son of the man who ruined your father. I am Harry Ransley."

The Earl of Enfield, Beth's father, had been a sober aristocrat, pleasant to his small family, taking an interest in his cows and mangelwurzels, until Lord Ransley crossed his path. Beth, a child when her father began the trek down the road to perdition, wasn't sure how it happened. Perhaps Ransley took him to his first whorehouse, or taught him to palm a card. Ere long, Lord Enfield owed Ransley a considerable sum, and had to sell timber lands to pay it off, but even money failed to sour the relationship, and they pursued their pleasures together, as merry a pair of disreputable rakes as could be found in Cromwell's England.

After a while, though, the restrictions of the Puritan land began to pall, and the two men scraped together what money they could and went to the stews and whorehouses of Europe. They pretended to serve the king in exile. *Send money,* they would write to their families at home. *Sell the lower acreage,* Enfield scrawled in a drunken hand, *and send the proceeds to* . . . wherever they were at the moment. The Hague, Paris, Lisbon, Beth never knew from one month to the next. Then the house was sold from under Beth and her mother. Just before they were forced out, they received word that Lord Enfield had died from a combination of pox and ague and an unforgiving liver. They never knew what had become of the money paid for their estate. Not long after, Ransley died in a duel, or a brawl, but in any event with a sword in his tripes.

Those two men, Father and Ransley, had been the chthonic gods and devils of the Countess of Enfield's personal religion, the hatred of masculinity.

"No!" she cried. "I will not let you be him!" Her eyes grew luminous.

"I am not him. He is my father. I am me, only me. Hush, hush!"

She was weeping with little gasping sobs. "He ruined us too, sweeting. My mother, a lady, took in embroidery to keep meat on the table. I have four sisters with no dowry. We live in the game-keeper's cottage while our erstwhile tenants tip their caps to the privateer who rents our manor for a pittance. I hate his memory too. But I mean to make amends."

"Oh, Harry," she cried, "do you really think I wouldn't know you out of all the world? Of course I knew you, the moment I saw you. I only pretended...I thought if I could have these few minutes with you, before I was forced to hate you, it might be enough."

"You do not hate me," he said gently.

"I thought of you for so long, after we were forced from our house. I imagined there might be some mistake, that our fortunes would be restored and our families reconciled, and you would come to the rose garden once more. No, I do not hate you. I'm afraid, if you stay but a moment longer, I will love you. But it cannot be. You, of all people! My mother curses your name daily. Oh, why did you come only to show me what I cannot have?"

Harry caught up her hands. "I cannot tell you how, but I will win my fortune and yours. For years I have thought of you, spoken your name in my heart. My mother and sisters, too. That we be cursed with such a father is bad enough, but that his poison should seep into your family...If you plunged a dagger into my heart, little Beth, I would not blame you. You have, though; I feel the stiletto's prick. Can I love you already? Madness!"

"It couldn't be love," Beth murmured.

"Oh, no," Harry said, with mock seriousness. "Call it duty, obligation, honor, to the world's face." He leaned close to her. "But we know better. Or I do, and I'll teach you what I know, if you are willing."

He kissed the swell of her breast above her bodice.

"Can this be real?" she asked, him and herself.

"We are real. This is real, even if we never meet again." He stepped away from her. He groaned; she whimpered; both in physical pain. "I have bad business before me," he said. "But at the end, should I survive, your troubles, your family's and mine, will be over. Will you be here when I return? Will you wait for me?"

She nodded, and he stepped away. "It may be a year, it may be two, but I will come for you, and right the wrongs of my father."

"Don't go!" she pleaded, reaching for him, but the iridescent azure of the rough glass-studded wall caught her hair, holding her back just long enough for him to escape. *If I had touched him,* she knew, *he would have stayed*.

It was a rape of love. He came from nowhere, ravished her heart, left her trembling and broken.

At last she made her unsteady way back to the hall. In the flutter of her passing, a torch flickered and leaped, and reflected on a silver hawk's beak in the shadows.

"What ails you?" Eliza asked, but it was too sacred for Beth to speak of yet.

Beth remained in attendance on the queen until she retired, then went with her friends to the room they shared, more elegant than that at Hampton Court, with wall hangings of alternating deep green velvet and pale green silk, and delicate carved walnut furniture from France. As before, they shared a bed.

Their things had been unpacked and arranged by Hortense and Prue, and of course no one could find anything.

"Have you seen my nightcap?" Zabby asked Beth.

"She's in her own world," Eliza said when there was no answer. "And a mighty fine world it must be. Look at her face, like Saint Catherine on the wheel." The saint was the only victim to enjoy that torture device—instead of having her limbs broken, she broke the wheel with the force of her own purity. She was beheaded instead—the executioner's ax felt no similar qualms.

Zabby examined her friend's face narrowly. Something had altered her drastically, though subtly. "Has . . . has someone died?"

"Yes," Beth replied, distracted. "Oh, no, of course not, though I almost think . . . to have him and lose him, all in the same instant, it's almost like death, isn't it? Not but what I'll see him again."

Zabby checked Beth's brow for fever. Though flushed, she was cool.

"I found him—he found me!"

"Who?"

"I dare not say."

"Is she intoxicated or am I?" Eliza asked, torqueing her torso as she tried, unsuccessfully, to reach her own laces. "For I can't comprehend a word she says."

Beth, laughing and crying all at once, twitched Eliza's laces free. "You write about love in your plays, but you don't know a thing about it. I do. I know it now. I saw him, and I knew him, and he knew me. He came looking for me!" She danced around Eliza with the unwound laces in her hands, twining her tall friend like a maypole. "He says I won't see him again for the longest time, and I hardly think I can bear it, but I will. Oh, my eyes are open now!"

Indeed, the world looked different, felt different, with a new sensuality — the costly green wall hangings seemed to call out to be touched; the very air dripped like crystal honey, sweet on her tongue. She had to move, to laugh, to sing, to look boldly into every eye, because she was fully alive for the first time. She felt like a madwoman, exultant, exalted by her madness.

The door creaked open, and Beth, thinking it must be Prue with their bath water, had an inspiration. "Prue," she said without turning, fiddling with the Venetian point trembling at her cleavage, just below the burning memory of his kiss. "You know everything that passes at court. What can you tell me about . . ."

She turned, and the merry smile froze, then crumbled in the face of that red-robed gargoyle, her mother.

"It's a short, sweet step from the girl who's groped in the palace to the whore who lifts her skirts for every poxy sailor on the quayside." Her voice was so sweetly reasonable that Eliza and Zabby, whose mothers were kindly ghosts, were almost expecting their friend to receive nothing more than a fond lecture. Surely Beth had exaggerated her mother's maniacal control, her strange combination of pander and protector.

But Beth, looking terrified, backed away until her legs hit the bed, and stood poised like a hart at bay, waiting for the deerhound to close.

The Countess of Enfield hobbled closer and made a maternal clucking sound that, with the syphilitic bobbing of her head, almost made Eliza laugh aloud. *Higgledy piggledy, my red hen,* she thought, *complete with a beak.* She stifled the sound in a cough and sidled to the door to leave them to talk in peace, grabbing Zabby by the arm. Beth shot her a desperate look, but the countess said, "Begone, you pair of hoydens. This is none of your concern." They slipped away.

"Drip, drip, drip," the countess said when they were alone, punctuating each word with a rap from the light lacquered rattan cane she carried. She stroked Beth's cheek, erasing the precious invisible kiss. "You're dry now, dry and clean, but let a man have his way and it will be juices and drippings all your life. You'll leak and squirt and spurt and sop — aye, my girl, all over." She ran her fingers coquettishly over her own bodice, showing her oozing sores. "And you'll die, bit by bit."

"But, Mother," Beth whispered.

"Defy me!" the countess roared, brandishing her cane. "Defy me and die in the streets, your body eaten from within while men use whatever scraps remain. Did you even charge him? If you want to be a slut, let me pimp for you. Your virginity will fetch a fair price — if you've still got it. Or, if you'd prefer, I'll slit your throat right now, to save you dying by degrees." She slid the cane across Beth's neck, and the girl cringed but could not flee. She knew it was useless. There was no escape.

"Please," Beth begged, and knew she was pleading for aid from her unknown lover, not her mother.

"You will sit on the dish, a tasty morsel to make their foul mouths water, but you must not let them taste! Not one lick! A taste leads to a nibble, nibble to bite, bite to devouring!" She shoved Beth backwards on the bed, then grabbed her ankle when she tried to scramble away. "Look the whore, to trap them, but let one have his way without buying you outright, and I'll flay the skin off you." Spittle flew from her mouth, and she twitched in rage. "Now take your punishment for acting the harlot."

The command was not new. Beth, swallowing heavily, obediently stood and turned her back to her mother. She dragged her skirts up above her hips and bent over the high bed, exposing her creamy white thighs.

Another woman might have been mollified by such a display of filial submission, but it seemed to drive Beth's mother mad.

"There is our fortune!" she screamed, hauling back with her cane and striking the tender flesh with all her force. Beth shrieked but didn't move. A deep purple-red weal rose instantly, and the cane whistled through the air again, this time drawing a line of blood. "Some rutting man will pay a fortune for that, and you think to give it away?" She struck savagely again. "You're trying to hold on to his touch, aren't you? But you can't! You can't! Not through this!" Again and again the cane fell, until Beth's thighs were crisscrossed with bruises and blood. "It always feels lovely at first, the kisses, the caresses, but it is the pain that lasts."

A final cut, and her voice was almost loving. "Forget him, my sweet, whoever he was. He's false. Marry well, for your family, for your name. One man's like another, in the end."

She whipped out a handkerchief, much laundered but impeccably clean, and draped it over Beth's bloody thighs. "There's blood enough for a maidenhead. Perhaps that will cool the heat of your sanguine humors." She chuckled and peeked at the gore underneath. "They'll likely scar," she said blandly, "but that shan't hurt your value. If ever a man sees them before your marriage night, I'll kill you, then him, then myself. Will so much blood suffice?"

She hobbled out the door.

When the sound of her knocking cane grew muted, then hushed altogether, Beth stood painfully, as proud and erect as her slight frame would allow. "I don't care what she says. He came for me, and we're meant to be together. I will meet him again. I will!"

Blood seeped through her skirt, the first autumnal red on her bright summer green.

Chapter 9

THE DREAM MADE FLESH

PARLIAMENT was in session . . . which mattered not one jot to anyone at court. All that concerned those wits and rakes, debauchers and debauchees, was that when Parliament opened, so did the theaters.

"Eliza, I have *five* fingers, you know," the queen said as her maids of honor pulled buttercup-yellow gloves onto her hands. Beth was already smoothing the kidskin to the queen's elbows, but Eliza was struggling to shove two of Catherine's fingers into one hole.

"Pardon, Your Majesty, but flay me, how can a body know what it's about when her dream is on the verge of being made flesh?"

"Flesh?" Catherine asked. Her English, though much improved, was not up to the complexities of Eliza's rapid speech. She thought the word had something to do with the sacraments, and indeed she saw that Eliza was aglow with agitated rapture.

"The stage, Your Majesty! The passion and the pathos of life distilled into a three-hour draught, the world compressed to a jutting apron."

Catherine had no idea how the world could fit in a cooking smock, but she smiled at her maid's excitement.

"Charles is most . . . happy? . . . with the theater. He says he loves it with all his cunny."

Beth gaped, the other ladies tittered, but Eliza only shook her head.

"Your Majesty, Buckingham has done it to you again. What did he tell you that word means?"

"This," she said, putting her hand on her chest. "Boom-boom, boom-boom. The organ of love, he told me. Did I say it wrong?" She looked around innocently.

"Damned whoreson! Pray, madam, pay no further heed to the duke. Imagine if you'd said it in an audience, or to the archbishop!"

"What does it mean?"

Smirking through her anger, Eliza turned to Beth. "You tell her, sweetheart. You've a knack for putting things gently. I'll shock her back to Portugal if I tell her what a cunny's for."

Blushing, Beth leaned into the queen's black curls and whispered in her ear.

"Oh!" Catherine said, then surprised them all by remarking, "The duke was right about one thing. It is what a woman uses to love a man."

The queen had changed a good deal in the past few months, or, if not changed, adapted. She dressed exclusively in English clothes, took part, however awkwardly, in the dances and masques, and even learned to play cards, though she still thought gambling a sin. She'd come to understand that patience and grace would serve her better than a show of temper — that was Barbara's forte — and though she still wept when no one was watching, and thought God must be annoyed that her prayers were ever on the same topic, she gave a convincing show of accepting her husband's infidelities.

"I'm still not sure playgoing is a moral pastime," Catherine mused as they powdered her throat and fastened pearl drops to her lobes. "Women flaunting themselves onstage . . ."

"Troth, Your Highness," Eliza said, "a woman will flaunt herself wherever she goes, even so mean a specimen as myself. When the king your husband granted charters to the two companies, he bid them present life in its true myriad forms. You'd not have a burly fellow of forty play dainty Desdemona, would you? You'll enjoy it, madam. Come, chin up so I can pin these roses to your bodice. There now, you're ready for your audience."

"Another word I use wrong," Catherine said, shaking her head. "I thought *we* are the audience."

"You are audience and performer and director all in one. You go to watch the play, and the people go to watch you. And His Majesty, of course. Then they go home and do their best to ape their betters."

"I'm tired of being watched," Catherine said.

"Then you should have chosen a different line of work," Eliza said, not unkindly. "You are like one of your popish icons, an object of devotion."

"Ah, but holy statues can sometimes work miracles. What do I do in this world?"

Eliza shrugged her broad, square shoulders. "That's for you to decide, Your Majesty. You have the third greatest power in the land—God, the king, then you. And God rarely bothers. Now where is that Zabby?"

"Where she always is," said Catherine with a sigh. "At my husband's side."

Eliza regarded the queen archly. "There are many threats to your happiness, madam, but you and I both know our Zabby isn't one of them. Here, turn toward the gueridon so I can see to paint your lids. Aye, I know, but you've finer eyes than that slut Castlemaine, so you might as well show them off now and do penance for vanity later. No one will notice if your knees are red from praying, but give them a weary eye and they'll say for weeks how unbecoming you've become. Tch!" She held up a hand to stop what she knew the queen was about to say. "You've beauty aplenty; only learn how to use it. Perhaps if you watch the actors tonight you'll have a lesson."

Zabby slipped into the room, dressed, more or less, though with a black smudge on her nose.

"Pardon, Your Majesty," she said, sweeping low.

"Please recall you are my servant, not my husband's," Catherine said in Spanish, and Zabby did her best to look contrite. But she'd spent a glorious morning in Charles's elaboratory, examining a specimen brought by a German alchemist, a pale waxy substance that gave off its own light, burning without heat, without being consumed. Because the effect was more noticeable in the dark, they'd extinguished the lamps, shuttered the windows, and huddled together on a workbench, hunched over their Lucifer light. Zabby had watched Charles at least as much as the specimen. His anxious, harried face had been softened in the glow, his cares erased. She remembered, acutely, what it was like to watch him sleep in those days when the danger of death had passed.

Staring into that morning-star glow, side by side, was almost like staring into each other's eyes, she thought, then chided herself for being as dreamy as Beth, who these days could hardly string a coherent sentence together without trailing off into the silence of some inner fantasy. It was science, no more, Zabby told herself, then set about tying the ribbons on the queen's garters. She felt Catherine's eyes on the back of her bent head and willed her own phantasms away. The king belonged to another, and even if he hadn't, his heart was chipped into so many fragments that she'd scorn the sliver that would be hers.

The maids of honor turned possession of the queen over to the more senior ladies and bundled into one of the royal carriages. Runners and criers paced the length of the splendid train, while liveried coachmen and foppishly clad Life Guards, the king's ceremonial protective force, held their wigs against the stiffening wind. More efficient guards watched from the sidelines in sober clothes, their pistols hidden beneath their jackets, but Charles had no fear of assassination. He could always read his people, and knew there was little risk of an individual attack. He was well beloved—as a king and as a man. The danger would come not if one man turned against him, but if ten thousand turned against what he represented, and Charles, trained by his early tragedy, would surely smell mass treason in the wind.

Then too, he was known to say privately, he was safe as long as his brother lived, for no one wanted him as king. A bad heir is a monarch's best protection.

However magnificent the equipage, gilded and plumed, it was really no more than a box tied upon a wheeled frame, the only mechanical cushioning being in the slackness of the ropes — which, if it made the ride a jot more comfortable, also considerably increased the odds the two parts would separate and tip the giggling, silken cargo into the nearest sewer.

Most of the audience arrived an hour or two early, since half the fun of a play was the before-curtain roistering in the pit and the destruction of characters in the boxes. But all chatter stopped when the king and his retinue entered. There were a few *huzzahs*, a whistle or two, a bleat like a billy goat (which for some reason brought a smile to Charles's lips), and then the crowd devolved into their previous gaiety.

"How does he do it?" Zabby murmured. "How is he god and king and man, all at once? See how they love him, like he is one of them."

"You've struck upon it, Zabby," Eliza said, fanning herself languidly against the heat and press. "He's like the Greek gods of old, with all the foibles of a man. I've read a thing or two of ruttish Zeus. He had lust and anger and laughter just like a man. People like their gods accessible, and your Charles has the knack of seeming so."

"Too accessible," Zabby said.

"Jealous?"

Her pale eyes widened. Had Eliza read her secret, the one she denied even to herself? "No . . . no, certainly not. I only meant that he rides with scant guard, he touches the masses to cure their ills, he walks through St. James's Park where any ruffian could accost him. He should hold himself apart."

"He wants love," Beth said. "Desperately."

Eliza laughed, thinking Charles had that aplenty, and Zabby was sure Beth was wrong, but before they could argue, the crimson curtain rose and a distinguished silver-haired gentleman stepped out. Slim and elegant, he twirled his mustachios affectionately until the crowd hushed, then addressed the audience directly.

"Slit my gizzard, I never thought I'd see the day!" Eliza gushed as Zabby strained to catch the actor's words. "Thomas Killigrew himself! He runs the King's Company, you know. I have a folio of all his plays. I weep every time I read *Claricilla*. How can so much genius fit in such a small, neat head? You'd think his skull would positively bulge with it."

The maids of honor were seated in the royal box (mostly to fetch syllabubs, fans, or a scented *mouchoir*) two rows behind Their Majesties and Highnesses, and their view was obstructed by piled curls and feathers. The Countess of Suffolk hissed at Eliza to hold her tongue, and Eliza muttered in a stage whisper that Suffolk wouldn't know a good play if it crawled up her petticoats. She canted herself this way and that, trying to get a better view, and at last stood up, hands behind her back like a soldier at her ease.

The movement caught Killigrew's eye, and he turned to speak the last lines of the prologue directly to the royal box—and, Eliza was sure, to her.

> *"He wed her, then away to war.*
> *Will she be true or play the whore?*
> *All unguarded, bound yet free . . .*
> *The married maiden's tragedy."*

In a dreamy voice—much the same as the one Beth had been using of late—Eliza sighed and said, "If only I could have a moment with him. If only he'd read but a page of *Nunquam Satis*."

She stood through the rest of the play, like any apprentice or cocklemonger at a shilling a head in the gallery. She had found her personal deity—not a virile, unattainable monarch such as Zabby almost unwittingly, certainly unwillingly, desired, or yet a mere man such as Beth adored.

What she'd felt before was no more than an infatuation with words on paper, a lusty green-sickness for a thing she imagined but had never experienced. Now Eliza had seen her heart's desire, and she knew that she was firmly, unequivocally, passionately in love with the stage.

When the curtain closed she clutched at her heart in a true tragedienne's expression of grief. She was so distracted on the way out that the queen was forced to resort to picking up her own dropped fan.

"My pardon, Your Majesty," Eliza said, elaborately contrite, and, under the influence of the recent exhibition, bowing with exaggerated drama. "But how can a soul do her duty when she's been glamoured? I vow I'm not responsible for a thing I do in the next hour—I'm under such a spell! What did you think, Your Majesty? Was it not a marvelous spectacle?"

"I couldn't quite follow it," Catherine confessed.

"It was rather simple, Your Majesty. As soon as the lady was married, her husband was sent to war before the consummation could take place, so of course the neighboring gallant made a play for her. To guard her chastity, the maid suggested the women switch places, and then to further guard themselves they dressed as master and manservant."

"Those pretty boys were females?" Catherine asked, baffled.

"Certs, and then the gallant dressed his page as a girl to sneak him into the lady's estate, and the lady, dressed as a boy servant, and the page, dressed as a girl, seduced each other, but were such innocents neither thought anything was amiss at the grand unveiling."

"And the marriage at the end?"

"The gallant married the maid, thinking her the lady."

"The married lady?" the queen asked, almost giving up.

"The maid—acting the lady—swore it was annulled."

"And this is called a tragedy?"

"Aye, for the absent husband it is, I suppose. The clever maid gets a step up in the world, the swindling gallant gets swindled himself, and the lady finds pleasure. Best of all, she can keep the lad as a servant under her husband's nose, once he returns."

It was a new world for Catherine. She was aware that none of it was serious, that the play was only an elaborate excuse for jokes and puns and clever verse, yet it grated on her that such obscene frippery should be held up as an example.

Even now, Charles was leaning close to Barbara, no doubt whispering some assignation. He supped with his mistress nearly every night, though the maids encouraged Catherine to host her own entertainments, even inviting the hated Barbara, just to keep him home. Why was Charles free to seduce where he pleased? What would he do if she took a lover? In the play it was expected that everyone would wear horns. If plays mimed life, why shouldn't she do as Charles did?

Chapter 10

THE TRANSFIGURATION

WHERE ZABBY LOVED she denied; where Beth loved she sighed and said nothing, guarding her treasure like a gentle dragon; where Eliza loved she fretted, drove herself and her friends to distraction, and, finally, acted.

"I'm going to see Killigrew," she told Beth and Zabby as they tied their hair in curl rags one evening. (Almost without noticing, Zabby found herself falling into these little tricks of the feminine trade—though she had a shabby copy of *Alchemical Principles* on her lap as she primped.)

"I don't think your father would like that," Zabby said. "You wouldn't even tell him in your letters that you'd been to a play."

"My father's a fine old fellow, but he doesn't understand the world . . . or me. But that's neither here nor there, because I won't be going to see Killigrew."

"I thought you said . . ."

"*I* won't be going—my cousin Mr. Duncan will." She leaped out of bed and tore through a chest, and when she stood she had what looked like a dead shrew on her upper lip.

"What in the world?" Zabby asked.

"A false mustache. And look. I have breeches, a coat and waistcoat, hose and boots—everything!" She stripped off her shift and began to struggle into the unfamiliar clothes. "Ain't I a sight? Will I pass, d'you think?" She spat, awkwardly, into the fireplace, took a few swaggering steps, and finally made a leg at the ladies. "Ah, I forgot," she said, and rolled an old glove before stuffing it down her pants, where it made an impressive tumescence. "Now?"

The transformation was amazing. "Clothes do make the man," Zabby said. "I wonder, did I look like that in Barbados? I wore breeches most every day."

Eliza put on her most raffish smile, puffed out her chest, and sauntered to Zabby's side. "Ah, my sweet," she said in as deep a voice as she could manage—it sounded like a croak, and she modified it. "It takes more than pants to make the man. It takes"—she made a suggestive movement of her hips—". . . bollocks. Clapping flesh-bells. Dangling—"

"Stop!" Beth pleaded. "However did you get like this? You, growing up in the country."

"And you at court, Beth dear, how did you stay so virginal? You blush at the name, but when you see the object, no doubt you'll be hot for it, bell and clapper, eh? Oh, we've seen your mooning eyes search the crowds, but we don't ask, do we, Zabby? Our

Beth will tell us in her own good time." She tapped the side of her nose. "But we have our suspicions, we do. That dark, oldish fellow we saw your mother the countess in deep talk with? The one just come from the Moorish lands, an Earl of Something, if I mistake me not. Briar, or Bramble . . . no, Thorne. The Earl of Thorne."

"No, not him," Beth said.

"Ah ha, I've caught you out! If not him, then another. Take care: your mother was none too happy the last time you let a man ogle you." They never knew about the beating. Beth wore double petticoats and a russet dress, and refrained from sitting until the wounds closed. "This Thorne, now, he looked a handsome fellow, if a half-century old. They say the old ones are easiest to cozen, and when their sight goes they'll never see what you're up to."

Beth, eager to change the subject, said, "When are you going to meet with Killigrew?"

"Oh, any day, after the play. He's sure to be backstage."

"And how will you get there? The queen won't let you go, and you can't take a carriage without her leave."

"I'll take a hackney, then."

"What, ride in a hired hackney all alone? A lady can't do such a thing."

"She's right," Zabby agreed.

"I thought you told us you used to ride all over Barbados alone," Eliza said.

"On the land we owned, certainly, which was enough to tire a horse. But London is different. There are cutpurses and highwaymen. Simona was telling the queen the other day about a devil of a scofflaw, one Elphinstone, who robs and ravishes travelers. The roads past the gates aren't safe, and who knows but what he'll strike in London itself. A lady shouldn't be unprotected in the city."

"But I won't be a lady," Eliza said.

"It's a foolish idea," Zabby said, "but if you must go, I'll come with you."

"My protector!" Eliza said, bouncing on the bed. "Oh, I'll surely be safe with Zabby the Mighty at my side. Will you come too, Beth? How sweet you'd look as a boy — and probably just as likely to be raped, in this Gomorrah London." She beamed at the expanding adventure. "We can be a trio of fopdoodles in from Essex to gape at the town. See a play, visit the bawdy-house, eat at an ordinary, fight a duel. Oh, yes, please, let us all go!"

The foolhardy plan grew, and even Zabby became excited, though she told herself it was only an experiment to examine life from the male point of view. With the help of Hortense's visits to the Royal Exchange and Eliza's bottomless purse, they outfitted themselves with an extravagant array of clothes: petticoat breeches that looked like knee-length skirts, linen shirts heaped with Flanders point, coats pinked to show a dozen underfabrics, cascading boot-hose. They quickly abandoned Eliza's initial idea of making herself as masculine as possible with false whiskers and a rough voice, and instead impersonated the dandy of the day, vain, effeminate, affected. Since they'd put it about that they were from the country, Londoners would excuse any flubs as rural gaucherie, thinking them merely new to fashionable society, not the gender.

Zabby even managed to procure them three swords, the slim rapiers that every man with a pretention to status carried and many — even the most delicate-seeming fops — knew how to use to deadly effect.

On the day appointed for their adventure, Eliza copied out the final scene of *Nunquam Satis,* blotted it carefully, and added it to the stack of pages already waiting in a box of gilt Spanish leather. "There," she said, patting the box. "My fortune and future."

"How can you say that," Beth asked, "when you already have nearly all a person could desire? Had I a tenth, a thousandth of your fortune, I'd be content. And as for your future, you have the leisure to wait, and a fond parent who will let you choose your husband."

"Bah! Husbands! Who wants them?"

"You speak as if everyone keeps a stable full of husbands," Zabby said, adjusting the ivy-patterned "cheat" waistcoat of her costume — ornate in the front, which showed, but plain in back.

"Now, there's a thought. If I could have a seraglio of mates, perhaps they'd not pall. But no, 'twould take more than a eunuch to control them. They'd be after me en masse if I bought a costly gown or smiled too long at some young buck, myriad voices of masculine nagging. Perhaps if I had them all gelt...but then what's the good of them? No, I have no wish to marry. What I want is to write plays."

"You can do that *and* wed," Beth said.

"By the grace of my husband, perhaps, but only under his suf-frage, until such day as I vex him — then he'll take away my ink. I'm chattel to my father now. A cow in a velvet stall, true, but a cow nonetheless. I'll stay in his barn because I know how to whee-dle him, but I'll be no other man's possession."

"You mean you won't marry at all?" Beth looked at her as if she were something monstrous, an aberration of nature. To marry was all Beth wanted. No, not even that. Desire, per se, didn't enter into it. It was the natural order of things that one day, and soon, she would tuck herself under the wing of some man. She might hope he was good rather than bad, wealthy rather than poor, but he would exist, as surely as she breathed. She might have some choice in his identity — and, in fact, had firmly chosen — but not the mere fact of his being.

Even Zabby was astounded by Eliza's bold proclamation. Zabby had always assumed that someday she'd discover a conge-nial mate — that's how she thought of him — and set up a house-hold with her own collection of beakers and books, chemicals and curiosities. She always pictured him (on the rare occasions when she *did* picture him) rather like her father, or perhaps like God-mother Cavendish's husband, sweetly solemn, gently philosophical. But now, feeling the stirrings of love for the first time, she became aware of a husband's other purpose, physical comfort, tactile com-panionship, bodily joy, children, and suddenly she couldn't quite envision finding any of those things in the paternal helpmeet she assumed awaited her.

She could, however, quite clearly envision doing those things with Charles.

They were flaunting their unfamiliar vestments and laughing at Eliza's ribald merriment when the door was flung open and Queen Catherine entered, alone. For a moment the girls froze; then, after puzzling through the etiquette of being both host and servant, male and female, curtsied. But a curtsy looks a great deal better in skirts than breeks, and their knees bent outward like awkward dancers.

For a moment the queen assumed her chaste maids had invited a trio of fops to their rooms, and it was in her favor that her first thought was how to shield her charges from scandal. Her second thought, upon seeing neither hide nor curl of the girls, was that the men were robbers. And at last, after Beth giggled, she realized what she saw. Zabby looked like a beardless *kouros,* Apollo perhaps, god of light and truth, healing and prophesy. Eliza, for all her foppish attire, was so well made that she might be Ares, though her amused mouth and high color made her more like tipsy Dionysus. Pretty Beth could be none other than Ganymede, ripe for ravishing.

"A masque?" Catherine asked, and to the girls' astonishment sat down on a brocade tuffet. It was unheard of for the queen to visit the quarters of her underlings, unprecedented for her to do such a homely thing as perch on a footstool. Beth, long schooled in court etiquette, felt a compulsion to lower herself so her head would be below that of her queen, but since the only way to do so would be to lie on the ground — and that didn't seem quite right either — she refrained from doing anything. "Life is nothing but amusement here," the queen added with a sigh.

"How may we serve you, Your Majesty?" Eliza asked.

"I need . . . an ear." She had to tell someone, and she couldn't imagine telling languid Suffolk or the scheming, catty dressers or other maids of honor. These three, though, reminded her of her childhood in the convent. She might be nearly a decade older than they, but she could occasionally forget her rank and status far enough to confide in them. They'd never broken her trust.

"I had an idea," Catherine went on. "I never should have, but I saw him caress Simona's cheek and I couldn't bear seeing him pick yet another one, one I'd have to look at day in, day out. So I . . . I . . ."

"You confronted him?" Zabby asked. She wished she could do the same thing herself, but it wasn't her place.

"I told him what is good for the gander is good for the goose, and then I asked him what he would do if I took a lover."

The girls gasped. "What did he say?" Zabby asked.

"He got very angry, and said a woman may be pardoned for succumbing to a king, because it would almost be treason not to, but for a queen to be unfaithful is itself treason of the highest order. Then I asked him what he would do if I had a paramour, and he spoke of the eighth King Henry. Which king is that, do you know?"

The maids of honor exchanged glances. "The one with so many wives," Eliza said at last.

"So many?"

"Eight, I do believe. Some divorced, some beheaded."

The queen's mouth made a little O, and she touched her throat as if her slender gloved hands might preserve it from the executioner's ax.

"Do you want to take a lover?" Zabby asked in curiosity.

"No, never, but if he can cut off my head for it, why can't I do the same thing to him? It isn't right! Why should I have to see his bastards fat and laughing in their cradles, and that young bendsinister Crofts acting like a kingling himself?"

"It is the way of the world, Your Majesty. Fear not: you'll have a cradle full of baby-fat soon enough."

"No, no, or I would be quick by now!" She covered her face with her hands. "Oh, why was I born a woman?"

"To laugh at men, Your Majesty," Eliza said gently. "There's naught for it but laughter. Against war, and plague and strife, one can but be gay and spite the devil. Take comfort in the knowledge that every man is the same, and every woman full of the same complaints. Your husband wenches well and publicly, because he is king, but the farmer covets his neighbor's wife — and his ass, too, in Scotland, from all I've heard — and the inn-keeper has his hand in the serving-slattern's placket."

"It cannot be true. Other men do not use their wives so, or no woman would wed. It must be Charles's particular sin. Other men aren't always pursuing a new conquest."

"Would you like to find out?" Eliza asked, and the others shot her warning looks. "These costumes aren't for a masque. We're going on an expedition, into the foreign land known as the World of Men. Clothed in native fashion, we propose to mingle with the savage tribe and discover its secrets. Will you don like garb and join us?"

Catherine's face grew wistful, distant. "When I was a little girl in the convent, a bit younger than you, my friends and I would barter our embroidered cambric handkerchiefs to borrow the milkmaids' clothes, and slip from the mother's watchful eye. Mostly we sported in the meadows, but once there was a hiring fair nearby. My friend Anna was hired to milk goats, and a farmer kissed my sleeve and said my lips were the color of a field poppy. When our abbess found out where we'd gone, we lived on bread and water for a week. But she never knew about the kiss. I always wonder if that farmer found another goat girl to replace Anna. She took holy orders a year later. Quite a different career!"

"Why, Your Majesty, what a surprising creature you are!" Eliza said. "Then you will come?"

She gave them the smile she used when she was alone, when no one could see her protruding front tooth. "You girls are under my care. I am your duena. I must be there to see no harm comes to you. Now, shall I wear a periwig or tie my hair up under my hat?"

An hour later, with Hortense watching the corridors, three very loudly dressed dandies and one dignified gentleman in an old-fashioned high beaver hat and gold-tipped sword-stick set out for an evening on the town.

"If what you say is true, and all men are thus, then never

again will I berate my husband for the foibles of his gender," Catherine said.

"And his rank," Eliza said. "As poor men have one shabby suit of clothes, so a rich man will have the choicest raiments, and many of them. I think, Your Majesty, that you must learn to look the other way, as does your husband when your courses come. Since married you must be, then enjoy your hours together, and forget him when you're apart."

Chapter 11

THE WORLD OF MEN

WHEN THEY ARRIVED, the play was in its final act, and carriages lined the street and around the corner, waiting for their noble owners.

"Boy!" Eliza called to a ragamuffin waiting for odd jobs — a penny to hold a horse, a shilling for a more important commission, delivering a love note.

"Ar, sir?" he said, tugging his lousy hair.

"How do we get to the tiring rooms?"

"You pay your two bob six for a pit bench and go round the back when the show's done."

But they didn't care to go in the theater proper, for fear of attracting attention. The queen's disguise might not fool the king's keen eye. "And if we don't care for the pit?"

"Well, a box is four shillins . . ."

"Here, then," Eliza said, and she pressed four silver coins into his grubby hand. "Take us round back, the way the actors go in, and sit in the box yourself tomorrow."

"Oh, very good, sir! But laws, no, sir, begging your pardon, and I'd prefer pork pasties to a box seat, if 'tis all the same to you." He skipped ahead of them so fast that they thought he was trying to take their coins for nothing, then skidded to a stop at a narrow wooden door. "Through here, if you please, and mind your 'eds." He lolled against the building-side as they passed through. The queen, last in line, heard him mutter, "Curse me, what a green pack of cullies." As soon as they were inside he scarpered to Madame Ross's brothel to arrange his cut should he later manage to lure the naïve country fops to her notorious establishment.

They slipped through darkened hallways until they heard a bustle ahead. All save the leads shared a general tiring room, and those playing servants, soldiers, nuns, and assorted extras lolled and chatted and powdered their noses, waiting for the epilogue that would signal the great influx of admirers.

"I know the third act was weak," a voice said archly from across the room, "but even if you can't bear to watch it, pray, henceforth do me the courtesy to eat an orange, or fondle a doxy to pass the time. Don't pour salt in my wounds by leaving your seats early."

"My Lord Killigrew!" Eliza breathed, and promptly forgot her companions as she minced (quite forgetting to strut, masculine-fashion) to her idol. "I assure you, it is a most excellent play. Which is it? No matter, if it is one of yours, or one you had your hand in. Oh, sir, you do not know how mightily I admire you, how very deeply I respect you!"

"From desolation to exaltation in an instant. It is too much for my confused humors. Save your flattery for the actresses, lad, and out of my way. I must see if that pricklouse Walter Clun flubs the final speech yet again."

But Eliza trailed after him with such a worshipful face that one of the actresses laughed. "Your friend will find his attentions better returned if he compliments Kynaston," she said, referring to the lovely boy actor who until recently played women's roles onstage, and still played them offstage. "Killigrew prefers ladies, as much as that sour old dragon can stomach anyone."

"Or he did until your sex came to the stage," an actor said to her, lounging in no more than a dangerously short shift. "With such a glut of breasts and thighs shaking at one, I almost find them to pall myself. Almost." He winked at Catherine. "Looking for anyone in particular?" he asked.

"We're just waiting for our friend," Zabby said.

"Suit yourself," he said, "though once the rabble comes in, you'd best move aside for the paying customers. Beck Marshall lacks a keeper at the moment, and bidding gets hotter by the day."

Hoots, whistles, and applause met their ears — if Clun forgot his lines, the audience didn't notice — and almost at once the tiring room was full to a press, first with the actors and actresses, and a moment later, the half-gentlemen and lesser lords from the rowdy pit. Younger sons, students, penniless wits, and moneyed idiots poured in to pester and praise their favorite actresses, to comment on the play, to exchange gossip. Most of them crowded around a dark-haired beauty in a spectacular headdress of egret feathers.

Feeling awkward, sure they'd be exposed at any moment, Zabby, Beth, and Catherine remained clustered tight near the wall.

"He'll read it!" Eliza shouted a moment later from across the room. "He likes the story line and I recited the prologue and he says I've a rare wit and a clever turn of phrase!" The crowd gave her amused looks, but she was all oblivious. "Let us celebrate. Odam's Ordinary, or Harrison's?" She'd heard gentlemen talk about those restaurants, though she'd never eaten in one.

"You're hopelessly out of date," said a voice at their elbow, and a plump, bright-eyed fellow with a massive curled wig set slightly askew insinuated himself into their cluster. "Charles Sedley, at your service. Sir Charles, if you insist, but not if you're paying. I am hopelessly poor, today at any event, but amusing enough to earn my keep. You gentlemen are obviously new to London, and need a guide. Buckhurst!" he called over his shoulder. "Come meet my new friends, Mister Someone, Mister Someone Else, and Sir I've Already Forgotten. They propose to let us drink to their healths all the livelong night."

"I'm game as a gamecock," Buckhurst replied, putting an arm around Zabby and Beth. "Where do they propose to take us?"

"They proposed Odam's, for apparently they want their tripes in a twist from his rancid oysters, but I think we'd do better at the Legge or the King's Head."

"Where is the King's Head?" asked Catherine, intrigued at the thought of eating in an establishment of that name.

Buckhurst and Sedley exchanged glances, deciding who should take such an easy jest. Sedley looked at his pocketwatch. "At this hour, I'd say buried to the nose in Lady Castlemaine's . . ."

Catherine turned deep scarlet, but fortunately the two libertines were too amused with each other to notice. Beth squeezed her queen's hand. "Do you want to go home?' she whispered.

"No," Catherine replied, controlling herself. "I came to see what it is like to be a man. I will not shrink from it."

"Eh, what's that the parson said?"

"He's a kinsman by marriage, from Italy," Zabby said. "He doesn't speak English."

"Well, then, let's away and show your solemn friend how an Englishman disports himself. Though I hear in carnal appetites the Italians are no slugabeds." Sedley elbowed his sovereign queen sharply in the ribs, took Eliza by the shoulder, and led them out of the theater.

The lad was back to holding up the building when they exited, and he grabbed Eliza by the coat. "Oi, gotchervirgin."

"Beg pardon?"

"At Mother Ross's. She says she has a peach plucked just for you, fresh from her mother's teat not more than twelve years ago. Only twenty pound for a maidenhead, fifty if you all want a go." He looked at the men dubiously. "There's more of you'n a minute ago. Might cost extra." He scratched his head. He'd never done math at such fantastic sums, pence and ha'pence being his usual lucre. "Hundred pound for the lot of you!" he said, holding out his filthy digits to strike the bargain then and there.

"Save the virgins for the connoisseurs," Sedley said. "Give me a good fatty piece of mutton that knows what it's about. But Mother Ross's sounds like as good a place as any to start the evening. What say you, flesh before supper? Lead on, lad!"

They picked up a few others as they staggered away, those who found no favor from their actress of choice, others with a keen ear for the clink of another's full purse. Catherine looked around, amazed, as the men accosted a flower-seller, plucking at her skirts but making recompense with the purchase of a pennyworth of dried heather. They were like hounds off a leash, without a master, doing what they would without fear of consequence. And these were supposed gentlemen. She recognized some of them, those on the periphery of the court who came to see and be seen, but rarely contributed wit or wisdom. They had scraped and bowed before her, impeccable of etiquette, making a leg to their queen as if she were an object of worship. And now they cried bawdery to every female they passed, shouted ribald abuse to a frail old couple traveling homeward in a coach. One scooped up a stone and hurled it at the cloudy glass of some respectable citizen's house.

And this not even full night-time, Catherine thought. She could understand a bit more license under cloak of darkness, or perhaps on a festival day, but this was just an ordinary Thursday, ordinary men . . . Did they all have the beast in them? She began to feel herself fortunate that her husband was at least truly a gentleman, unfailingly courteous, never rough, moderately discreet. If a common man could behave thus, what might not a king do? He might have a seraglio, or entertain himself by burning down villages.

Beth, feeling safe in her disguise, watched it all without surprise. A habitué of the court, she had seen every manner of vice and depravation, knew that the cleverest minds used their knowledge of Latin to quote lewd epigrams and the bravest swordsmen used their skills not to defend their country but to kill a man over a minor slight of honor. People no longer shocked her. She was just innocent enough to believe that, despite the ready example the world held out to her, there might still be one good man, who would love her alone, tenderly. "Yes," she told the queen, "all men are surely alike." But she held a private caveat: *except for my man, my Harry*.

Eliza had one arm around Zabby's shoulders and she whispered commentary as she ate it all up for future plays. "The infamous Madam Ross's brothel. See how it appears no more than a housefront, when untold wonders of debauchery parade inside. There, the sign of the oyster, by which you know it. Zabby-heart, I do not think there's another female in court who's seen the inside. 'Tis not so fine as Madame Cresswell's, they say, being of a more boisterous character, but of wide fame nonetheless. Don't you feel like an intrepid explorer?"

But Zabby just felt debased. The theater had been bad enough —loud, stinking, false. What was to Eliza a miracle of man's contrivance was to Zabby a gaudy, ugly mockery of nature. The actresses' faces were ghastly, painted flat chalk white as though the very skin had lost its soul, and their manner was even more contrived than that of the court ladies. She did not like this world of forced, loud laughter, pretended sentiment obscenely coupled with the most mercenary ambition, the play of desire and con- quer, resist and acquiesce, that had no joy in it.

But she did not condemn it. It was another aspect of mankind, and what was man but a part of nature, subject to natural laws? She'd never seen people behave thiswise on Barbados, but unless all London suffered from some mass sickness — a miasma in the vapor or an ill humor in the water — all that she had seen must be contained in every human soul, and therefore must be studied.

So she watched Mother Ross's quick, appraising eye as they all entered her stew; saw the flash of coin the lad palmed and pocketed; sniffed the air for that same scent that lingered on the queen's sheets, magnified; spied the quickly composed counte- nances of the bevy of girls who, like any others, had their bread to earn.

Mother Ross greeted Sedley and Buckhurst like the old friends they were and clapped her hands smartly together. An elfin girl with loose ginger hair brought a bottle and glasses on a lacquered tray and deftly served them, not spilling a drop even as she danced away from opportunistic gropes. When Sedley, catching her mid- pour, managed to handle her hip familiarly, she kept her compo- sure long enough to finish the job, snatched up a little knife from a tray of apples, and with a dart like a heron's strike snipped off one of his silver buttons.

She tossed it in the air, laughing, then slipped it into the re- cesses of her skirt. "I get silver for every feel, gold for a taste," she said tartly, "and those who steal from me get robbed in return."

"And how much for your virtue, pretty Nell?"

She gave him a piquant wink and said, "I have no virtue, sir, but if you mean my maidenhead, why, you couldn't afford that treasure." She looked at the others, her gaze lingering curiously on the queen and her maids. "Perhaps you fellows could form a pool, and I'll draw straws for the lucky winner." She laughed again and sauntered off, swinging her narrow hips. Her body looked all of thirteen years old, but her eyes were as cynical as Mother Ross's.

"Now, who for you, good sirs?" Mother Ross asked her regulars, adding in a very audible aside to the disguised ladies, "Something special for you, I warrant, not the usual *rem in re,* eh? Enjoy your cordial. I'll not be a minute heaving these rakes atop our scullery maid, the poverty-struck popinjays."

Like customers at the Royal Exchange, the men picked out their beauties. Sedley chose a buxom blonde dressed as a milkmaid, with short skirts and tight stomacher and no shift at all. Buckhurst, of a mind for something exotic, picked an ebony wench who Mother Ross had discovered at the docks and dressed in rabbit furs dyed with leopard spots.

When the others had been disposed of, the bawd turned her attention to the newcomers. Her bright eye confirmed what the lad had said — wealthy, green sons of country squires on their first trip to London, aping the mode of men about town. *Cubs of a bumpkin,* she quoted to herself, *licked into genteel form.* Desperate to appear civilized, they would buy anything if told it was fashionable, financed by Papa's good turnip crop. And Madame Ross knew exactly what to sell them.

She sidled closer and looked up at Eliza, evidently the leader of the rubes, and therefore, in her vast experience, keeper of the fattest purse. "I have a treat for you, a rare pastry, soft and buttery, a bun as yet untorn. Are you in the mood for a delicious little morsel, noble sir?" It never hurt to flatter the yeomanry with a grant of rank. "She's virgin and clean, I trow, natural daughter of a nobleman who left her to my tender care. She's been like a daughter to me, but even a daughter must earn her keep when she comes of age. What say you, sir? Do you fancy the taste of ginger? She's sharp, but if there's ever a one to tame her, it's a strapping buck like yourself. Or perhaps another of these gentlemen? Her honor is yours for . . ." She reckoned up their clothes, their lace, their swords, and said with confidence, "Fifty pounds!"

The girls looked at each other uncertainly. They all wanted to leave now, slip out while their companions were otherwise occupied (and occupying) and make their way back to Whitehall.

Mother Ross wondered if they'd not been to a brothel before. Now, there's an idea, she thought. Country outposts of my establishment.

"Perhaps you'd care to step into my private chamber, and I'll show the lady, the young lady, the child, the infant, in." She ushered them into a room hung with deep crimson, flames flickering perilously near the loose material. "I'll bring her in, but no sampling, mind, not without payment upfront." She was suddenly businesslike. "Many gentlemen have been asking after her. If you don't seal the bargain tonight, like as not the duke himself will be after her." Which particular duke, she did not say, but implied with a significant nod that it might be the notorious Buckingham himself, or perhaps even the king's brother, the Duke of York.

A moment later the red-haired serving girl slipped in and leaned against a chair back. "Well?" she asked, staring at them each in turn. "Which is it to be?"

"Are you the one she is selling?" the queen asked, forgetting to pitch her voice like a man's.

"No one's sellin' me . . . sir," she said with a little smirk. "Only a small part of me." She slanted her eyes provocatively. "Very small. So, who's the lucky gentle . . . person, eh?"

The disguised ladies looked from one to the other, torn between mirth and disgust.

"Do you mean," Eliza asked, "that woman would actually sell the . . . honor . . . of a child your age?"

"I'm old enough," she said, puffing out a chest that was barely there. She was in fact nearly fifteen, but her slight, lissome form helped her pass for the child so many customers favored.

"Oh, blessed Mary, we must save her," the queen said.

Eliza sighed. "What is your name?"

"Nelly Gwynn," she said.

"And do you want to work here? Would you rather do something else?"

"Been selling herrings. M'sister Rose has a cart, but herrings ain't what they was." She shook her head sadly at the thought of a world in which a herring could depreciate. "So I took to serving spirits here. But a girl must advance, and so, good sirs or whatever you may be . . ."

"You mean you really would give yourself to one of us?" Zabby asked. "For money?"

"Aye," she said, laughing, "for all you could do to me, unless there's something new under the sun. Wherefore do you dress like men? Are you nuns come to chastise the world's wantons?"

"You knew?" Beth gasped.

Nell patted Beth's cheek smartly. "Your chin's as hairless as my . . . Ah, I'll have done with lewdness, now the secret's out. What's your game, then?" She lounged in the chair, curious.

"We've come to see what men are like, away from us," the queen said.

"And?"

"We find them worse, and better," she replied. *For at least my husband would not buy a child,* she thought. *Would he?* "When we go, does another man come for you, little one?"

"Aye, tonight, tomorrow. Such is life." She shrugged her skinny shoulders.

The queen called her ladies to her and consulted them in hushed tones. *Oh, my,* Beth said. *But we cannot save them all,* Zabby protested. Eliza chuckled, shook her head, and said that they might as well be hung for this lamb as a piece of mutton, and took something from the queen.

"Here you go, sweetheart," Eliza said, tossing her a glittering emerald ring. "From my mistress. Don't go pawning it, or flashing it around. It's your chastity belt, until such time as you have another dwelling. If any fellow offers you insult, show him that and tell him you're under the queen's protection."

"Gemini!" Nell said, privately thinking that she'd yet to hear the offer she found insulting.

"Though officially I suppose you'll be under *my* protection. Tell your bawd you have a keeper and you're off the lists. Tomorrow we'll find a place for you."

And so, the queen and her maids of honor found they'd acquired a collective mistress.

They might not have been so concerned for Nell's virtue had they known that, with the judicious use of alum and a sponge soaked in sheep's blood, her virginity had been sold three times in the last week alone.

Eliza, under the name of Duncan, took a pretty set of rooms over the Cock and Pie Tavern at the end of Maypole Alley, just a stroll away from where Killigrew was supervising the construction of his new theater on Drury Lane.

The girls fretted over Nell as if she were a pet spaniel. Zabby thought she should have plain, serviceable linsey-woolsey clothes, to help her avoid temptation, while Beth wanted to dress her like a doll. The queen sent her a gilded diptych of the Virgin and the Magdalene, so she'd have before her examples of purity and repentance. Eliza, more practical, brought in masters to teach her fashionable speech, dancing, singing, the Spanish guitar.

And like a spaniel, Nell had only to implore prettily to get her way. She complained of being lonely, and after some resistance they let her sister Rose call on her.

"But mind you, you're a kept miss now," Eliza said. "No gentlemen visitors."

A week after giving Killigrew her play, Eliza had met with him again, still in masculine guise, strolling with him as he shouted instructions to laborers at the new theater. He decided to produce her play — with a few alterations — and took the promising lad he too knew as Duncan under his wing. Eliza snuck out to meet him at least twice a week, and she used Nell's rooms as her headquarters. Eventually, she invited Killigrew to meet her pretty mistress, and Rose happened to stop by with a friend from Madame Ross's, then Charles Hart and Walter Clun came in search of Killigrew, and it became a regular party, with oysters and a venison pie ordered from Odam's Ordinary (which turned out to be quite good, despite what Sedley had said). Before long, Duncan and Nell were a popular couple among the actors and demimonde. Nell's wit remained cleverly coarse, but now it sparkled with Latin and French and court gossip. Eliza was living, firsthand, the decadent life she wrote about.

Zabby and Beth disapproved — Beth on the grounds of propriety, Zabby on those of her friend's best interests. "What will your father say if he knows you're consorting with whores and players and writing for the theater?"

"People don't talk about what they don't know about," Eliza replied, supremely confident.

The queen knew nothing of this, but freely allowed her maid of honor to visit their rescued virgin.

"And how does our pretty, pure Nell this night?" Catherine asked when Eliza, a bit tipsy, snuck back into Whitehall near midnight one evening.

"Oh, her singing improves immensely, as does her dancing. I watched her practice for many hours."

"Good, good," Catherine replied drowsily as her maid of honor, now in a bodice and skirt but smelling of tobacco, undressed her hair. "In a few years we will find her a suitable husband. It is a fine act of charity, is it not?"

"Indeed, Your Majesty."

She did not mention that Nell had been dancing a sarabande on a tabletop for a cheering crowd of players, whores, and poets, or that the songs she sang were lusty street ballads. *The world is what it is,* Eliza thought, and she rather liked it that way.

Chapter 12

THE GIRL WHO SAYS NO

CHRISTMAS WAS A TIME at which the court honored the birth of their savior by showing off their choicest silks and most costly jewels, and by concocting merry hijinks and amateur theatricals. They played children's games, groping each other in blind man's buff, and concluded with the merry pastime of slip-the-marriage-vow in dark corners and private rooms.

The queen kept a smile tacked onto her face as maids of honor to her and her sister-in-law Anne frolicked in a mummery of pastoral seduction, ending with Winifred Wells dancing the fashionable new minuet with a pillow stuffed under her skirts. There were uncouth shrieks of laughter when her gravid stuffing became dislodged, and Buckingham solemnly declared the pillow a stillbirth and handed it to the king for dissection in his elaboratory.

Catherine had been married seven months and still had not conceived.

"Charles's own mother did not bear a living child until she'd been four years wed," Beth said softly when she saw how much the girls' tomfoolery affected her queen, and how well she hid it. "Then see how many babes she had? There is time aplenty, Your Majesty."

"So says the witch under the stones," Catherine said. "Yet every day is torture."

Across the room, Barbara was eyeing the giddy young girls with indolent superiority. She was pregnant again, standing with her hips thrust forward to emphasize the barely visible bump. Though her husband, Palmer, had made a pretense of claiming the first two, he'd rarely been within fifty leagues of his wife in the last year, and the king was already acknowledging the unborn child as his own, fondling her stomach in public, saying he fancied this name or that. To the world, she was absolutely secure in her position as *maitresse-en-titre,* the official mistress of the king, but she was always keenly alert to anything that might change her fortunes.

Zabby came reluctantly to the king's presence chamber from the elaboratory, where she'd been puzzling once more over the Lucifer light. The German alchemist had told them, after the king's jocular threats (for who can ever be sure if a king is in jest, when he laughingly threatens to hang you for treason?), that it was composed from the substance of the human body, showing that the light of the soul glows from even the basest matter. Pursuing it later, they captured Zabby's breath in a glass balloon. They waylaid the Duke of York's physician after the unpopular heir's quarterly bleeding. They refrained from collecting feces, thinking no element of the soul would choose to reside in such an odiferous substance, but set aside several basins of the royal urine. Zabby had been scraping the salts left after evaporation, but a servant rapped on the door and summoned her before she could decide how to proceed. The queen was adamant that all of her attendants enjoy themselves on Christmas day, whether they wanted to or not.

Zabby came through the door and lingered, her mind still in the elaboratory, not noticing who was standing beside her until it was too late to leave without giving dire offense.

"You smell of piss," Barbara said. Zabby owned privately that it was probably true and bit back her sharp retort. "Is that what you get up to with him, then? I still can't fathom you, miss, but I don't fear you. Ah, you should have heard the wagging tongues when you appeared from over the sea, trapping him in that inn with your perverse lust, but I always knew he'd return to me. I have what I need of him, and he of me, and no doxy of the moment will interfere with that."

She slid her eyes sidelong at Zabby. "D'you know, since you've arrived he's been another man entirely. Calmer and sharper all at once. You must suck some poisonous humor out of him, eh? He used to rise, nights, in my bedroom, and pace for an hour, muttering to himself, but now he sleeps like a babe till sunrise. If you did that to him, my thanks."

"You really care for him, then?" Zabby asked the older woman skeptically.

She laughed, sharp and strident, and not a few heads turned and marveled that the rivals for the king's scepter were closed in conversation. "Does it matter one whit? He's the king, you chit, and I'd act the same whether I despised him or adored him. Oh, don't look so shocked. You'd be doing . . . whatever it is you do for him in that stinking magician's lair of his . . . even if he was a poxed-up blubberous lout, because he's the king." Her voice softened and her eyes half closed in what Zabby realized, with a jealousy that made her want to claw the other woman's face, was a memory of ecstatic passion. "Lucky for me—for us—he's handsome and considerate and fashioned like Old Rowley himself." She winked at Zabby, and the girl blushed, hating Barbara but coming closer than she believed possible to liking her too, because of her obvious deep affection for the king.

"No, you don't worry me one jot," Barbara continued after a moment. She flicked out her fan and covered her face as she spoke, so only Zabby could see where she looked. "I scent a storm in the air. Do you see that pretty little piece of insipidity there?"

Zabby followed her gaze and saw the newest maid of honor, a girl about her own age who had served the king's beloved sister Minette in Paris: Frances Stewart. Zabby didn't have a high opinion of her—the girl had an annoyingly high-pitched giggle and childishly skipping movements, and enjoyed such pastimes as blowing bubbles and crafting houses of cards. Zabby thought she might even be simple, and as much as she pondered her at all, thought only that it was lucky the girl was pretty, because she certainly couldn't make her mark any other way.

At the moment she was dancing with Charles, or rather, he was trying to entice her into a dance and she was tripping away like a tipsy wood-nymph.

"I give you advice from one whore to another, Zabby," Barbara said lightly. "Never trouble yourself over the girls who say yes. They're a dozen to the half crown, everywhere, like slugs on a rhubarb. A man wants a yes, aye, but he needs more than that, and that's what we can give him. *Nulla puella negat,*" she added, surprising Zabby, who didn't realize it was only a common saying: No girl says no.

"Fornication's no novelty to him," she went on, "though you've apparently come up with something bizarre to please him." Zabby bristled, wishing she could tell the world once and for all that she and the king were not lovers. But then how Barbara would laugh at her!

Barbara smiled as pleasantly as if they were confederates, two admirals, perhaps, discussing how best to serve their monarch's interest on the high seas. "It's not you I have to worry about, nor you me, so long as you mind your place and never interfere with mine. Our danger lies there." She nodded to where slim, golden Frances, now blindfolded for blindman's buff, was letting herself be spun around. She stumbled unerringly into the king's embrace, felt too low and guessed him to be Eduardo, the queen's Portuguese dwarf, mistaking a fortuitously fondled bump for his nose. "For she says no."

"Has he propositioned her?"

"Are you blind? He's been after her for months now. She giggles and simpers and lets him paw her a bit, then pretends to be shocked and says not without marriage. She works him to a frenzy and then sends him away. Then he slakes it on us. Haven't you noticed? There's her fortune sitting like a cat in her own lap, and she won't reach out to stroke it. She's either the world's master idiot, which is what we must hope for, or a thousand times cleverer than you or I."

"What do you mean?"

"Oh, I curse the day I married that blighted Palmer. If not for that . . . Well, I deceive myself. He needed Catherine's money, and the people wouldn't have stood for anything other than a princess, so he'd never have wed me even if I'd been free. But if the queen remains barren, and Frances keeps saying no in that way that seems to mean *yes, if only,* what do you think he'll do? They say she has a drop of royal blood, if you dissect the escutcheons well enough, and if she's virgin, too . . ."

"You mean he could cast off the queen and marry Frances?"

"That's her game, if I smoke her right."

"He wouldn't do it!"

"If he gets no heir on his queen, he just might. It's been done before, and no one can stomach the thought of James as king. Poor Catherine!"

"Poor Catherine? I thought you despised her."

"Ah, well, one cannot despise a mouse in a trap. She had no say in her life. Not everyone is captain of her own vessel, like us. Besides, what would I be without her? She's my safe port."

"How do you mean?"

"Charles is bound to a childless, plain woman, so of course he loves elsewhere. But say he had a tart little baggage like that Frances to excite him, and give him children. Why, if she played her cards right he'd drop us all like blistering roasted chestnuts. I need Charles to stay bound to his yellow Portuguese bat. And he probably will. He likes things to be easy. Keep an eye on Frances, though. Together you and I should be enough to carbonado her." She sighed. "If it gets too serious, we can always hire someone to ravish her. I doubt he'd be interested in spoiled goods, particularly for a queen. Well, back to business."

With a wave of her fingers she sailed off and caught Charles expertly in her clutches, whirling him away from the pouting Frances, promising him untold delights. It didn't look to Zabby as if they had anything to worry about.

What a merciless, terrible woman, Zabby thought. All the same, there was something admirable about her. She was analytical, practical, almost scientific in her pursuit of power. With what cold precision she'd tossed off the scheme to have Frances raped, as though such a crime was but an inconvenience on the path to fulfillment, like the stink of urine in the quest for the visible soul. What a shame Barbara could not be a statesman, or a general.

She didn't realize that in her own way, Barbara was.

Zabby stayed aloof for the rest of the festivities. She used to think the petty machinations of the court ladies beneath her notice, schemes of love and vengeance, but now she studied them like the natural history lessons they were. She saw Simona flirt simultaneously with four men, but after close observation Zabby realized it was all for the sake of a fifth, the Duke of York, whose interest increased in proportion to his competition. She watched Suffolk move among the foreign ambassadors, whispering a word here, granting a nod there, which struck Zabby as odd because she knew the mistress of the robes had no interest in politics. Then she remembered the woman had the queen's ear, and as Catherine adjusted to court life people were beginning to court her favor too, thinking her word to the king might win them whatever they desired. She saw a something glinting change hands—a fine pair of diamond ear-drops from the Italian ambassador in an exchange for a message Suffolk would never deliver to the queen, that the queen would not comprehend, in any event, that her husband would not listen to. Gossip, bribes, blackmail, were the favored currency of the day.

Godmother Cavendish's advice came back to Zabby. *I'm cleverer than any of them,* she thought, *and I have Charles's ear. I could have ambassadors seeking my counsel. I could scheme to have funds sent here, withheld there. I could make such a fortune as to build my own elaboratory, a library surpassing the king's, gardens full of wild beasts, alchemists and philosophers at my beck and call.*

Zabby thought she didn't care for money. The truth was, she simply had no wish to spend it as these empty-pated fops and wantons might. She could have money and power surpassing them all.

Why, look at Barbara. To the nation's displeasure, Charles had granted Barbara all of his Christmas presents that year. So the clocks from the Netherlands, the Titian, the baubles and Bibles and pearls and plate from ingratiating courtiers and merchants all went into the royal mistress's coffers, to be turned to cash, and thence to silks and jewels. What Zabby could do with that money! Her family had always been comfortable, but now, musingly, in the haze of the wassail bowl, she dreamed of extravagance: her own sort, a spendthrift riot of science and learning.

And all I have to do is take part in this vice and madness, she thought. *I could be the most powerful woman in London, in England.*

If the world worked out exactly right — and if I helped it along — I could be queen!

She'd been holding a goblet of raspberry cordial, viscous and rich as blood. When that thought struck home, the vessel slipped from her nerveless fingers, splashing Catherine's hem with sanguine crimson. With a stifled cry, Zabby fled from the room.

She started for her own chamber, but at the last moment whirled, knowing it was all too likely one of her friends would seek her out there. Where to hide with her shame? The elaboratory, of course. Anyone might stumble on her elsewhere in the palace, but no one save Charles ever visited the elaboratory at night, and it was unlikely he'd be torn from the festivities by the lure of chemicals. She dashed down the hallways, her heels clack-clicking, and tucked herself away in her sanctuary.

Feverishly, she forced herself to work. There was a cured skin of a serpent waiting to be stuffed, and she spent some time coaxing it into lifelike articulations. If she could only focus on science, perhaps she could subdue those shameful thoughts.

But she looked into the snake's dead, hollow eyes, thought how fine a pair of emeralds would look there, once it was mounted, and from there began to mull once again over what she could do with a fortune, with power.

How easy it was for her agile mind to light upon the notions that would make it acceptable — preferable, even, the best and most rational course. Catherine was not happy at court. She preferred the solemn silence of the convent. Charles wasn't a brute; he'd not concoct some petty treason to behead her for. No, he'd simply point out her unsuitability, her barrenness, and send her back to Portugal. Where she'd be happy, Zabby added. And then, whom else would he choose but her? Not Barbara, married, and enough of a termagant to frighten Charles away from a permanent union in any case. Certainly not that insipid, giggling infatuation of the moment, Frances. And not, she was sure, some fat German princess or Spanish infanta. Who understood Charles? Who had nursed him back from the grave? Who shared his passion for books, for science, for beasts and plants and ships? Only Zabby.

"No!" she said aloud. "I couldn't." But that wasn't true, and with a certain pride she amended it. "I wouldn't."

Still, the possibility loomed, and she could find no way to banish it utterly.

Me, queen! Me, with the riches and learning of the nation at my command! The idea glowed before her like a sun, and she stared, though she knew it would blind her.

It would be an honorable way of having Charles, she thought.

No, not honorable, but in the eyes of the world, to be a wife was a better thing than to be a whore. *If I were his wife, my passion for him would be right and proper. I could yield to it, as often as I cared to.* And as Barbara herself said (and who should know the ways of men, if not her?), if Charles had a true friend and helpmeet in his wife, he would not look elsewhere for his diversions.

I could do it, she thought, *just to show that I could. The world might be a better place for it.*

For a moment it seemed to her no more than an experiment. Given such a set of variables, with such forces acting upon them, would the anticipated result follow? Never had she been faced with a hypothesis without attempting to prove it.

She stroked the snake's supple scaled leather and recalled a time on Barbados. She'd been twelve, as apt a student of her father's natural philosophy then as she was still, marveling at the firm, sleek quicksilver bodies of dolphins sporting in the outflowing tide. They swam, like fish, but their eyes were quick and keen like a human's, and once when she'd perched in the bow of a swift skiff and reached out her hand, a dolphin riding the forewake had puffed hot breath into her palm. Fish, she knew, are cold, so what could a dolphin be, with his warmth and canny eyes?

She'd asked a fisherman to spear her a specimen for study and dissection. He'd been reluctant to comply, because dolphins are luck to sailors, but she was the little mistress and at last he came to port with a slack body tied alongside his boat. Zabby had been so heartbroken to see the beast dead, its eyes as lifeless as any fish's, its body as cold as any corpse, that she'd insisted the poor creature be given a proper burial. The slaves dug a hole on the beach and she'd strewn it with hibiscus, hating herself for what she'd done.

Then her father found out, and with very gentle words explained that in the pursuit of knowledge — as in the pursuit of anything that is worth the chase — there is always pain and sacrifice. *What's more,* he pointed out, *would you see the creature's death be a wasted one?* And so she had him dug up and together she and her father dissected the dolphin.

Had the knowledge been worth the sorrow? Would power be worth the pain she would cause?

The door opened, and Charles said her name. Of course he would know where to find her. Of course he would seek her out.

Ask me, she begged without turning. *Ask me to be your whore, so that I may say no, so that you may desire me all the more. Or ask me so that I may say yes, and you may tire of me before I do irreparable harm. I want . . . I want . . .*

She did not know what she wanted, but she wanted it with all of her heart, with all of her body.

"What a pretty little jilt you are, sweetheart," he said, looking her over with a slow, sweeping gaze that made her tremble. "Come, the court must see me dance with my favorite mistress or they'll all think we've fallen out, and make your life miserable." He held out his arm.

She wanted to rage at him, tell him he'd already danced with his favorite mistress, Barbara, and tell him she refused to play his foolish game any longer. She wanted to pound him with her fists and meet his mouth with hers, to bite him, tear at him, to envelop him.

But she only put her hand lightly on his arm and went back to the presence chamber for her dance.

Chapter 13

THE HIGHWAYMAN

SLEEPY-EYED BUT MERRY, the maids of honor piled into a gilded palace carosse before the May Day sun rose. The city teemed with hopeful young girls—and some not so young, who never lost hope—who flocked to the fields and commons outside London to gather May dew, a sovereign tonic for the complexion, sure cure of freckles, pimples, moles, wrinkles, and smallpox scars. They would spread their handkerchiefs or clean shifts over the damp grass and squeeze precious drops of fairy balm into stoppered vials, then wait anxiously for male attention to confirm their new beauty.

"And you must gather it yourself," Winifred said, "else it doesn't work."

"There's no rhyme or reason to that," Eliza said. "It's only that if you buy a pint off some Royal Exchange 'pothecary you can be sure 'tis no more than well water with a bit of sweet clover steeped in for effect."

"But how is it that dew will do such wonders if gathered one day, but nothing if gathered on another?" Zabby asked. The custom didn't exist on Barbados, where sea bathing and coconut cream were all a woman thought necessary for good skin. "A carrot isn't healthy if torn from the ground one day, and unpalatable the next."

"You should pray May dew works at all," Simona told Zabby. "Or does His Majesty extinguish all the lights before he makes use of you? The Spanish have a saying: Any spittoon when the mouth is full."

"Have you wheedled James into spitting into your filthy gutter, then, miss?" Eliza asked, referring familiarly to the king's brother. There was a rote to all their acerbic raillery by now, and none of the girls took it very seriously. Spiteful Simona could never quite school her tongue, which dropped steady insults as a scored tree drips sap, yet she was forever making little overtures to Zabby, trying to do her small favors, because she, like everyone, believed her to be the king's mistress. Zabby paid attention to neither of these behaviors.

The queen did not accompany them, saying she didn't believe in such heathen flummery (though she swore by an unguent supposedly made from the fat of a boar and a she-bear taken in the act of generation). The girls dressed for the occasion in peasant costumes, at least, the way they imagined a peasant might dress if she had an unlimited supply of money. Their skirts, daringly above the ankles, were wool, to be sure, but of a weave as tender as a baby's cheek, the petticoats trimmed with embroidery, and the stockings beneath them clocked silk. Tight black stomachers laced in silver ribbon and drooping straw hats bedecked with roses completed their outfits, and it was only a shame that the male half of the population had little interest in May dew. Curious, jealous female faces peered into the passing coach and wondered if their betters were mocking them.

They had a chaperone, the half-blind, mostly deaf Lady Bridget Sanderson, mother to the maids, eighty if she was a day. She earned a comfortable pension by sitting quietly in corners, fiddling with her rings and frowning at odd intervals just to show she was wise to her charges' giddy, hoydenish ways.

Eliza and Simona continued to fling their barbs at each other, just to keep in practice, while on either side of them Zabby and Beth gazed silently out the windows. Beth, as always, was thinking wistfully of her beloved Harry. As time passed it seemed more like a dream, and she worried that each time she replayed the encounter she added something or stripped something away. Had he truly said he would find her? In her memory there was the crucial word *soon,* but soon had come and gone. Did he say he would see her, or contact her? She couldn't quite recall, and so every day she waited for some page or washing woman to slip a note into her hand. But nothing had come, not a word or a sight. She desperately wanted to ask after him, but lived in such mortal terror of her mother that she dared not do anything that might get back to her. For a woman without the means for bribes, the Countess of Enfield had a remarkably efficient spy system within the court. Beth assumed the rest of the world was too terrified of her to deny her information.

He will come, she chanted in her matins. *He loves me,* she whispered in her vespers. And every night she dreamed of him, clasping the proxy limbs of Eliza and Zabby beside her, though to her secret shame she could hardly remember his face. He had more substance than the shadow savior of her early fantasy, but he was still hardly more than a handsome fancy. *I know it takes a man a long time to make his fortune,* she bargained in her prayers, *but please, may I see him just one more time, even if he is still poor?*

Beth thought about her love all the time, and chided herself if he slipped from her thoughts even for an instant. Zabby, in turn, had learned the terrible impossibility of trying not to think about something. One can ignore, one can lose interest, one can forget, but apparently one cannot purposefully not think of a thing. To make the effort is to think the thought, and the battle is lost in the first muster. Though Zabby marshaled all of her considerable mental forces to drive away the notion, it returned time and again to mock her with its logic.

Yet she had done nothing to further it. As far as she was able, she went to the elaboratory only when she knew Charles was elsewhere, playing at Pall Mall or taking his customary morning walk up Constitution Hill. Still, he found her often enough, and his flirtatious pleasantries were enough to make her heart race. She deliberately ignored his bawdery, feigned ignorance of his innuendo, and forced their conversations into purely scientific lines.

Charles never ventured beyond talk, never touched her except to brush her fingers when taking a vial from her hands, or hold aside her tumbling pale wisps when she bent over a steaming concoction.

I wouldn't have him out of wedlock, she told herself time and again, *and I wouldn't displace the queen to have him in marriage. But why won't he at least make the attempt?* Every other woman, from loyal, sheep-faced Winifred to that clergyman's daughter to the insufferable giggling Frances, was apparently worth the chase. Why, then, did he (despite her effort to avoid him) always seek her out, always look at her admiringly, always make his little jokes that could be taken innocently or indecently . . . and yet never attempt to seduce her? What was wrong with her? For the first time in her life she spent a long time before the mirror, tucking combs under her locks to bolster her curls, placing decorative black patches just so, anointing herself with orange-flower water, all to no avail.

I don't want him to, she thought as she stared out the window, *but why on earth won't he?*

They were well outside the city now, deep in the rolling fields. The six matched flaxen chestnuts thundered ahead of the carriage as the coachman searched for a solitary oak, reputedly the best place to gather May dew. Suddenly another horse pounded along-side, matching their pace. *How thoughtful,* Zabby mused for a moment. *Charles sent outriders for our protection.* Then the man flashed her a black-toothed grin, pulled a shining constellation of stars from his saddlebag, and whirled them around his head. No, not stars. Something she'd seen only in old manuscripts: a morning-star flail, three spiked balls swinging from chains attached to a cudgel. He winked at her, hung off the side of his mount like a Scythian, and smashed the carriage's gilded axle.

The horses screamed as the drag caught them, the back ones stumbling in their traces and the lead beasts in their panic trying to rear even as they ran. The listing contraption tipped sideways and shuddered to a halt.

"Stop your bellyaching long enough to get your arse off my face!" Eliza shouted to the wailing Simona. The girls were tumbled on top of each other but unhurt, thanks to the masses of cushioning petticoats and the stomacher boning that would probably keep a mule kick from snapping their ribs.

Eliza struggled to the top of the heap and pushed open the door of the capsized coach. A large hand in ornately scrolled gloves took hers, and she said, "Many thanks, sir, and if the coachman's still breathing, would you put a stop to it? You'd think the king's servant could make sure the wheel was sound. Oh!"

She finally noticed the pistol. It wasn't quite pointing at her, but its proximity was enough to make her queasy.

"Have you any cream for me today, my pretty milkmaid?" he asked, and now she noticed the mask, a hood of softest velvet covering his hair and his face down to the nose, with eye holes stitched in gold thread. She couldn't help but notice too that what she could see was remarkably handsome: broad, curling mouth; crinkling, merry eyes that somehow took away the gun's menace...while she looked in them. Then the cavernous barrel loomed, and she replied, shaking, "I'm afraid all my cream's soured into clabber."

The coachman, footman, and the spry teenage postillion rider had been dragged down and huddled in the grass under a third man's gun, muttering curses but too frightened to meet the marauders' eyes. The masked man helped the maids of honor out. Simona screamed until the black-toothed thug dangled his morningstar in front of her face, then she settled into a whimpering heap, throwing her apron over her head like a real peasant. Winifred looked like a soldier at his execution, knowing exactly what she was in for but willing to take it bravely, as was her duty. Zabby and Eliza each thought she should do something but wasn't sure what. Eliza had grown accustomed to playing the dashing blade, but she never thought to use one, and that day her only weapons were hairpins. Zabby was perfectly comfortable with guns, knew the rudiments of fencing, and could hurl a tolerable harpoon, but she had even fewer weapons, for she'd worn her hair down.

Frances, pale as birchbark, cowered behind the mother of the maids. Her eyes were dead and her body rigid. She too thought she knew what would happen to any young lady captured on the open road by a band of highwaymen. Zabby felt a rush of sympathy for the girl, whose plans (if she was canny enough to have any, as Barbara thought) hinged on her chastity. However infatuated, the king would never have her, not as a lover and certainly not as queen, if she'd been ravished by three criminals in a roadside ditch.

Beth emerged last of all, and Zabby clung to her, thinking to offer comfort, for wasn't Beth in the same position? She might not be angling for the throne, but her marriage prospects depended on her purity.

But of all the girls, only Beth was serene, for she had seen the mouth, the crinkling eyes, and they were enough to reconstruct the face she thought she'd forgotten. She patted Zabby's cheek reassuringly and smiled at the highwayman.

"I know who you are!" Mother Bridget crowed. "You're the one they call Elphinstone!"

He bowed, and Zabby noticed he had a courtier's flourish. "Your servant, madam," he said. "And you, likewise, gentlewomen." He turned to Beth. "And you, my lady." To her he bowed lowest of all. "As my reputation precedes me, it will save me my customary speech." He winked at his fellows. The one with black teeth chuckled, while the lean man with the pistol rolled his eyes to the heavens. "Your jewels, my dears, or ... something else. I'll have payment one way or t'other."

"You can see they have no jewels," Mother Bridget snapped, brave, for she knew even the most desperate criminal wouldn't bother ravishing her. "We're May-Daying. Young man, do you know what fate awaits the man who molests the queen's own maidens? Begone, gallows-bird, before His Majesty's Life Guard is upon you."

"Peace, madam. I have no fear of the noose. But if life's to be short, why, then, it must be sweet. You wear no jewels, but every woman carries a choice treasure wherever she goes, and in the finest purse." The other highwaymen guffawed. "Now which shall it be?" He stroked his beardless chin contemplatively as he paced before them, making a show of looking them up and down. Eliza tried to pull Beth back so he wouldn't notice her, but Beth evaded her grasp and stood at the fore. "Only the loveliest lass will do for Elphinstone, a girl of unsurpassed beauty, charm, grace."

Frances gave a stifled cry, sure he must mean her.

Elphinstone stopped in front of Beth and took her hand.

Shows you, Frances, Zabby couldn't help but think even as she lunged between them. "No, not her!" she cried. Eliza joined her, and Elphinstone stepped back, raising his pistol.

"You have loyal friends, my lady, but tell them to step aside. Now." His voice hardened.

"Please, Zabby, Eliza, do what he says," she said.

"Sir, if you're a gentleman . . ." Eliza pleaded.

"I've seen a gentleman slit another gentleman's nose to the bone for an imagined slight. I've seen gentlemen ravish other gentlemen's wives in their own houses. I've seen gentlemen sell their families for a bottle of brandy and a poxed whore. Do you still ask me to be a gentleman?" He smiled ruefully. "I'm no more than a man today." He took Beth's hand again and gently pulled her from her friends. "I claim one dance from this beauty, nothing else. A dance in my arms is your ransom. Do that, lady, and all go free."

"Gladly, sir," Beth said, and followed him to the far side of the carriage.

"Better her than me," Simona said, recovering as soon as her own skin was safe. "What will her demon mother say now? Ow!"

Eliza had pinched her. "You know what these peasant louts mean when they say a *dance,* don't you? They dance in the haystacks, they dance behind the hedgerows, they dance with their sheep if there's no skivvy about. They say Elphinstone has never left a maidenhead intact, that indeed he'd prefer it to jewels and gold."

"Can't you do anything?" Eliza pleaded with the elderly coachman sitting on the ground.

He looked at the pistol, then at the slowly pendulating morningstar, and said nothing. One more year and he'd have his pension. He didn't want his widow to enjoy it without him.

"Music!" Elphinstone barked from around the carriage, and, in the most incongruous sight, the barbarian became Pan. He slipped his flail into his wide leather belt and from under his coat produced a double pipe. He licked his lips, leaving a smear of black on them, and struck up a merry tune. Zabby strained to hear what was happening on the other side of the carriage, but the music drowned out whatever they were doing. She thought she heard a sound, perhaps a sob, though it sounded more like a laugh. She bit her lip and glanced at the third robber. He was tapping his foot to the lively jig, but his pistol still covered them. Perhaps if she and the others rushed him, only one of them would perish... but as she had no guarantee it would be Frances or Simona, she dared not risk it.

As soon as they were out of sight, Beth flung herself into Elphinstone's arms.

"Oh, Harry, Harry! My love!" She kissed his masked face.

"Did you wonder why I'd kept away so long? Whether my heart was still true?"

"You couldn't be false," she cried, and kissed him again. She'd been practicing on her pillow so often that kissing felt quite natural by now.

Suddenly she pulled away and slapped him across the face, where the kisses had only just settled in.

"Perfidious wretch! Elphinstone? I know what they say about you! The Lusty Highwayman. You're just like your father, and mine, and every man! Did you have every wench you waylaid up against the carriage door?" She drew back to strike him again, but he caught her hand easily, then let it go.

"Go on, hit me again, lemman," he said cheerfully. "A blow from you is sweeter than a hundred honeyed kisses from a . . . no, please, I jest!" He held up his arms to fend off further attack. "I've never kissed another than you, my darling, I swear. Ye gods, because I haven't blacked a lady's eyes yet they call me a ravisher. I'm no brute, but believe me, I'd rather have gold than a bit of houghmagandie any day, except from you, dear Beth."

"You mean it isn't true?"

"What, rape a woman in the middle of a road, with carts full of ploughboys and soldiers passing every few minutes? You're sadly misinformed about my trade. A robber must be swift as a peregrine. I take my life in my hands to dally with you now, Beth, but I'd risk the Tyburn dance for a chance to be with you."

"Then why does everyone say it of you?" Beth asked.

"Because the world will say something about everyone, given half a chance. I suppose I smiled at some countess, or kissed a dowager's hand when I let her keep her wedding ring, and now

I'm a gallant of the road, the robber seducer. I warrant it makes my job easier, for the women all keep their husbands from fighting me, while the men are all too eager to give up their coin in place of their wife's honor . . . or their own. Every criminal needs a legend. D'you suppose Robin Hood really gave to the poor? Perhaps he did once and a story was born. Now, hush, and doubt no more, my love. I moved heaven and earth to discover when you would be on the road, but I dare not meet you like this again. But there's another way, if you are brave. Do you know the mulberry grove?"

Beth returned, flushed, and with all eyes on her the highwaymen made a practiced escape. When they were nothing more than a distant line of dust, the coachman finally mustered the courage to shake his fist at them.

"I'll see you drawn and quartered! Ravens will eat your guts, and your maggoty head will stand on a spike, you accursed whoresons!"

Only then did Beth fully realize what occupation her lover had chosen, and what fate would await should mischance catch him. She fainted into her friends' arms.

They cut one of the horses from its traces and the postillion lad was sent to Whitehall. However, as he had fouled his small clothes in the initial attack, he was too ashamed to go in by any of the main passageways and lurked behind the kitchens until someone noticed him. So the maids of honor waited a good hour by the roadside before anyone rushed to their aid, subject to the curious stares of the populace. A goat-girl offered them ladlefuls of milk, a timid swain dropped a pretty bouquet of violets at their feet, but no one pursued the dread highwaymen.

At last two coaches came, and riding hard on a bay before them all, the king himself. He saw Beth, conscious but prostrate and weeping, and Frances, who was now bored but burst into fresh tears at the sight of Charles and the renewed thought of what could have occurred, but he strode straight to Zabby and said, "Tell me what happened, and no concealment."

She tried to pretend he came to her because he loved her best, but she knew it was because she was the only one of the maids whose judgment he could completely trust. His next words confirmed it. "Did the blackguards touch her?" His eyes flicked to Frances, as if he couldn't trust himself to look at her and find her soiled.

"No," Zabby said spitefully. "Your Frances buried her face in the mud so they wouldn't notice her. They took a fairer flower: Beth."

He had the decency to look guilty. "And did they . . ."

"It was only one, the man they call Elphinstone, and as far as she will say, he offered her no insult."

"Though they say the man will ravish grandmothers, big-bellied matrons, anyone. Are you sure? Neither she . . . nor Frances?"

Disgusted, Zabby pulled away, in time to see the Countess of Enfield step from the first carriage and stoop over her child. Shoving Eliza aside, she took Beth by the shoulders and pulled her up, looking her over.

"You stupid, stupid girl!" she shouted, shaking her. "How could you let this happen? Spoiled! Spoiled! And not a mark on you. Before you let yourself be violated you should have fought with all your strength, so he would be forced to ruin your face to have your honor. Did you give in because you feared bruises and blood?" She slapped her.

"My lady!" Charles said, endeavoring to restrain her, but loath to touch her. "The child was not harmed, as far as I can tell."

"Not harmed? Better her face should be scarred, her bones sundered, than her one treasure stolen from the family. Why didn't you fight him, you slut? Your skirts aren't even torn. Did he lift them so easily?"

"Mother, I swear . . ."

"What good is your oath when all the world will know you were alone with that Elphinstone, and for all I know every scurvy cutthroat in London! Your Majesty, I believe there is a physician in the second coach?"

"Yes, when word came I didn't know if anyone was hurt."

"And he is your own physician? Is he the one who verified the queen?"

"Whatever do you mean, madam?"

"Her chastity. Is he the one who checked her, or did you use a midwife?"

"My queen was never subject to such an indecent . . ."

The countess made an undignified snort. "Took her word, did you? Like as not she's barren now because she had a dozen abortions before she came to you. Ha! Ignorant wretch, even with a crown on your head. You there!" she called to the portly little doctor as he stepped out and Charles tried to decide whether to charge the countess with treason. "Here's your patient. Tell me if she's been raped."

It took some time for the doctor to be made to understand what the countess required of him, first because Beth, with her quicker apprehension, realized and began to wail, and second because it was utterly out of his customary line of work. He could let blood from a vein so neatly that his patient wouldn't even feel it, make the suction of a red-hot glass cup almost pleasant, slip in a clyster with buttered fingers, but he had no truck with what lay between a woman's hips and thighs. That was a midwife's territory.

"Are you incompetent as well as a fool?" the countess inquired as the doctor stammered his protests. "It is quite simple. Is she virgin or not? Go, straight away, and tell me!"

"Do you mean you intend me to perform an examination here? The girl looks untouched."

"Here! Now!" She had enough sense to add, "In the empty carriage will do, I suppose. It has curtains."

Struggling weakly, weeping mightily, Beth was half coaxed, half dragged into the coach and closeted with the physician for a good ten minutes. She emerged red-faced and disheveled, her eyes firmly on the ground.

"Well?" the countess demanded, hands on hips. The sun glinted off her shining hawk's beak, blinding the doctor, and he knew in his heart that, whatever had been his findings, he'd not risk the wrath of this horror by declaring her daughter not intact. He knew what so often happens to the bearer of bad news.

"I am pleased to inform you," he declared to all present, "that your daughter is still a virgin."

For a brief moment the countess looked almost human. A relief that might have been maternal washed across her face, but Beth knew better.

"The family fortune is still in its purse, Mother," she said grimly.

"And a good thing, too," the countess said, "for I've found you a suitable husband."

Once again, Beth found solace in unconsciousness.

Chapter 14

THE COLLECTOR OF BEAUTY

T HE EARL OF THORNE made no move to greet mother or
      daughter as they were shown into his library two days
later. He was so immobile that for a moment Beth thought he was
only another statue, albeit smaller than the dozens that towered in
the grand room, Grecian nudes twice the size of life. *They belong
outside,* she thought. *They're trapped in here, without the sun warming
their marble shoulders.*

She spied him at last only because he was clothed, and if anything even more handsome than the classically muscled statues,
for all that he was nearing fifty. She'd always thought beauty and
youth went hand in hand, and as much as she thought about her
own looks, expected to lose them after a few years of marriage.
But this man was as well preserved as one of the king's specimens
steeped in strong spirits, unnaturally young despite his years.

The earl's face was like the death mask of a young man, cast in unlined bronze, without expression. His black hair lay in neat, unmoving waves. He blinked heavily, once, making Beth start, as if she had seen a corpse become reanimated, and then very slowly he began to descend the spiral staircase leading from the second-story alcove he'd just quitted. Before the door shut, Beth caught a glimpse of richly ornamented volumes, a rolled scroll, another marble nude, much smaller, still classical, but more along the lines of a Pompeii bathhouse than an austere temple.

He stopped before them, his face immobile. It was his habit never to speak first.

Beth's mother dropped the barest hint of a curtsy, excused by her ailment from any elaborate show, and said, "Here she is, then, my lord. My treasure."

"I see," Thorne said, and continued to regard them without apparent emotion.

"Tell his lordship how pleased you are to make his acquaintance."

"Mother, I . . ." But she broke off at a dangerous look and said, mechanically, "I am so pleased to make your acquaintance."

"Pleased," he said, as if to himself. "Are you, now? I have made a study of pleasure since I was only a bit older than you, Lady Elizabeth. My own, not that of others." He took a step closer and examined her. She wanted to squirm away. "Is that what pleasure looks like, then?" He turned from them and took a book from among the hundreds on the shelves. "You may leave us now, Lady Enfield."

Beth's mother rapped her cane smartly on the marble floor. "I will not, sir! My daughter is alone with no man."

"Save footpads and cutpurses," he drawled without looking up from his book.

"Blast and damnation! The king's own physician swears she was not touched. Isn't that enough for you? The girl is pure, and any man with eyes can tell she's the most lovely thing in England. Now, anything you wish to say to her must be in front of me, and if you slander her good name once more, we leave this place."

Beth had never heard her mother sound afraid before. A stranger would have seen only fury, but Beth knew her mother better than anyone, and she could hear the desperation behind the snapping indignation.

"Very well. Come here, both of you." He plucked a dark hair from his head and used it to mark his place in the book, then led them to a statue of a young woman.

"Hero," he said. "Kept in seclusion by her parents to be a virgin priestess of Aphrodite, as if there could be such a thing, but myths, like men, become corrupt over time." He permitted himself a chuckle. "In my early days as a collector I occasionally trusted my acquisitions to another, a scholar of some repute. He'd made several small purchases on my behalf in the past, which pleased me, so I entrusted him to procure this Grecian beauty for me. The price was exorbitant, but he vowed it couldn't be had for less, and a doge was bidding against me, so I paid freely, with a large fee for his efforts. Imagine my surprise when I removed my statue from the straw and found this!"

Not understanding, Beth said, "But it's lovely."

"It is a forgery, sculpted not above fifty years ago!" He looked at her as if she were an ignorant worm. "I've kept it all these years to remind me of two things. First, to always be sure what I acquire is worth the price I pay."

He stopped and stroked the statue's bare breast. After a very long pause, the countess asked, as he'd meant her to, "And the second thing?"

"To severely punish those who deceive me. Look here." He circled to the far side of the statue where the virginal stone was marred by a reddish substance. "When I finally found the deceitful scoundrel, I broke his head against hers. False she may be, but sturdily made." He sighed. "I had to throw away a fine Turkish carpet, though. Brains never quite come out." He smiled broadly for the first time. "Now, let us see. Where to begin?"

"I won't marry him, Mother. I can't!" Beth was still hot with indignation at her second examination in as many days. This one was less intimate but far more disturbing.

"Nonsense," her mother said. She was in a prime mood, and while Beth's protests would usually earn her a slap, now the countess was positively jovial as they bounced in the carriage back to Whitehall. "He has fifty thousand a year at the very least, a house in London, a castle in Cornwall, a palace, from all I hear, somewhere in Italy. He's settling a thousand a year on me, which I don't care a fig about, but it shows he's a gentleman who does things thoroughly. And as for you, dear, why, you'll never want again! Think of it!"

She did. She thought of her mother free from worry and care, perhaps even happy. She could have the best physicians, sea-soaks, and patent unguents, possibly a cure.

And what will I have? Beth wondered. *A husband I don't love. Can't love. Not even if dear Harry didn't exist.*

"Mother, how could you have let him do that?"

"He'll be doing it soon enough after you take your vows, that and more. There's no escaping that, if you marry a beggar or a king. It's not taking liberties so long as I was there to make sure he didn't go too far. You heard what he said about that flummery statue of his, the brazen hussy. Ah, but I've done a fine job keeping you pure, my girl, haven't I? There's nothing amiss with you, firm, tender fruit that you are! What's a press and squeeze here and there? He had to be sure of what a splendid creature he's acquiring. He took the royal physician's word on your chastity — you can be glad of that at least."

"And you'd probably have let him examine that, too," she said under her breath.

"Perhaps I would, ungrateful chit! Do you know what it will mean to you...to me...to the family to unite with Thorne? That's worth a feel or two."

"I felt like a pig at the market."

The countess laughed. "And what a pink little squealer you are. But save your blushes for your wedding night."

"I told you, Mother, I won't marry him."

The countess glanced out the window to be sure they were unobserved, then dug her nails into Beth's arm. "What is it, you fool? Do you think you're in love with some fresh-cheeked page or beribboned court popinjay?" She got so close to Beth's face that the silver hawk's beak touched her nose. "Who will have you, eh? Oh, they'll pet and praise and hope for a tumble behind the stairway, but who will have you to keep? Look at us, look where life has dragged us. You'll never have another chance like this, and I swear, by my blood and bile, if you foul this prospect I'll kill us both!"

"But Mother . . ."

"Not a word!"

Beth stroked the half moons on her arm and stared out the window. Perhaps if she told her mother about Harry, about how much money he had already, she'd listen to reason. She snuck a glance at that hard raptor face.

No, there was no reason in her. And Beth knew within her own heart that it was an unreasonable suggestion. What, marry the son of the family's greatest enemy, with the blood of a rake in his veins, and the hangman's noose around his neck? Even if Harry came to her laden with gold, her mother would never consent.

In their too-brief conversation he'd implied he had masses of it already, and certainly the court was all abuzz with tales of his exploits. Now that the queen's ladies had been attacked, everyone with a pretense to fashion was claiming to have been stopped by the notorious Elphinstone, though they were chary with details. To say he'd taken their jewels would imply he had no interest in their charms, but though he was popular, no lady would — quite — boast of having lain with a highwayman.

Beth knew the lascivious rumors weren't true, simply because her Harry had denied them. Still, she couldn't help but feel a twinge of pride that the man she loved was so desired by other women. Pride, and uncontrollable jealousy. She'd almost lashed out at Barbara when she'd joked openly before the amused Charles that she would take to riding the byways unprotected just to meet this rare specimen.

Gentle Beth had no compunctions about being in love with a highwayman. "I've never killed anyone, or harmed a man who hasn't sought to harm me first. And I rob from none but gilded coaches," he'd said, kissing her. "No widow's mites for me; only the riches of lords and aldermen. Do you think they miss a ring or a few coins?"

"But what if you get hurt?" she asked, clinging to him.

"'Tis a rare man who will risk his life for coin," Harry replied. "Besides, I've become a story, soon a legend. Everyone is pleased to be part of a story. They pay now so that, snug by the fireside in years to come, they can tell the tale of me. Most think it a fair price for an adventure."

"But what if one day..." she'd begun, but he'd stopped her fears with yet another kiss.

No, she had no fear for her lover's soul. How could she fault him his occupation when all around her men made their living by pimping to the king, stealing from ambassadors, and blackmailing their neighbors? The sole virtue her mother preached was chastity, and that only because it was in her best interests. Beth knew for a fact that her mother was enmeshed in the complicated palace spy system. Penniless, they had survived since their ruin on the coins passed for a whispered secret or a muttered message, or larger sums for the promise of silence. Many an illicit lover had slipped out of his lady's chambers in Whitehall only to find a silver hawk's beak glinting in the torchlight. Hush money was safer than a duel. Beth wouldn't put it past her mother to pick a pocket, if it was convenient.

But she did fear for Harry's neck. As they drove back to the palace, their carriage slowed, then halted, stuck in a crowd. "When you're married you'll have runners to beat these rabble back," the countess said irritably.

Beth heard a bell toll, and with a start of foreboding realized where they had halted: St. Sepulcher's Church.

A booming basso rang out. "Repent with lamentation, O ye condemned sinners, and you, good people, pray for the miserable souls of these criminals for whom the final bell hath tolled." A black-clad minister was having his moment of glory as, before him, massive dray horses pulled an open cart upon which sat four bound men and one woman.

"Crow's meat," her mother said sourly. "Can't they haul them to their just rewards at an early hour so the streets are cleared for decent folk?"

Their driver edged them to the far side of the road as the cart and the cheering (and jeering) followers passed. The nooses were already tied snugly around the prisoners' necks, and their hands were bound before them in praying position, whether they repented or not. They perched atop their own coffins.

One, a scruffy fellow with blackened teeth who reminded her

of Harry's cohort, caught her eye as they came abreast. He pursed his lips in a whistle, then winked at her. Some of the pedestrians caught it and laughed; a prisoner was expected to put on a good final show. The end often went easier for him if the crowd was pleased. But Beth could see a sheen of sweat on his brow, and his hands in their hempen cords trembled.

She watched them until her mother jerked her back into her own troubles.

"I suggested an early wedding date, within the month at least." Beth gasped. "But he must go abroad for a few months, so it will have to be after. He'll be back in October or November. Now, listen here: whatever objections you might have to Thorne, get over them. He's the best you'll get, and we're damned lucky he'll have you."

"Why does he want me?" Beth asked. "He doesn't know me." *Of course,* she thought briefly, *neither does Harry, really, but that's different.*

"Have you looked in the glass lately, pet? You look like I did as a lass, and they said I could have had my choice of husbands. Of course, I had no choice, and neither have you. I daresay you'll meet a better end."

"Why isn't he married already?"

"Oh, he has been, a time or two. Or three, perhaps. I remember one wedding just before the old king was killed, a grand affair. She was a dark-haired lass, not much in the way of family, but pretty as a kitten."

"What happened to her?"

Her mother shrugged. "Died in childbed, I suppose. It was abroad, though. Then there was another, an orphan Lady Somebody."

"Where is she?"

"What, do you think he keeps them in a closet, like Bluebeard? She's dead and buried too, of course, else he wouldn't be marrying you."

"And there was a third wife?"

"Stop plaguing me, child. Life is brutal; people die. But not I! Look what your father did to me, and here I am." She patted her daughter's arm where the nail marks were turning purple. "You have my blood, my spirit. Whatever he gives you, you'll endure, as I have. You're like me, my girl. You'll do well. I'm so proud of you!"

With a shudder, Beth realized how terribly her mother loved her, and how terribly hard it would be to escape that love and find a love of her own.

But I'll do it, she swore. *I'll never marry that earl. I'll marry Harry or . . . or . . . die trying!*

She was to meet him that very night.

Chapter 15

THE LUCIFER LIGHT

AFTER MONTHS OF LABOR, of trial and error and noxious fumes and blistered hands, they had finally recreated the German alchemist's Lucifer light. Zabby shaded the specimen with her body and peered at the uncanny green-white glow. There was light, but no heat. Fire, without apparent consumption. All from the king's urine, the distillation of a luminous piece of his soul.

He was not there to see it.

In the beginning he'd been as enthusiastic as Zabby, meeting her by appointment every day and often colliding with her in the elaboratory when they both got the whim to work at odd hours. He was dedicated to finding the soul light, and, Zabby told herself, to finding it with her. But lately under the lure of the elusive Frances Stewart, his scientific passion had all but vanished, replaced with an unsatisfied passion of the flesh. He had no interest in his soul.

Now here it is, whether he cares or not, Zabby thought with triumph. *It is his work as much as mine. I just had the final inspiration. Once he sees this, he'll remember his first calling and forget all about Frances.*

As she dashed through the cool corridors of Whitehall with her glowing specimen held before her, she told herself she was doing it for science, for discovery. *When he sees it,* she repeated to herself, *he'll remember what is truly important.*

"Knowledge," she whispered aloud.

Me, she could not help thinking.

She asked the servants, the courtiers, and finally her old friend Chiffinch, who told her with averted eyes that Charles was in the climbing rose bower in the gardens.

Chiffinch was page of the backstairs (that is, the private passage to His Majesty's personal rooms), a job that encompassed spymaster, wine steward, and pimp. He was particularly known for the last, handling assignations with clerical organization and utmost discretion. He'd seen women come and go—mostly go, except for Barbara, and her time would come sooner or later—and Zabby was not like any of them.

She ran with her skirts gathered high above her knees, her pink stockings looking fleshier than real flesh ever had. She was laughing, forgetting all her past fretful hours, putting aside, for a time, that troubling scheme for power. Here was something pure —knowledge! Discovery!

There it was, a bosky cave, a sweet bower of roses climbing upon an unseen frame to make a perfumed nook. It was a notorious place for lovemaking, but somehow Zabby never thought . . .

She caught herself at the sound of voices.

"I'll do anything!" Charles's deep, virile voice said. "A dukedom, a county, my heart, my soul!"

Zabby clutched the glowing vial to her own heart. *She* had Charles's soul.

"There's only one thing I desire in this world," Frances said primly.

"Name it and it's yours." His voice was hoarse, as if he'd been pleading for hours.

"I want to be an honorable wife. I'll have no man under other circumstances."

Charles groaned.

"I can't, don't you see? If I were free I'd marry you, but it isn't possible. Sweet nymph, I promise you'll be queen of my heart. You'll never want, never hear an ill word spoken of you. Please!"

"Never without marriage," she said.

"But what of love? Love is better than marriage."

Zabby stepped out from behind her wall of roses into the sunlight at the bower's mouth. Charles was on his knees, his breeches muddy, while Frances looked a tall, sulky child.

"Animals," she whispered, not in derision but in pure fact. There was no escaping it. *Whatever else we are, we are beasts too,* she realized. *Gluttony, lust, greed . . . they are not mortal sins but the stuff of our flesh and bone. There is nothing more natural.*

The real sins are the human ones. Pride. Jealousy. My sins.

"I've found it, Your Majesty," she said, formally. "The light of your body. Your soul." She held out the vial and, when he did not take it right away, let it slip from her fingers. The glass splintered on the sunbaked cobblestones, and the lumpen waxy ball, its light dulled by the summer glare, rolled to the king's boot. He stared after Zabby as she walked slowly away.

A moment later there were shrieks and cries of "Fire!" Zabby hadn't gone far enough in her experimentation to know that phosphorus is combustible at moderately warm temperatures. In a moment the dry grass caught, and soon the bower was engulfed in flames.

"Yet it is not consumed," Charles said wonderingly. Indeed, though the sere grass around the bower sent flames licking skyward, the well-tended roses were too green to catch easily. The outer buds singed and curled into blackened capers, but after the first flare the fire subsided to creeping embers and writhing smoke, leaving most of the full-blown roses untouched.

"Witchery!" Frances said, and for an instant Charles lost his temper.

"Never speak of her so again!" he snapped, and made as if to leave her. But a word and a pout brought him back, and they went to blow soap bubbles for spaniel pups to snap at.

"You may not be the king's doxy, but you play the part of a jealous mistress well enough," Eliza said as they settled into bed that night. "They say you set a spell on that chit Frances, or else tried to murder her, no one's sure. Even Barbara chuckled at it, though the queen took it amiss for some reason. Perhaps 'twas the talk of sorcery; you know how papists are. You'd think she'd be glad to have someone fight her battles against Frances, and as she knows you're nothing to Charles, she shouldn't mind one bit . . . Zabby? Zabby, dear heart!"

It was too much. She could keep her secret no longer.

"I love him! I love him!" she cried into her goosedown as Eliza and Beth embraced her. "I've tried so hard not to, but I can't help it. Why? It seizes me and shakes me like a rat, and never lets me go."

"Oh, sweetheart, the king's an easy man to love. Why, half the court . . ."

"I hate them! Every single one. Barbara, that sniveling idiot Frances, even, heaven forgive me, the queen. Oh, the poor queen. She must know. It was an accident, truly. I didn't know it would catch fire, but now she must believe I did it for jealousy. I didn't, I swear, but oh, if Frances had burned I would have been glad!"

"You don't mean that," Beth said placidly.

"But I do. Is this what love does to a person? I thought love would be something pure and ennobling, but it must be a curse from the devil himself if it makes rational beings behave like mad beasts, like criminals." She looked up, wild-eyed. "Save me from love."

"If you love him, really love him, then there's nothing you can do," Beth said.

Eliza stared at her. "What, you too? Don't tell me you've succumbed to that black earl's charms. It never does to love one's husband. In fact, the experts—the playwrights, that is, who are expert in all aspects of the human condition—believe a certain degree of hatred and contempt is vital to a happy marriage."

Beth ignored her. "Zabby, look at me. If you truly love him, it will never leave you. Even if there is no hope. Even if the world laughs at you."

"You've grown wise a mite too swiftly," Eliza said. "No half-century earl can inspire that sort of rumination. You've found yourself a young buck. Who is he, now? That captain who's been giving you sheep eyes, or perhaps the Russian ambassador?"

But Zabby and Beth were locked together, face to face, thought to thought. Each had loved in isolation so long, and now a great dam had burst. Beth had yearned for a confidante, but never thought to look for one in stolid, sensible, impermeable Zabby. "It's like a pain, isn't it, like hunger when you smell the feast? And a terrible fear all the time. It's not happiness, no, nothing like. Perhaps it is almost-happiness, or something beyond, something that is peace and terror all in one. Peace because you have found the reason for your life, and terror lest it be taken away."

"Yes," Zabby said, "and the schemes I can't control, and the jealousy. I'm not this person. I don't want this love. I should have gone away at the start. I should leave court now."

"It would follow you, though you never see him again. When I hadn't seen Harry for—"

Eliza caught Beth's slip. "Harry...hmm...Lord Stargate's

a Harry, and there's the eldest Paget. Who is it you love, Beth?" Zabby's outburst had unnerved her, and she wanted to change the subject to something more believable. Beth in passionate love she expected, but if rational Zabby could be torn asunder by her emotions, why, then, no one was safe.

Except me, Eliza thought smugly.

"I . . . I can't say."

"Well, good thing you're marrying an old man. I know nothing of that Thorne, but anyone past forty must be easy to cozen." It seemed such a tremendous age to Eliza. "Marriage is but a business, a woman's only business, so it seems to me she must find love elsewhere. Perhaps a few may be fortunate enough to love their work, but for most it is no more than a way to keep the body fed and clothed. The heart needs other food."

"I'm not marrying Thorne," Beth said.

"But your mother is telling everyone it is all arranged." Eliza was quite practical when it came to anyone's marriage but her own. "He's astoundingly rich, from all I hear, and you'll learn to bend him to your will in a fortnight, and have all the lovers you care for."

"He's not like that," Beth said. "There's something hard and dark about him, unnatural. He makes my skin crawl. I don't think he's the sort to let anyone control him, or even sway him. I was only in his company for a few minutes, and I hope never to be again." She shuddered.

"Are you running off with your mysterious Harry? Your mother will only have you hauled back and annul whatever you've accomplished, though then perhaps the earl won't have you after all."

"That would be a mercy."

"Indeed? Are you so pleased with your poverty? I don't mean to sound hard, Beth, love, and you know I want you to be happy, but it seems to me marriage isn't the way to achieve happiness. I mean, it matters little who you marry, so long as he's well off. If you marry for love, you'll only be brokenhearted when he takes a mistress or spends his days with dogs and horses, but if you marry a mere man, not a lover, why, you're each free to follow your own heart, apart. At least, so it goes on the stage."

"But life isn't the stage," Beth said. "You have no idea what it feels like to love someone. If I marry Harry I'll be joyous forever. If I don't, I'll die. That's that."

"Now who's talking out of a play? No one dies for love. Every woman must marry. What, lead apes in hell?" This was the proverbial fate of an old maid. "It is the way of the world."

"Even for you?" Zabby asked. Her outburst vented, her tears brushed aside, she looked as calm as ever, her large tawny eyes examining Eliza quizzically. "I thought you had no wish to marry."

"Oh, I'll pick a likely old duke someday, one with three or four wives buried and a slew of heirs, one who won't trouble me with childbearing and gives me free rein to write."

"But will he let you dress in a man's clothes and carouse as you do now?" Zabby asked. "A husband is a master."

But Eliza wasn't concerned. "I have practice enough managing my father. He wants a noble son, and grandson, but he made a vow on my mother's deathbed not to marry me off against my will, and so long as I play the Puritan with him, he's easy enough to control." She affected a prudish voice. "Marry him, Father? But he takes the Lord's name in vain. Him? Oh, laws, no, Father, he once hunted on a Sunday. No, he'll never force me into a marriage. I'm free as long as I want to be, and I'm enjoying my life. When carousing and gambling and the company of loose women begin to pall, I'll settle down with my nice gray gentleman. But for now, I do what I like!"

"Every person does what he likes," Zabby said. "Only some decide they like to give in to what the world wants."

"And what does the world want for you, Zabby?" Eliza asked.

For me to be queen, she couldn't help thinking. *For me to rule heart and mind at Charles's side, and lead England to a glorious age of understanding.*

"The world wants me to go to sleep," she said with uncharacteristic crossness, and pulled the linen sheet over her face.

"Then you'd best give in," Eliza said, and began to get ready for her night, stepping out of her petticoats and replacing them with a pair of snug breeches. "Ugh, I liked the full ones better, but times and fashions change. Here, Beth, hand me that waistcoat and my sword, would you? Don't fret so, Beth, and certainly don't listen to me. I know so little of the world." She laughed at her own sarcasm, for she thought herself the worldliest of creatures. "Does your lad have money?"

"Some, and bound to get more."

"Does he have a title?"

"I suppose. His father was a lord."

"Eldest son? Then tell your beastly . . . I mean saintly mother and bed the boy before she can say no. Now, is my periwig straight? I'm off. Tell Catherine I have a headache tomorrow, if I'm still asleep when we're called for. The way Nelly pours the brandy, I'm sure it will be true. Shows what an early education can do. Dream of your Harry, Beth, and you of your king, Zabby."

"What's the use?" she said from under the covers. "He doesn't care a fig for me."

"Oh, at least one fig, my dear. You could have him with a snap of your fingers."

Zabby peeked out. She knew Eliza was just saying it to make her feel better. She knew she was too odd-looking, too awkward to attract Charles. She was smart, but not witty, and wit was what counted at court. That or otherworldly elfin beauty such as dim-witted, giggling Frances possessed. No, Zabby knew she was useful as an assistant in Charles's elaboratory, nothing more. Oh, perhaps he was grateful to her for saving his life, but gratitude is a far cry from love, or lust.

She tossed and fretted beneath the covers for an hour, irrationally cross with everyone, even dear gentle Beth lying as still as a marble odalisque asleep at her side. *She may have to face down her dragon mother,* Zabby thought, *but if she's brave she can have her Harry, whoever he is, and the world will think no worse of her in a month's time. There's no hope for me.*

At last, Zabby drifted into a fitful sleep, and as soon as her breath came evenly, Beth slipped out of bed, pulled off the shift that covered her gown, and left to meet her lover.

Chapter 16

THE LOVING FATHER

*E*LIZA SWUNG her golden watch as she strolled through the torch-lit streets to Nelly's house. *What a fine thing it is to have a kept woman,* she thought. Even if she did no more than provide a cheerful room and a soothing voice, and of course a cover for Eliza's own masculine disguise. She began to appreciate why a man might want to keep something soft and pretty and always merry for his own private enjoyment, to chase away the cares of the world.

Not that I have a single care, Eliza thought gaily as she walked. But she was worried about her friends.

Why doesn't every woman choose to live like this? she wondered, not troubling to think that she could do what she chose because she had money and leisure. *Every lass should put on a pair of breeches and seek out companions solely for their lively wit and conviviality.* She didn't mind at all that none of her companions (save Nelly) knew she was a woman. She didn't want to be appreciated for her womanly charms, such as they were, and knew that no matter how clever and poetic she might be, when she was clad in a gown a man would always see her handsome dowry first, her bosom second, and her talent last of all. But out here in the world of theaters and coffeehouses and rowdy inns, they heard her words first and hardly noticed her person. She could craft a subtle compliment or barb it with a malicious twist into the most cutting insult. She could extemporize satire on the court or praise the reigning beauty, to the delight of her audience, so that they didn't care about her face, never looked under her weskit for bound breasts, and if they noticed she had a full purse, it was only in gratitude that her wealth could extend a pleasant party for another hour or two.

She'd been giving it a great deal of thought, and now resolutely decided she'd never marry at all. *Why should I?* she thought complacently as she smoothed her coat before letting herself into Nelly's suite. *Even an old fellow might put his foot down if he knew what a merry life I lead when the sun sets, and I'll have no man's foot on me! What good is a husband except to make money or give one a title? I've got the first, and don't care for the second. Heirs? Mayhap when I'm a doddering old harridan of fifty I'll adopt a splendid young buck and make him my heir. Or Nelly here.*

"Hello, my sweet!" she said, and gave Nelly a kiss on the cheek. "Ye gads, what a sty this place is."

"Sorry," Nelly said with an impish grin. "I never had an instant to clean up from last night." There were walnut shells on the floor and shrimp tails on the table, and every candle was burned to a stump with trailing widow's weeds of beeswax. "You should really hire me a servant."

"A servant knows all her master's secrets, and I don't want anyone knowing the master is a mistress and the mistress a free woman. At least, I trust you're still free. You have been declining their offers, haven't you?" Despite the public knowledge that the supposed Mr. Duncan had Nelly Gwynn in keeping, a great many men propositioned the delightful girl.

"Mostly," she said. "Sedley gave me this." She held out a gold ring with a little winking diamond chip. "But I haven't done anything to earn it yet."

"That cheap frippery shouldn't buy him more than a smart slap. Don't succumb to that impoverished beggar, my lass. If you mean to sell yourself, aim as high as you can. I see great things in your future—we all do, the queen included, or we wouldn't trouble ourselves with you. You're comfortable for now, and will be as long as you like. Take some time to look at the board before you make a play. Now, where shall we go tonight? Are there any parties? No? What about that show they've been crying up for the last week. *Quarrell's Miscellany,* that's it. Now slip your stockings on...no, not that pair, you sweet slattern. You'd think you were kept by the pig-man. Find a set without holes. Thank heaven you're so lovely that no one cares if your hair's a mess, but do wipe that smudge of coal dust off your nose. There!"

Nelly was careless as a fairy, and always assumed she looked stunning—and she did.

When they stepped out onto the street, Eliza flung back her head as if she were about to howl at the gibbous moon, and took a great breath of the foul London air. "I'd rather be a London commoner than a prince of Araby," she said, and stumbled over the cobblestones when she tried to walk with her head up to the smoggy stars. "Isn't it a grand life?"

"Are you tipsy already?" Nelly asked.

"Only on life. Oh, how glorious to be free! Is that the theater?" she asked a moment later. An inked sign was pasted on the wall, advertising a variety show starring Pious Philadelphia, depicted with a high stiff collar and a prim mouth.

Nelly looked at it dubiously. It didn't strike her as her sort of entertainment — or Eliza's. "Perhaps this is a better entertainment for a Sunday morning," she hinted, but Eliza dragged her in.

"Come on, the doors are about to close. Trust me, from what I heard, you won't be disappointed."

They nudged themselves a bit of space on an already crowded bench and swayed to see the dimly lit stage. Most of the men wore low-crowned hats that didn't interfere with the tiered seating, but the fellow in front of them wore a high Puritan hat. Eliza nudged the portly man in the kidney with her boot and said, "Doff your cap, sir. The lady can't see."

The man half turned, then snorted dismissively when he saw it was no more than a fashionably dressed youngster, and said, "I remove my hat before my God and my king, young man. Tend to your own cares."

He was obviously a provincial; a town man would have offered either a more polite response or one far more cutting, with his hand on his sword to follow cut with cut. An ill word could lead to a duel . . . or an anonymous midnight assault that might end with a lopped-off ear. Honor was a fine point, and one never knew when the fop sitting behind might be a deadly swordsman.

But the Puritan had nothing to fear from Eliza. Though she wore a sword, even if she had the skill or the inclination she was in no state to use it. She had shrunk back, clutching Nelly's hand painfully, her eyes wide with shock. She knew that profile, that voice . . . why, she knew that very hat, black beaver with the bit of Flanders point, steamed to curl just so to sit above a set of prominent ears.

It was Eliza's father.

She was terrified. She might have told her friends she had her father under her thumb, but now that he was unaccountably here, in the flesh, she grew weak at the thought of what he'd do to her if he found her out. At the very least, he'd take her back to the country, and that was as good as a death sentence to Eliza now. He might have her thrown in an institution. Like many of the courtiers, she'd toured Bedlam, laughing at the crazed inmates who thought themselves birds or clouds, the men who swore they were women, the women who strutted like men. No, however furious, he'd never open himself up to that kind of shame. He'd have her quietly bundled into a coach by three strong ruffians and carted off to Scotland to be kept under guard for the rest of her life. Then he'd marry some hussy and get himself a son, and forget all about her.

"Are you unwell?" Nelly asked her benefactress.

Eliza took a deep, shuddering breath to steady herself. To rise now would attract unwanted attention. She was just glad the theater was too dim for her father to recognize his own daughter in male guise. There was nothing for it but to hold fast and wait for the end of the show, when she could leave quickly and be lost in the crowd.

As the show progressed she began to gain a measure of confidence. He'd never recognize her, and if he did, why, she was such a deft hand at cozening the fond old fool, she'd just spin him some fabulous story and he'd accept it. What could she say, now? Something near the truth — that she was here on the queen's orders. He'd certainly ask the queen about it himself, and the queen was not adept at lying, but if Eliza could get to her first and give her a little coaching, she'd certainly confirm that she and the ladies in waiting had taken an interest in saving an unfortunate girl from the degradation of the streets. Yes, that had a pious ring to it. Almost assured now, she settled against Nelly and tried to enjoy the show.

I'm as free as ever, she thought. *Even though my father sits before me, I still manage to do exactly as I please, and the devil take any who stand in my way!*

The first act featured a man who played the viol with his feet, which struck Eliza as unnecessary because he had a perfectly good set of hands. His music was atrocious, so perhaps he found people more forgiving of his instrument's caterwauls when they were produced with the wrong appendages. Then came a man with a pair of marionettes, and he was likely very good, but he spoke in

Italian and she couldn't follow the plot the jigging dolls acted out. Then a man swallowed swords, a woman ate fire, and a dwarf did nothing at all save be diminutive.

Last would come the main act, the Pious Philadelphia.

In front of her, Eliza's father spoke in querulous tones to his companion, a man whose face Eliza could not see.

"This isn't at all what I expected, Lord Ayelsworth. The handbill led me to believe this was to be a performance of hymns and devotions, yet all I see are tricks fit for a heathen and freaks of nature."

The young man pulled at his collar and said, "Believe me, sir, I had no idea. I am as flummoxed as your good self."

Ayelsworth . . . she knew that name from somewhere. It rushed back to her: the insincere compliments, the blob of ink on his multihued petticoat breeches, the look of terror when she obliquely threatened his cods. It was her most recent suitor!

She hardly recalled him as a distinct entity. So many men had courted her, or tried to, for a day or two at most until she drove them away. He was like every other — vain, egoistic, dandified, a parrot of popular wit without an original thought in his head. What on earth was her father doing with him?

"Ah well, it makes me appreciate a quiet country life . . . and yet it makes me yearn all the more to have a hand in state affairs, so that perhaps in years to come, London and all of England can learn to find pleasure in more decorous pastimes. Why, damnation aside, can you imagine the cost of keeping London alight at all hours of the night? A nation that goes to bed with the sun would save money enough to feed the destitute and fund an army!" Her father shook his head, gray wisps of hair a trembling nimbus in the candle and rushlight. "How long, d'you think, before I can make a difference? You say once you are wed you can get me a position close to His Majesty?"

"In a heartbeat, sir."

"And I won't have to do anything . . . degrading?"

"You won't have to do anything at all. Particularly if all you care for is a job title and access to the king. A sinecure without a salary is as easy to come by as a bawd in a brothel. Er . . . ahem . . . as a novice in a nunnery. Once I marry your daughter you'll have a real connection to the throne. I'm thirty-third in line, you know. Ah, no, thirty-fourth, because my great-uncle's new bride has whelped a boy, but you know how precarious childhood is."

Eliza's face became ghastly, and she didn't hear the rest. Marry that poxy Ayelsworth? Was her father mad? Senile?

She almost leaped to her feet on the spot. It had been an easy matter to dismiss him once. Surely she could do it again. Then she remembered her clothes, the hour, and the fact that she was in the company of a woman who, while not exactly a whore, would certainly be taken for one.

It would be a weak position for attack, to say the least.

She took a deep breath, glad she wasn't wearing boning and busk that would have prevented it. It was vexing, certainly, but she could talk her way out of it as soon as she saw her father under more appropriate circumstances. If necessary, she could even hint that she was on the verge of arranging an even more splendid alliance for herself, or that the queen valued her service too much to let her go for at least another year. Failing that, she could threaten Ayelsworth's cods again. That did the trick to a nicety almost a year ago. He just needed a reminder.

Somewhat calmer, she settled down to enjoy a round of juggling before Philadelphia came onstage. After all, he couldn't force her to marry. She had to sign the paper and speak the words, and no manner of threats or cajolement could induce her to say "I do" to simpering, mealy Lord Ayelsworth.

"Are you certain she will marry me, sir?" Ayelsworth asked. "She seemed . . . reluctant before."

"She was but a child. By now she's likely struck with the green sickness herself, and eager to be wed. But if not, no matter. I've put up with her objections long enough. No one was good enough for her. At that rate I'd never have grandchildren — and proper heirs! What use is a girl, after all, except to get boys?" Eliza's fists clenched. "Get a few sons on her and she'll forget she ever objected to you. By then I'll have the king's attention and finally put my fortune to some use for this poor benighted nation of ours. For England's sake, I must have access to the court, and the only way I can do it is by allying Eliza to a nobleman close to His Majesty. You wait, Lord Ayelsworth. In a year or two you'll see some changes here. No more debauchery and license. Why, I heard the queen was once seen in trousers! Pah! They say she's barren, too. Perhaps I can convince him to do as Henry did and get himself a good, honest, fruitful English girl for his bed and bride. They say there's a Frances Stewart . . ."

But supplanting a royal, even an unpopular queen, was treason, and Ayelsworth steered the conversation back to his reluctant wife-to-be. "What if she protests, or pleads her case with the king?"

Eliza heard her good, honest, loving Puritan father laugh and say, "A draft of datura, two strong men to bind and carry her, a fast carriage, and you can have her wedded and bedded before she knows what she's about. There's no annulment then. Keep her drugged and you can even get my first grandson for me before she can naysay you. I've waited long enough for her to make up her mind. She's been so carefully raised, almost cloistered, that she fears consummation like the devil. But virginity does no woman any good for long. What's a treasure that's never spent, eh? Won't have my girl be a medlar, rotten before she's ripe!"

Ayelsworth chuckled and Pious Philadelphia stepped onstage, prim and saintly, as assistants assembled a sort of box around her lower half.

Eliza didn't know what to do. She wanted to crack their two heads together. She wanted to dissolve into tears. She wanted to flee and she wanted to leap on the stage and denounce her father for a hypocrite who preached goodness but planned to have his daughter drugged, kidnapped, and raped.

But she did nothing, because she realized what she should have known all along: she was powerless.

She might don masculine guise and strut through the night. She might write as well as any male playwright, with her work to be put on by the King's Company that very autumn. She might have the mind, and the courage, to do anything her heart de-sired . . . and yet because she was a woman, she could be raped into marriage and, once bound, not be able to do a thing about it. *Why, even the king would take my father's side,* she thought bitterly. *He needs my father's money. He'll forget that I've cared for his wife, that he's danced with me and exchanged pleasantries.*

What her father had proposed was not strictly speaking legal, but it was a common enough occurrence. Young girls with for-tunes were cajoled, coerced, and yes, even abducted into giving themselves and their fortunes. And most of the time, at least one parent was complicit. Marriages were arranged, and though in theory consent was necessary, in practice a proposal was less a case of *Will you?* than *You will.*

"The Pious Philadelphia will now recite from the Bible, be-ginning with the forty-fifth Psalm," said the announcer. "She is so holy, so devout, so pure and saintlike in her nature that nothing will distract her from her devotions. As the Christians in Rome prayed with the light of heaven in their eyes even as lions rent their bones, so does Philadelphia ignore mere flesh and keep her mind on higher things."

"This is more like what I came to see," Eliza's father said, and settled back with a saintly air.

"Now we but need three volunteers from the audience, to test her faith. You sir, and you, and yes, you lad, if you can free your hand from your miss's pocket. Do whatever you wish, gentlemen. I vow she won't know or care."

"They're plants, you can be sure," Nelly whispered.

The three men crouched and disappeared behind the box that obscured Philadelphia from the waist down. In thrilling, heavenly tones the top half recited:

> *"With myrrh, aloes, and cassia your robes are fragrant.*
> *From ivory-paneled palaces stringed instruments bring*
>   *you joy."*

From below, hidden, came stirring and sound that indicated something quite worldly was occurring behind the box. Philadelphia kept reciting the psalm, but her breath began to come quickly and her eyes rolled in an extravagant mummery of conflicted pleasure. The audience cheered and loosed loud catcalls, but true to her advertisement, Philadelphia never stopped reciting.

> *"Listen, my daughter, and understand; pay me careful heed.*
> *Forget your people and your father's house..."*

A woman was supposed to leave her father with tears and cleave unto her husband and his family, in biblical times as now, Eliza thought. *Well, I've done the first, at least.* She stared hard at the grizzled patriarchal head, hating him, hating herself because she could not hate him as a man hates his enemy, his equal, but only as a slave hates his master, the cur hates the spit boy who puts coals to his paws. Because hating him was the only thing she could do. He had might and money and, for all practical purposes, the law behind him.

Philadelphia's phrases, rising, gasping, reached her piecemeal through her misery:

"Then the richest of the people will seek your favor with gifts ...

They are led in with glad and joyous acclaim ...

I will make your name renowned through all generations;
Thus nations shall praise you forever."

No, I'm not a slave, not a cur! Woman I may be, but I am man enough to best a worm who would have his own daughter raped to further his designs. I swear on my life, I will never marry that befouled Ayelsworth, or any other man my father may choose. That is not my destiny. Fame! Renown! The praise of the nation! I will be a playwright. I will live my own life, as I choose to live it, Father, in skirts or breeches, in a palace or a gutter, with the money you give me or with the money I earn.

Because I can write damned fine plays, Father, she thought fiercely to the gray head. *And I warrant I can act in them too.*

Furious (and yet still desperately afraid), she posed for herself one final test of her resolution.

"Good lord!" her father said when, belatedly, he realized the mock-holy burlesque Pious Philadelphia was enacting. "What cloaca of vice have we stumbled upon!" His voice drowned out the next biblical piece, the Song of Solomon. "Blasphemy!" he cried as the crowd hissed him down. "Sinners, hellfire awaits you!" He stood and frowned at the audience, which had nothing but contempt for old bugbear Puritans.

"I had no idea, sir!" Ayelsworth said, terrified lest his prize slip away. "Od's fish, a man can't even trust the Holy Book these days, I vow!" He tried to steer Eliza's father away before the man could become any more incensed.

"You've disturbed my lady once, sir!" growled a low voice from behind him. "Pray leave this place now, before she has cause for further complaint and you have need of a chirurgeon."

Eliza stood squarely with her hand on her sword. Her father, without looking up, started to shuffle away, looking suddenly old and diminished.

"Are you a man, sir?" Eliza said. "Do me the honor of looking me in the eye as I chastise your bad manners."

He looked at her without recognition and tremblingly doffed his high-crowned hat. "I beg your pardon, sir. I'll be going."

She stared at him a long moment, then sat down and composed herself as her father and Ayelsworth took their leave.

I can best him, she thought. *Whatever was I afraid of?*

Through the commotion Philadelphia never stopped her throaty recitation as the concealed men kept up their subterranean endeavors below her skirts.

> *"The joints of thy thighs are like jewels,*
> *the work of the hands of a cunning workman.*
> *Thy navel is like an round goblet, which wanteth not liquor;*

thy belly is like a heap of wheat set about with lilies.

Thy two breasts are like two young roes that are twins."

Eliza looked at pretty, witty Nell and whispered aloud, "I will never marry a man."

Nell shrugged in agreement. "Why bother?" she said, looking up at her friend. "You have all you need already."

"Do you mind us leaving now, Nelly? There's something I need to talk to you about."

Chapter 17

THE MULBERRY GROVE

ZABBY WOKE when Beth closed the door behind her. In a trice Zabby was on her feet and tugging up the breeches she'd saved from their night masquerading as men. If she wanted to catch Beth she'd have to hurry, and it was simply too hard to put on a gown quickly, and alone. She'd look disheveled and half dressed and everyone would assume she'd come from an assignation, with the king or an illicit lover. But in a few heartbeats she had breeches, shirt, and waistcoat neatly on, and struggled into high black boots so she didn't have to fiddle with hose. A knot in her pale hair, a feathered Cavalier hat perched on top, and she was following Beth's footsteps down the hall.

She lost her for a moment, then heard the click of her friend's heels down a servants' passage that led out of Whitehall. She followed partly for the sake of curiosity, but mostly from a desire to keep Beth out of trouble. Her dreadful mother was always watching. If Beth was sneaking out for a whispered word of love, Lady Enfield might catch her and...Zabby didn't know about Beth's savage beating, but she knew her mother would stop at nothing to keep her untouched until her marriage.

Skulking in the shadows, she followed Beth westward through the darkness, over smooth-rolled grass and the bowers of the king's gardens, and beyond.

Good Lord, St. James's Park at this hour? By day it was a place for genteel strolls and flirting dalliance, frequented by the king and his courtiers; by night it was a hotbed of lechery, where moss and grass and tree trunks served as beds.

Zabby quickened her step as she caught sight of shadowed couples half clothed and giggling in the shrubberies. No, dear Beth, this is not love! What, to rut in the mud with your Harry? If he is a gentleman, a man of honor, he would never ask you to meet him in St. James's Park by night.

From somewhere near she heard a muffled protest and then a gasp—of joy, of pain? *I must be honest with myself, if with no other,* Zabby thought. *If Charles reached out his hand from there in the thicket and drew me into the mud, I would go, and willingly. Curse love! Curse lust! Curse this body of mine that is virtuous only because it lacks the opportunity for vice!*

Beth was a ghostly luster of moonlight on silk far along the path, and Zabby hurried after her. *Let her swive in the park, then, if it is with the one she desires with all her heart. Who am I to tell her no? Perhaps that is love: resignation to degradation. But I'll stay long enough to see her safe in his arms.*

The black mulberry trees were in full fruit, and the ground beneath her squelched in the droppings of the riot of birds who had gorged themselves on the berries. *She'll have to clean her gown herself in the morning,* Zabby thought, *else the maids will know where she's been.* The violet-black juice was very distinctive. This was the only grove of the exotic trees near the palace, planted by James I in hopes of starting a silk industry in England. He hadn't done his research — silkworms prefer the white to the black mulberry, and though the trees thrived, his plans for domestic silk manufacturing failed.

"Oh, Har . . ." Beth squealed, her voice suddenly muffled by a kiss or a cautious hand. Zabby pressed herself against a bush, straining to hear, to see.

"My love, my light," a masculine voice said, then broke off. "Hush, we haven't time for that." But from the audible sound of kisses and Beth's delighted moans, they evidently had a bit of time after all.

Zabby heard more murmured prattle, and thought, *That is exactly what Beth would say to one of the king's spaniel pups.* "Darling," "precious" . . . Shouldn't love be grander — or silent? The words of love struck Zabby as banal. She wouldn't have breath or brain for words if she were in Charles's arms.

"Mother says I must marry that vile Earl of Thorne," Beth said more clearly when the nuzzling ceased.

"Never fear, my heart," he replied, and Zabby saw a glint of very white teeth. "I almost have enough now, for you and all my family."

"I don't need much, Harry, and if you should be caught . . ."

He laughed. "They don't want to catch me, love. I'm safe. Soon, very soon I'll put that business behind me and I'll just be another fireside legend. There's only one more thing I have to do, one more prize I must capture."

Zabby thought he was referring to Beth.

"And then we can be married?"

"As soon as I've done that last thing I'll take you away, from your mother and that vicious Thorne. I've heard a tale or two of him. But Beth, I must not take you like a common thief. I don't know that you owe your mother any special consideration after the way she's treated you, but you are under the queen's protection, and I am a man of honor who treasures you too much to carry you off like a baggage. I must ask the queen's permission to marry you."

"Oh, but Harry, you can't just walk into court! Not with a price on your head."

"You forget, no one knows who I am. But you're right: if your mother were to see me, even if she didn't know I'm your suitor, there'd be trouble. Maybe I can find the queen when she's away from the court. Traveling, perhaps."

"Oh, yes! We're to go to Tunbridge Wells and then Bath in a month or two to take the waters. They're said to be a sovereign cure for barrenness. Will you be done with your last bit of business by then, do you think?"

"I should be, if I play my cards well."

"And then we can be married?"

"Once I find the queen alone and get her leave, I'll carry you off on the fastest horse I possess."

"Oh, Harry, you really do love me, don't you?"

There was a long silence, and Zabby assumed they were kissing again.

At last he said simply, "I need you, my Beth."

Oh, thought Zabby, *those are better words than* darling *and* sweetheart, *the common cant of every flirt and adulterer.* To be needed—now, there was something worthy! A traitorous body might succumb to fleeting desire, to sharp hunger and sudden satiety all in the course of a few moments—the hunt, the kill, the gorging, the repletion—but a need is profound, lasting, visceral.

And so Zabby looked with deep, shameful envy at the young lovers clutching each other in the shadows. She'd thought they were children playing at love, their lust a fleeting touch of skin, excited nerves. Then he'd said *I need you,* his voice shifting from playful to deadly earnest, and Zabby believed that her friend had found the happiness of life. To be the beloved's needful thing, to be his bread, his water, his air, his rest.

Some deep devil part of her hated Beth for her luck, but the rest of her was blissfully happy for her friend and vowed to help her in any way possible. She thought the couple needed her assistance.

How foolish of them to meet in St. James's Park. It was such a common place for trysts that if Beth were seen coming from the park she'd be immediately suspected and condemned, by gossip if not fact, and whispered untruths could be more damning than verity proclaimed. It was clear that the naïve couple needed the guidance of someone more clearheaded. The lad was no doubt determined and ambitious, having evidently found some way to make money, but if he pressed Beth into meeting him in such notorious locations, her mother would catch her eventually, and flay her.

Shall I talk with Beth? she wondered. *No, she loves him so deeply, she'll fly wherever he bids her. I'll find out who he is and tell him to be more circumspect. Those children might wind up happy if they're a little careful now.*

Zabby, disappointed in her own love, felt infinitely wise.

When the loving couple parted (and joined for another farewell, and parted again with lingering backward looks), Zabby left Beth to find her own way home. She meant to follow Harry, but he lingered in the park, so Zabby remained hidden, waiting, still debating exactly what to say.

Before she could decide, another figure emerged from the darkness, a large man with blond hair so elaborate that it had to be a wig.

"Did I give you enough time alone with your inamorata? Was she willing? Oh ho, don't look so stricken, you with your gallant reputation! I don't mean was she willing to quiff on the turf."

Zabby thought the voice was familiar.

"The queen goes to take the waters soon, and Lady Elizabeth will be with her."

"Good."

"Her love and her hand are all I desire," Harry said.

"Sweet heaven, are all young creatures such fools? She'll lose her looks after the first baby, her gentle temper after the second, and you'll hop from one mistress to the next ever after. Love? Pah!"

"I own, before we met again in the flesh she was but a means to an end, a way to restore my family's good name. But now that I've tasted her sweetness, I must have her."

"You could have had her this night."

"No, I can't be like that."

"You're a man— you *are* like that."

"My family wronged hers, and I must make amends."

"Well, I suppose a fellow must get heirs, so go, be fruitful and multiply. Only, a family devours a fortune, so take care lest you come to me for another job." The unknown man chuckled.

"It is shame enough I do this vile thing. Henceforth, I'll live lawfully and in peace with my bride."

The unknown man made a noise of disgust. "Just remember you're not to meet your sweetheart again until the queen goes afield. It's too risky. That mother of hers has a spy system to rival my own, though how she does it is beyond me. Do you know, I spend near twenty thousand pounds a year in bribes and payoff, and she, on the strength of nothing but her own foul visage, discovers nearly everything that passes in Whitehall. Perhaps I ought to recruit her. Now be off, and don't contact me until the thing's accomplished."

Harry strode off into the night, and the other figure stood a moment. He gave a short, sharp laugh, whispered, "Fool!" then turned on his heel and walked past Zabby back toward Whitehall.

She still could not pierce the darkness enough to see his visage, so she followed him, through the park, the gardens, and into the palace. He strode without hesitation through the labyrinthine halls—evidently he was a resident or regular visitor, but who? Who would help a young man win a penniless girl, yet speak so cynically of love? Was he an uncle or patron, determined to help a favorite have his whim, even if he personally disapproved? At least he'd done the couple the service of telling them not to meet until they could be honorably married. What a noble idea Harry had, to petition the queen herself for Beth's hand!

Zabby's rosy thoughts collapsed in confusion when the unknown man let himself into a door she recognized all too well—the private chambers of Barbara Palmer, Lady Castlemaine.

Immediately she was full of suspicions, nebulous but certain. Barbara had never helped another human being in her life, unless it was to somehow further her own ends. Zabby recalled the time she'd rushed to help the injured boy— surely that had been only to win the goodwill of the people. And when she'd seemed to confide in Zabby about the threat of Frances Stewart, why, that wasn't camaraderie at all. Barbara wouldn't hesitate to get rid of Frances, Zabby, the queen herself, to ensure she continued her reign as the most powerful woman in the land.

If Barbara—or any friend of hers—was involved, then surely something sinister was afoot. Why would Barbara help Beth?

Or Harry Ransley, a very minor lord no one had heard of? She must have some ulterior motive. Perhaps she saw Beth's beauty as a threat. Certainly Beth was far lovelier than Frances Stewart, though it wasn't the kind that drew every man's eye. A man didn't notice Beth immediately, but when he did . . . Perhaps the king had finally realized there was a greater beauty than Frances among his queen's ladies in waiting. If Barbara had the opportunity to help Beth get married and farmed safely out to the country, she might spare herself future competition. Perhaps that man was simply her agent.

She waited a while, but no one emerged, and finally Zabby crept off to bed. Though she couldn't imagine Barbara being up to any good, she couldn't clearly see that her meddling was doing anything bad. If her will was advanced by giving Beth exactly what she wanted, why not let her practice her machinations?

Still, it bothered her, and as she snuck back into the room and tucked herself beside the blissfully sleeping Beth, she wished she knew who that familiar man had been.

The next evening Zabby had her answer — one that served only to raise more questions. While the highest of the high, and the syco-phants who continually reminded them of their lofty status, gath-ered in the king's presence chamber, Barbara turned her attention from her monarch and lover to her cousin (and, some said, lover) the powerful Duke of Buckingham. He was third in rank, just be-hind the king and James, Duke of York, but far wealthier than ei-ther of them. He was a provocateur, a plotter, a poet, the king's closest friend since boyhood — and the only man to ever scheme against him and live.

He was another creature like Barbara — self-serving, with an intense love of power. Unlike Barbara, he had a particularly keen mind and was always using it to make trouble. Barbara contrived only for her own gain; Buckingham plotted for sheer love of a good plot. He was a periwigged Loki.

His shoes — the foppish slippers favored at court, red-heeled, with bows at the toes — were stained dark purple-black near the sole. Her own boots had been tinted a similar color. She was certain it was mulberry juice.

Zabby gasped, so that the queen, under her ministrations, gave her a concerned look. "Only a pin, Your Majesty," she said, and stared hard at Barbara and Buckingham, calculating. Buckingham was the right size, as large as the man she'd seen the night before, and he favored an expansive golden wig with trailing curls. It might not have been him — or he might have been in St. James's Park coincidentally, for his own purposes — but it was too likely for her to dismiss. What's more, the man had let himself into Barbara's room without a knock or announcement, something only a relative (or lover) would do, not a hireling.

If Barbara was involved, mischief was afoot; if Buckingham had combined forces with her, it must be downright evil.

But no, it could not be. Who would want to harm poor sweet Beth? And what harm could they do to her by granting her fondest wish? Zabby's mind, easily as keen as Buckingham's but less well versed in the subtleties of treachery, could not unravel it.

Then, with a little laugh, she chided herself. *Why look for intricacies and evil when the simplest answer will likely suffice? Didn't Papa say that while you should explore all avenues, the most probable solution will be the most obvious? Harry must be doing some important job for the king, and Buckingham, as the king's dearest friend, was playing messenger. And afterward he merely paid a visit to his cousin Barbara, who had nothing to do with any of it.*

Still, she could not help but be worried that the court's two most notorious troublemakers were in some way involved with the fate of her innocent friend.

In the morning, Eliza, dressed more soberly than usual, sat ensconced with her father and Lord Ayelsworth. She kept her head bowed and a modest little smile on her face as her father spoke to her quite sternly.

To his surprise, she responded gently, "Why, of course I will marry him, Father." To her personal disgust she managed a shy, seductive glance at her beau under batted eyelashes. Her acting was progressing apace. "I would never go counter to your wishes, particularly when they so closely follow my own. Only..." She looked up to her father appealingly. "Please, may we wait until after the queen returns from taking the waters at Tunbridge Wells and Bath? I have sworn to serve her, and she would be so vexed if I wasn't there to dress her hair. She says I'm the only one who understands how to place a comb."

He laughed and patted Eliza on the head. "Ah, what a loyal little featherhead I've raised. Combs for the queen! You'll soon have a host of other duties as a wife and mother, no doubt more pleasant than sticking tortoiseshell in a popish poll. Still, there's no harm in waiting a month or two. When will the queen return?"

"In October. I'm not sure exactly when."

"Then let us plan the wedding for the middle of November, the second Sunday. Will that give you time to buy enough pretties for your trousseau? Here, my dear." He was positively benevolent now, and Eliza felt a fleeting qualm at deceiving the old man. He handed her a purse fat with coins. *Buying and selling,* she thought. *My body, my loins, my generation. All for sale on the open market, and I'm not even the seller.* "Buy what you wish," he said. "There's plenty more where that came from. I mean for my daughter to be happy!"

She had to bow her head to hide a most unfilial snarl. She remembered the father who had petted her as a little girl, who bought her books and ponies and ribbons in every color, wind-up automatons and foreign songbirds to entertain her. *He thinks he loves me,* she thought. *He really thinks it is for the best.* She hated him for his ignorance.

She controlled herself, and simpered at Ayelsworth, who laughed nervously, his hand still hovering protectively near his cods.

That evening she dressed as Mr. Duncan and confirmed with Killigrew that her play was to be performed upon the court's return from its peregrinations. Most of the players would be traveling with the court to amuse the ladies as they took the restorative waters.

Next Eliza tracked down the owner of her little apartment at the end of Maypole Alley and, after a bout of strenuous dickering, managed to secure a ten-year lease in exchange for the sack of gold that was supposed to buy her stockings and embroidered smocks for her husband's pleasure. She put the lease in Nell's name, just in case it ever came to the law. After all, Mr. Duncan didn't exist.

"Ten years of safety," she told Nelly.

"Of lodging, anyway. If you don't have money, what will we do for food?"

"Oh, I'll manage some way. I can sell a play or two a year, and maybe act."

"I'd love to act," Nell said wistfully.

"Well, why don't you? All of the players adore you."

"The men do, anyway."

"Well, they're the ones who make the decisions. For now."

"My sister Rose said the theater is looking for another orange girl this season. I could do that for a time, to tide us over."

"Only, an orange girl's next door to a whore. Don't forget you're in Mr. Duncan's keeping. I don't want you earning any extra money that way. Mr. Duncan will be mighty jealous." She smiled, but she was only half joking.

"I wouldn't mind, you know, if it brings in money."

"I have a bit of my own, don't forget, dear, no matter if the worst happens. Two hundred pounds a year or so, plenty to get us by if we're careful. Be patient, have faith in me, and before long you'll be living like a queen."

"I don't see as the poor queen lives so very well. I'd rather live like one of the king's mistresses."

Eliza laughed and kissed Nelly on the cheek. "He's the only man I dare not be jealous of. If His Majesty wants you, Mr. Duncan won't object to parting with you." She didn't think Mr. Duncan had a thing to worry about.

Chapter 18

THE HEALING WATERS

*T*HE THREE ELIZABETHS did not forget their sorrows while the court was on pilgrimage, but they managed to defer them. Eliza and Beth had been granted a temporary hymeneal reprieve, and each planned to make the stay of execution permanent.

Eliza, filled with an excited dread about what she planned to do, was preternaturally lively and witty, and many of the courtiers went home after an afternoon's converse with her to scribble down her epigrams and later claim them as their own. In years to come, she'd discover lines in plays that sounded awfully familiar.

She danced and joked, gambled and gamboled, and lived as high a life as she could manage in skirts. Her father had returned to his estate, but Ayelsworth, parasite that he was, had naturally followed the court and plagued Eliza with unwanted, awkward affections until she actually bribed two penniless younger sons to become his disciples and pretend they thought him a mortal god of taste and brilliance. Thus encumbered, flattered into obedience, he spent most of the day spouting off his own silly opinions and utterly missing the two men's yawns. They weren't such good actors as their employer, but they did their best to earn their money, and Ayelsworth was fooled and distracted enough to leave Eliza in peace.

At Tunbridge Wells, Eliza took one swig of the chalybeate waters and spat it out.

Ayelsworth, who had broken free from his feigned admirers, giggled and said, "You ought to drink it, my lady. 'Tis said that taking these waters all but guarantees conceiving a son."

She looked at him evenly for a long moment, so that he flushed and began to stammer—he still wasn't sure if she was Puritan or wanton, and didn't much care, beyond what it might mean for his chances of consummating the union and securing her fortune. Then she said, loud enough for those standing nearest to hear, "How ignorant I am—I thought children were gotten in quite another way. Then surely, sir, I should avoid the waters now. Or would you prefer me to come to our wedding big-bellied with a son?"

Ayelsworth slunk away, red and confused, and Eliza dumped the remainder of her water on the ground. "It tastes of nails," she said to the small crowd around her. If the water stank and tasted of eggs and iron, she wouldn't drink it, no matter how good the world said it was for her.

Beth spent most of her time with the queen, living in a dream of love. Despite formidable protest, her mother had been forced to remain behind. These travels were for the king and queen's pleasure, and their pleasure would be marred by that woman's presence. So, though several hundred rode with the entourage, Lady Enfield was told to stay in London, albeit in slightly more diplomatic terms. She ground her teeth and poked her silver beak into the face of every courtier she thought might change the royal mind, but in the end she could not quite defy the order. She did, however, closet Catherine alone before the journey and once again promise deadly consequences to anyone who allowed Beth to fall to ruin.

Beth, blessedly free from scrutiny, reveled in thoughts of her lover. She sat by Catherine's side for hours on end, playing with her hair and talking, in a confusing abstract, about love. The queen, who had heard of Beth's ambitious engagement, smiled indulgently. She knew little about the Earl of Thorne, but if the girl waxed this enthusiastic about him in the months before the wedding, it was sure to be a happy union.

Beth had already received a coded message from Harry telling her he would meet her in Bath, and they would arrange their elopement from there. Beth waited patiently for the day her lover would come for her.

And what of Zabby? At Tunbridge Wells she rediscovered the king who was her friend, and enjoyed that so much, she sometimes forgot for minutes at a time that she loved him.

Tunbridge was little more than a spring with rough rooms on either side, one for the repose of ladies, one for gentlemen, though as might be imagined there was much commingling. Southborough was the nearest town, but rather than try to lodge in this cramped and unfashionable place, Charles had decided to emulate kings of old and established the entire court on the downs in gaily flapping tents and pavilions. Standards fluttered in the air, and the whole thing was lovely and vastly inconvenient, romantic and almost intolerable. The good parts, as always, were experienced by the upper crust — starlit nights, cool breezes, rambles, a sense that one was on a gay adventure — while the bad parts — hauling water in for washing, hauling the night soil out for dumping — were borne by the servants. If not for their constant labor, the place would have stunk unbearably within three days, and no doubt the whole court would have died of dysentery.

As it was, the king and his friends lived as they imagined King Arthur had on his promenades and pilgrimages. He rode hard across the downs, and though there were no stags to bring to bay, he took his greyhounds and lurchers out to course for hares. He also renewed his interest in falconry and, though he didn't catch much, enjoyed riding for a time classically posed with a harrier on his wrist.

Zabby was with him all the while, riding as hard as Charles, full-skirted but astride, the wind whipping her white-blond hair. When they hunted they always had companions — to Zabby's dismay Frances had a good seat and looked splendid in a habit, side-saddle — but Zabby managed to lure Charles into other pursuits where they were not likely to be followed for long. They explored the spring, speculating about its origin, its properties, examining the water and surrounding earth through the lenses he brought with him. They hired a local farmer to show them the ruins of a Roman villa and, much older, the weathered battlements of a hill fort. Other courtiers, eager to ingratiate, always started on these expeditions but even for king and country couldn't maintain their façade of interest for long, and after a while, Zabby invariably found herself blissfully alone with Charles.

She succeeded in schooling herself, never revealing by word or glance or touch that she desired him, and Charles treated her like a sister . . . or perhaps a favorite younger brother, because he never would have allowed his sister, Minette, now a princess of France, to slog barefoot through creeks, digging the banks for arrowheads.

One day they rode their mounts to exhaustion to see an ancient giant figure of a horse carved into a chalk hillside. They sprawled on the opposite hill, talking about what tribe could have carved the elegant white beast, and for what purpose.

"I suppose there was a horse god, or they killed a horse as sacrifice," Zabby conjectured.

Charles disagreed. "I think perhaps they made it simply because it is beautiful and men love to gaze at loveliness." He was looking at her when he said this, and Zabby's heart gave a great saltation. Charles touched her hair. "Almost as pale as the chalk," he said, and she didn't know if it was compliment or criticism or mere observation.

Charles lay down and took her hand in his. She stiffened. But a moment later he was asleep in the sunshine, and she kept perfectly still, shading him with her body, for more than two hours.

"I love you," she whispered to her sleeping king.

Catherine too was having a marvelous time, mainly because Barbara was still at Whitehall, though this satisfaction was somewhat marred by the fact that Barbara had recently given birth to her third bastard by the king. Then too, while Frances was frequently riding or hunting with the king, she was never, as far as the queen knew, alone with him. Tents made for pleasant dalliance so long as no one worried about keeping it a secret, and she was sure she would have heard if Charles had finally convinced Frances to yield. Timidly, Catherine had begun to employ her own spies, and though they gleefully reported that Charles was still sedulously courting her young rival, they assured her that the maid was maiden still.

She knew Zabby was often alone with Charles, but if she had any suspicions, she fondled her seashell and fought them down. She believed her husband, and yet . . . there was something in the girl's eyes when she looked on her sovereign—a wistfulness, a devotion. That same look was in Catherine's eyes, if only she knew it, and it would never leave them, not all her life.

While at Tunbridge, Catherine discovered a pastime that perfectly suited her early training in the convent—fishing. Her childhood and youth had been spent gazing placidly over verdant scenes, sitting in the shade, deep in contemplation, and it was a short step to place a rod in her hand. She was accustomed to hours of solitude and patient silence, and so she had the serenity to wait for the fish's pleasure. What's more, the countless hours of embroidery allowed her to tie a pretty fly, and it was not long before she was happily casting her line into merry creeks and still ponds, in such prayerful repose that it was sometimes a shock, practically a disappointment, when a fish finally struck. Charles joined her frequently, though he preferred more active pursuits, and these were some of the happiest days of Catherine's life, when he sat beside her, scarcely talking, stroking her arm occasionally.

They retired early, and he spent every night in her tent.

By the time they quit Tunbridge Wells, Catherine had begun to suspect that she might at last be pregnant. She mentioned it to no one, though, not even her trusted maids of honor. She didn't realize that most of the court followed her monthly courses so closely that they suspected almost as soon as she did.

Chapter 19

The Quickened Queen

CATHERINE WAS NOT A NATURAL HORSEWOMAN, but in an attempt to show she was as good as Frances, she donned her tightest habit and rode a large, handsome leopard-spotted gray for the last leg into Bath. She trotted at Charles's side all the while, smiling blithely, but unfortunately the beast had an awkward gait and she wasn't skilled enough to correct it, so by the time they rode into the city of creamy gold stone, her thighs felt like they'd been ground under a pestle.

The three Elizabeths, seeing her distress, lured her into the thermal baths, and she found these so soothing, she visited every day. Wearing long, full shifts that billowed about them, they would soak by the hour, gossiping (another sport for which the queen was acquiring a taste), singing, and helping the queen perfect her English. Sometimes Simona or Winifred joined them, but the older ladies thought it was a barbaric habit that would disrupt the humors.

"A good wipe-down with a damp cloth every other day is enough for any modest Englishwoman," one of her ladies sniffed. But Catherine loved to let her muscles melt, her vision blur in the steam, dreaming of a warm nursery filled with happy children, while outside the baths the first frost settled on the grass.

She drank the heavy ferrous waters too, with each sip feeding the baby she knew grew inside her. She ate the sweets and pastries the city was becoming famous for, and her slim figure grew rounder. Charles began to pay attention to places he'd previously overlooked.

One morning, Charles had risen betimes for a game of tennis, while Catherine lazed in bed. She sent the chambermaids away and only the three Elizabeths remained.

"What would you like to do today, Your Majesty?" Eliza asked as she rummaged through the queen's jewels, holding them up to her throat and thinking how well they'd look against Nelly's creamy skin. She passed along a pair of fire-laced opal drops to Beth, who fixed them in Catherine's earlobes. "Lady Southesk is setting up tables for gleek this morning." The card game was currently in fashion at court. "I believe some of the ladies are going riding, and there's a party going to Lord Bartlett's estate to tour his gardens."

"It all sounds dreadfully dull," Catherine replied.

"What would you like to do, then, Your Majesty? Maybe a bit of archery?" The queen was becoming quite a sure shot with her light bow. Like fishing, it was another pastime that required patience, and she had that to spare.

Catherine rose and stretched, deciding, and suddenly Beth let out a little shriek. "Oh, Your Majesty!" She pointed to a red blot of blood on the white sheet. "We had all hoped that you'd at last..."

Catherine's hand went to her throat as if she were choking, and then dropped to her belly, now ever so slightly rounded. "No! It cannot be!" She fell to her knees, keening a prayer, then stopped abruptly in the middle of a plea to the Virgin and got to her feet.

"Take the sheets away and dispose of them. Say nothing to a soul. This is a small matter. I'm told breeding women often bleed a bit." But her lips were pressed tight and she was scarcely breathing.

"Then it's true? You're pregnant?" Beth asked.

Catherine nodded, ignoring the gripping sensation low in her abdomen. *Misfortune is like the devil,* she thought. *To acknowledge it gives it strength. A bit of blood is nothing. I know I carry Charles's child.*

"But I've not yet told Charles," she confided to her maids of honor. "I wanted to wait until I was certain. And then..." She gave a little forced laugh. "If he knew, he'd bundle me home and coddle me for eight more months, and I'm having such a good time here." She swept the sheet off the bed and scrubbed with a handkerchief at the russet stain on the down-stuffed mattress underneath. A sob escaped her again.

"Don't worry, Your majesty," Zabby said. "I've midwived many times at home on Barbados, and what you say is true: there is often blood early on. Most of the time it means nothing." *And the rest of the time it means a miscarriage,* she thought.

"How is it that you've midwived?" the queen asked, astonished.

"We have hundreds of slaves on the estate," Zabby said, "and perhaps three doctors on the whole island. Many of the slaves and bondswomen are competent midwives themselves, but if there's no one else, or if it is a difficult case, I assist. I've birthed babes, foals, pigs."

"But a foal isn't the next king of England. Oh, what should I do?" Despite her best efforts, her desperation was evident. "Should I send for the physician? If the gossips think I've miscarried, they'll never let me live it down. What good's a barren queen?"

"You're not barren, Your Majesty," Zabby said firmly, all the while thinking, *If the queen gives birth, there's no chance for me.* Then, *What if she dies in childbirth?* a demon voice whispered in Zabby's brain, barely audible. She pinched herself hard on the thigh and buried the thought under a thousand blessings. "Perhaps you should send for the physician after all, just in case."

But Catherine, though frightened by those crimson spots, didn't want to let a lack of faith doom her. If God had granted her a child, He would be offended if she doubted Him. She tended to think of God as the ancient Greeks regarded their pantheon, having capacity for a few petty human emotions. If she let a little blood shake her, then her child might be stripped from her, just to teach her a lesson. Blessed Mary might forgive her fears, but God would punish her.

She forced herself to be cheerful. "No, let us disport ourselves. Archery, did you say? Fetch my quiver and let us go to the green."

But though her courses didn't come, Catherine continued to bleed irregularly, a bit on her petticoat, a bit more on her bedclothes. She kept it secret from the other ladies, but at last she got her favorite maids of honor, her confidantes, together, and sobbed wretchedly.

"Tell me what to do!" she begged of them. "I must give him a child—I must! It is my only duty in this life, and if I should fail . . ."

She thought Zabby would have midwife lore for her, or Eliza some jest to cheer her. But it was Beth who said, timidly, "There is a shrine nearby. I . . . Someone told me it is the shrine of one who protects mothers in difficult times. Women go there to ask for an easy birth. We can go there, just the four of us. No one else need know."

"A shrine? To one of the saints?"

Beth knew it was not, but she didn't think the queen would be willing to pray at an old Celtic altar. "I think so. I don't know which one. The local women swear by her."

"I'll go!" Catherine said, starting up and scrubbing away her tears. "Where is it? I'll have my coach made ready."

"Can your coachman be trusted, Your Majesty?" Beth asked. "Does he gossip? Everyone near Bath knows why women go to that shrine, and if you don't want anyone to know you're quick . . ."

"You're right. We can hire a coach."

"The women say no man is allowed to approach the shrine," Beth said. Harry, in his latest message, had been very specific that she should get the queen alone. *If there's a coachman or footman there, he may be your mother's agent,* he told her. *She has spies everywhere, you know. He might try to stop us from eloping.*

She didn't call it lying. *Subterfuge* was a better word. She never would have believed she'd have such a knack for it, but love gave her courage, loquacity, a swift and crafty mind.

Zabby gave a gasp and pretended she'd just stubbed her toe. That midnight conversation came back to her. Of course — this was it! Their dear Beth was going to join her lover tonight. He'd get the queen's blessing and carry her off to a life of love and delight. Oh, lucky Beth.

She thought of Charles, of the love she would never have, and forced herself not to notice how haggard and unwell the queen had been looking lately.

"We'll go straightaway!" Catherine said, gaining hope.

"Not this morning," Beth said. "Tomorrow, late, when the others are dining. They say . . ." She wracked her brains for something convincing. "They say if you visit the shrine near nightfall, you will receive a dream from the saint that will tell you what you need to know."

"Very well, then. Tomorrow."

That would be quite enough time for Beth to get a message to Harry.

Chapter 20

The Shrine of Sulis

*I*T WAS BRISK the next evening, but the day had been sunny enough that the sharp scent of late-blooming verbenas and pinks still rose from the roadside to fill the air. Catherine and the maids bundled into a pony cart Eliza had wheedled from one of the local families, who loaned it gladly when they learned their queen was to ride in it. Why, once word got around, they could sell horse and cart for twice their price, as souvenirs of the royal visit...though perhaps it would be better to keep it themselves, and tell guests they sat where the royal rump once rested.

This outing had none of the festival atmosphere of their last evening adventure. They dressed somberly, the queen in deep indigo with a high neck, and no jewels. Even Beth, after much debate, decided a serviceable gown of sturdy make was better than silks and finery. Harry had told her they would have to ride hard for a while before they'd rendezvous with a coach, and proceed from there to a secret chapel where he had a minister prepared to marry them by special license. She packed an inconspicuous bag with her most minute treasures — her yellow gloves, a length of the emerald ribbon that looked so becoming tied in a bow at her throat, a swirled turquoise brooch Eliza had forced on her, swearing it wasn't her color.

Under her dress she wore layer upon layer of her finest petticoats and sheer shifts, some gifts from the queen, some of which she'd painstakingly embroidered herself. She didn't think her Harry would mind if she had a plain dress, but she rather thought he'd like her to have pretty underthings.

The ponies fretted and shivered their withers as Zabby drove them out of Bath. They were used to a clean, warm barn and sugar from the daughters of the house, and shied at shadows along the roughening path. There was a queer yellow half light in the air as the sun descended and warm day met cool night.

"It looks like a poisonous vapor," Catherine said, and told them of a sickening mist that rose from a marshland not far from her convent and periodically devastated the town perched at its banks.

Zabby was too distracted to tell her that the disease likely came not from air but from water befouled by their waste. Beth thought only that the mist might make her curls come undone. What if she looked so bedraggled that Harry decided he'd made a bad bargain and rode away without asking the queen for her hand?

They rode for almost an hour — and could have walked nearly as fast, if that had accorded with their dignity and footwear. The ponies usually pulled children, with a plump nurse or elderly groom strolling at their head, and only managed a trot under protest. Even then, their short legs made a great show of lifting primly and elegantly high, but accomplished little in the way of distance with each stride.

"Here, I think," Beth said, touching Zabby's arm.

"You think?" Eliza asked.

"He said turn at the little ruined inn. Yes, there." They could just see the skeleton of what had once been a building, long since burned out and overgrown with dying bracken.

"*He?*" Catherine asked. "I thought this was a shrine for women. What does a man know of it?" She nervously smoothed the midnight silk that lay flat over her stomach, flat where it should have bulged. Her belly still fluttered with what she was certain were the kicks and caperings of new life, but there was an ache, too, which in recent days slowly tightened around her like a snare.

"Oh, well..." Beth had run out of lies, but suddenly they were there.

The land dipped down sharply into a close copse, and Zabby pulled the ponies to a halt. Where the vegetation thickened stood the tumbled remains of a dry stone wall.

"It must have been badly built," Eliza said. "All the ones I've seen have stood for centuries."

They left the rig loose—it was obvious the ponies would never exert themselves without provocation—and picked their way along the narrow path that led into the little wood. It was just the sort of place a vixen would have liked to make her den, secret and dry, but the path was marked by many shoeprints and the flotsam of human passage: pipe ashes, torn laces, scraps of paper. No fox would have dared dig her earth here. Still, it felt wild, and though they knew the main road was nearby, it seemed to the girls that they'd stepped into something primeval.

Zabby ran her hand over the crumbling, lichen-covered stones. "Perhaps this wall *did* stand for centuries," she said. "Look at that. Surely it is Roman."

She pointed to a worn squat stone with the barest impression of having three sides.

"A grave?" Catherine asked, crossing herself.

"A terminus, I think. A Roman boundary stone." Zabby crouched down and could just make out the letters *DSM*.

A few more steps brought them to the shrine.

"Is that it?" the queen asked. "It looks more like a well. Which saint's can it be?"

A low oval wall of flaking stones surrounded a navel that descended into the earth deeper than any of them could see in the failing light.

"I think I know whose shrine this is," Zabby said. "Lady Bartlett was telling local legends over dinner a few nights ago. Don't you remember? *Dea Sulis Minerva*. This must be a shrine of Sulis. She was here before the Romans, Lady Bartlett said, but was so important to the native Britons that the Romans adopted her as an aspect of their own Minerva rather than offend the locals by banishing her."

Catherine recoiled. "What have I done? A false pagan god? We must leave at once!"

"Oh, Your Majesty!" Beth cried. She reached out to restrain her queen and stopped herself just in time. "Wait . . ."

She looked desperate, and Zabby realized that if the queen left, Beth would lose her chance to elope with Henry. She squeezed Beth's hand and whispered, "I know about your young lord, my dear. Don't worry, I'll keep her here."

To the queen she said smoothly, "Your Majesty, don't leave just yet. Now that we've come all this way, you must consider — will you pass up a chance to bear a child?"

Catherine stared at Zabby, alarmed.

"Oh, I don't know that there's anything to it, and it is, as you say, naught but a pagan shrine, but think on this: For centuries, millennia, women have been coming here to ask for the help of Sulis. Would they still come, generation upon generation, mother and daughter, if there was not some small sign of its efficacy?"

"But it is a false god. Why, to even be here is almost a sin."

"Forget Sulis, Your Majesty," Zabby said. "What if there is some other explanation? We know that the waters at Bath can cure certain ailments. The ancients thought that was the goddess — now we say it is some essence in the water, no more. Perhaps the same holds true here. Look at that hole — it seems to extend to the bowels of the earth. What if it emits some rare and precious vapor, a healing gas? They call it Sulis, but it may be only science. If women who come here say they have easy births, then why not try it? Forget the reason, and look at the facts."

Catherine hesitated, returning to her old nervous habit of counting the rosary on her fingertips. If there was any chance, and she failed to grasp it . . .

"Will you go first?" she asked her maids of honor.

Eliza laughed. "Allow me," she said, blustering forward. "If a sinner such as I ain't stricken down immediately, you three should be safe."

Zabby thought of her own secret sin, and wondered.

"What do I do?" Eliza asked.

Beth stepped up, casting Zabby a quick grateful glance. "I'm told you kneel at the shrine and . . ."

"I will not pray to a pagan god!" Catherine said.

"I don't think you have to pray, Your Majesty, and who's to hear it anyway? But they say you lean over the opening and ask for something, then make an offering. Something small, a coin or ribbon. Like a wishing well."

Catherine lightened at once. "Oh, a wishing well. There was one near where I grew up. A mere harmless entertainment." It never occurred to her that her natal well might have begun life as the holy site of some long-forgotten goddess. "Go on, Eliza, and if you're smitten, I'll pray for your soul." She gave a nervous laugh.

The girls and their queen retreated out of earshot while Eliza knelt by the shrine.

Eliza chuckled at herself; she scarcely believed in the religion of her birth, and certainly gave no credence to some old goddess who hadn't the good sense to drift forgotten into the mists of obscurity like a dowager when the new bride arrives. But it was not long before her keen sense of the dramatic took over, and she imagined herself not in the moment but on a stage, the rocks only plaster, the hole descending below the proscenium, where some actor thin and nimble enough to play the part would presently rise, wraithlike, to murmur strange prophesies in iambic pentameter. She found her voice, and who knows but that she didn't fool Sulis herself?

"Spirit of the waters, goddess of this holy hole..." No, that would never do, unless this was to be a comedy. She leaned over and stared into the shadowy pit, trying to find exactly the right words for her monologue, something that would make the audience, if there was one, shiver with delicious premonition. Before she could frame the words, she found herself growing dizzy, and swayed above the pit as if she would pitch forward.

Give me strength, she begged Sulis or herself, God or the world. *Give me the courage to leave comfort and safety and family and cast myself on the mercy of the audience as a playwright and a player. I have been my father's coin, a golden thing he'd spend to buy the ear of the king. Let me be my own coin, a ha'penny, if only it is one I can spend as I wish. Give me the words to astound the world, the voice to thrill them, and please, let me have no regrets when I have thrown away wealth.*

She bent her head to the well and stared into the blackness, looking, listening for answers. But Sulis, like every goddess and every woman, gives her answers in her own good time, and Eliza heard only her own surging thoughts.

On impulse she unclasped an emerald bracelet from her wrist and let it slither from her fingers like an asp into the depths. She thought she heard it brush the sides, but she never heard it hit bottom.

"Oh, well," she said aloud. "If it doesn't work out, I can always come back here with a grappling hook on a cord. Likely every lady with a hankering is as madly generous to Sulis as I've been. If I'm poor, I'll just fish up their wishes."

Beth stood and brushed off her skirts, lighthearted again, and thought how to turn that last line into poetry.

"Here I am, unblasted and uncursed," Eliza said blithely, returning to her friends. "Go on, Beth. Your turn at the altar."

Beth blushed fiercely and caught Zabby's smile. "No, you go, Zabby. There's nothing else I wish for." She peered through the boscage, waiting for Harry.

"There's nothing I wish for either. You go, Your Majesty."

"Nonsense," Catherine said, still a little afraid of the shrine, delaying as long as possible. "Why, a girl of sixteen must have as many wishes as there are stars in the sky. Pick a worthy one and go."

The command of a monarch could not be refused, and Zabby went slowly down the path. Her desires were not stars but one single burning sun that dimmed all else with its brilliance.

She did not kneel but stood defiantly above the maw, peering into it, wondering at its secrets. She had no real faith in anything she could not observe or theoretically surmise, but all the same she had time and again seen the efficacy of folk wisdom. The slaves on her father's estate packed cobwebs into freely bleeding cane-knife wounds and the flow quickly ceased—far faster than if they had stuffed them with cotton. They said the web is accustomed to being knit by the spider, and knits the wounds as well, but Zabby knew there must be some other mechanism. She didn't understand it, but she knew it worked. There must be some property of this well, or cave, or pit . . .

She dropped a pebble into it and heard no splash, no sound at all. She bent and put her face to the gap. With a faint susurrus the earth exhaled in a warm, sweet breath, a gust that made her gasp, inhaling deeply of the cloying gas. She felt lightheaded, but cogent enough to think, *Yes, a vapor, I was sure of it,* before reclining, half conscious, beside the shrine. The hot, honeyed smell was gone, and she knew she should move before it returned, but the worn stones were oddly comfortable, and she began to think, or dream—she was not sure which.

If Catherine dies in childbed, Zabby thought, for the first time not at all troubled, *Charles will marry again. He has to—there cannot be a king without a queen, a kingdom without an heir. Will he wed that simpering golden fool? Not if I have anything to say about it. And I will. Alone, in our elaboratory, I will have him to myself, as no other scheming hussy of the court ever does. A baron isn't much, but it is enough— Frances's family is no better. And then, once he is mine, he will never even think of her again. Not her, not Barbara . . .*

It was not a wish, a possibility—it was a vision, an oracle, a certainty. Bemused by that intoxicating breath churned from miles below, she saw herself as queen, her hand in Charles's, ruling together, shining such a light of knowledge and progress across the land as would never be dimmed.

Her head spinning pleasantly, she tilted to look down the hole once again, smiling at the unseen forces, breathing the earth's breath. Then she remembered: an offering. *What do I have precious enough to give?* She had a pretty garnet ring, pins with bits of topaz in her hair, but they were only minerals, and surely the deep beneath had enough gems. She was a bit confused now. Was it a well, or a goddess? A mouth? A scientific curiosity? No matter. There was one thing so precious, even pure science would value it, a worthy sacrifice to achieve her ends. She reached into her pocket and pulled out the silk scarf of the tempest-tossed sailors. She kissed it fervently, feeling Charles's lips in the weave, and loosed it to spiral like an ash tree seed until it was swallowed.

She lay in her waking dream a while longer, the silk kiss lingering on her lips, until merry voices called her, teasing, and even Catherine jested that she must save some of the well's wishes for her poor queen. Zabby sat dizzily, then rose, the trees marching in a widdershins dance before settling into their rooted places. She had a sudden fierce headache, and felt ill.

What have I done?

A bare moment later, she could hardly recall. She felt for her scarf. It was gone. So that much was true. Tears came then; the scarf had been her nightly bedmate, the confidante of whispered secrets.

The memory of her wish returned to her in bits and pieces. *No! I don't really want that! I take it back!* If she could retrieve her offering . . . She returned to the chasm's lip, then pulled away. She couldn't risk breathing that vapor again.

I swore I'd never even think of that. I cannot go near the shrine again. One breath, and I lost control.

She felt, acutely, how near to the surface her desires were. She thought she'd fought them so valiantly, beaten them until they cowered, but they were craftier and subtler than she'd ever imagined. She was afraid of herself, of what she would do, could do.

Zabby took great gulps of pure air, backing away, but she could not get that final image out of her head: standing at Charles's side, his queen.

She turned, and found the only obstacle to her success standing before her with her brow furrowed. "Are you unwell?" Catherine asked.

"Oh, Your Majesty!" Zabby cried, and fell at her feet.

"What is it, child? Did you make a foolish wish? Don't fret — this is all a jest. I'm sorry we came here. What was your wish, then?"

"I . . . I wished something about you."

"How kind!" Catherine said, and Zabby dug her nails into her palms. "Did you wish I would bear a son?"

Zabby gathered herself together. *She's right — it is a jest, a superstition. I breathed noxious fumes and hallucinated, and now I feel unwell. I haven't cursed this noble woman. I haven't lusted after a married man, my sovereign.*

I haven't hoped with all my heart that poor Catherine is indeed with child, so that she may die trying to bring it into the world.

She sniffed and hastily wiped her eyes. "I *do* wish you would bear a son," she said, equivocating. "I wish all of the best things in life for you." With a superstition she never knew she had, she cast her thoughts back to the chasm, hoping this new, controlled, conscious wish might undo the one she had made in her moment of drugged weakness.

"Then I suppose I'd better add my own feeble wish to it," Catherine said, and started for the shrine.

"Your Majesty, don't!" Zabby said.

Catherine looked back.

"There is something there, coming from the hole. It made me dizzy. It made me think things I shouldn't."

Catherine, misunderstanding, seeing her flush, sighed and said, "You'll find when you are married, such lusty thoughts are quite natural. Now ready the ponies; I'll only be a moment."

Watching her disappear into the little wood, Zabby knew exactly what Catherine would wish for. She wouldn't have a thought for herself. Not *Let me come safely through delivery*. Not *Let me live to bear him many children and watch them grow to take his place*. Simple, good woman that she was, she would think only of one thing. *Let me bear him a living son*. That done, she would have no care for her own life. Her duty in this world would be accomplished.

This business of wishing and praying and offering is falderal, Zabby thought. Still, she fervently hoped Catherine would, through cleverness or chance, frame her own wish in such a way as to undo Zabby's.

It must have been the aftereffects of the chthonic gas: Zabby was suddenly sure that someone, some thing, had indeed heard the shameful wish of her inmost heart and, maliciously, granted her the power to make it come true.

A moment later the queen came out, coyly smiling, and Zabby knew, unequivocally, that if she wanted to, she could be in her place.

"I have made my wish, for what good it will do," the queen began, but before she could say more, they heard a low, rhythmic rumble of rushing hooves. One of the ponies did her best to rear in alarm, but she was so stout she only managed a hop and then tried to dance sideways.

"Riders?" Catherine asked, unconcerned but hoping vaguely that Charles had been worried about her, discovered her whereabouts, and come in search.

Beth broke from her friends and rushed down the path, lifting her skirt to show layer upon layer of petticoats, colored and plain, as she ran.

The horsemen thundered into sight. At their head was a laughing young man with a wide, handsome mouth, flashing white teeth — and a black silk mask over his face and hair. Two others flanked him, leading fresh horses.

"Harry!" Beth cried, and reached up to him as his horse came to a dusty halt. But he swung down, pausing only long enough to say, "Where is the queen?" before striding past her. He spied Catherine before Beth could answer.

"Into the saddle, m'lady," one of the other men said.

"But wait. I must be with him."

"We leave within the minute," the man replied gruffly. "Mount or stay behind." He held his cupped hands for Beth to use as a step and settled her awkwardly astride.

"Why so soon?" she asked, baffled. "I must say goodbye to my friends."

The man held the reins and said nothing. He watched Harry and the other man approach the ladies.

"Your Majesty," Harry said, bowing with elaborate Frenchified elegance, his leg forward, flourishing his hat. "I must ask that you accompany me."

From the saddle, Beth strained forward to hear with what magnificent words her beloved would beg the queen for her hand in marriage.

Zabby knew him before she recognized the others. "Elphinstone!" she cried, and willed herself to step between the highwayman and her queen. Logic intervened, saying, *What can you possibly do against large, armed men?* From the direction of the shrine, leaves rustled in a laughing sound. *This is it,* the residue of intoxicating fumes said in her brain. *Your chance to be queen.*

She did nothing as Elphinstone's henchman lifted the queen bodily and carried her, shrieking, to the horses.

"Did she say no?" Beth asked stupidly as Harry swung into the saddle behind her.

"Tie her! No, don't strike her, but gag her if you must. Oliver, take her on your horse. Hurry!"

"For the love of God, I am with chi . . ." Catherine began to say, but a roll of linen was shoved in her mouth and she was hauled belly-down across the front of the saddle.

"Harry! What are you doing? Harry!" Beth screamed at him, twisting in the saddle. She knew, suddenly, surely, what was happening, but she sought for some other explanation, however implausible. The queen had forbidden their marriage, and this was some impulsive scheme to convince her. Harry's henchmen had turned against him with a treasonous plot of their own, and any moment now Harry's sword would fly to his hand and he'd chop off all their heads, rescue the queen, become England's darling, win full clemency, be granted an earldom . . .

"Hold tightly, my love," Harry said, and spurred his horse forward. Beth struggled to dismount, catching at the reins and trying to disentangle her legs, but Harry held her pressed firmly to him with one arm. The horse, confused by spurs telling him to run and the reins ordering him to halt, reared and danced, and the other highwaymen hesitated, unwilling to fly without their leader.

And still Zabby did not act, wishing she at least had a dagger to plunge into her own unworthy breast.

Eliza, however, had nothing holding her back. With a deep, houndlike bay she flung herself onto the ruffian who had the queen pinned across his lap, dragging at Her Majesty's indigo skirts with one hand and stabbing him in the back of the calf with her cloak pin. He kicked her and she fell back, breathless, but was up again, gasping curses, in an instant. The other rider, heavyset, with black teeth, got between them and shouted, "Let's go!" He forced his horse to shoulder into the other, the queen's legs between, to push him down the path. Eliza lunged at him, too, trying once again to reach her queen, but he dropped the lead of the riderless horse he was guiding across his saddle and caught her hand.

"None of that now, miss," he said.

Miss being a term for little girls and whores, Eliza took even greater offense, and this time wisely kicked the horse, who bolted away with his rider but without the spare mount. He caught up with the others, but his horse was already limping.

"Zabby!" Eliza cried.

Zabby watched the Queen of England bouncing away to her doom, trussed like a capon, and all she could see was a vast empty space, the vacuum chamber of Charles's elaboratory, waiting for her to fill the void.

"Zabby!" Eliza cried again. "I can't ride well enough to follow them."

Zabby didn't seem to hear her. She had a vision of Charles looking down at her, amused, in the elaboratory . . . no, in his private apartments . . .

"You are a good rider — you can go after them. Zabby! Do you hear me?" She snapped her fingers in front of her friend's face. "They have a lamed horse, and not enough fresh mounts. Maybe you can catch them. Zabby!"

She couldn't move — she was in a trance, one she knew she had the power to break, but she would not. She knew that what she desired, what she had against her will wished into the pit of Sulis, made her as despicable as any of the scheming half-whores of the court. Like them she was willing to do anything to get the man she desired, to rise in prestige and power. She hated herself, but she could not help rejoicing as she watched the queen's abduction. Sulis had accepted her offering and granted her boon. It was out of her hands now. She was worse than Lady Castlemaine.

With that name, it came back to her in a rush: the midnight rendezvous, the last task Harry had to perform, the wicked, scheming Buckingham. The visit immediately afterward to the palace suite of his cousin, Lady Castlemaine. Barbara, the king's chief mistress. Mother of his sons. The woman whom many people thought of as the de facto queen.

Zabby might allow a pagan goddess to guide her into evil, but never the despised Castlemaine!

The trance-image changed, and now it was Castlemaine standing at Charles's side, laughing at the world, a crown on her head.

Still not quite knowing what was real, Zabby got her foot in the stirrup and called to Eliza as she mounted, "Ride for Bath and tell the king!" A heartbeat later she was low over the horse's neck, urging him after the highwaymen.

Alone, Eliza looked at the fat, lazy ponies, thought of what the king would do to the bearer of bad news, and said in tragicomic tones to the unseen audience that followed her everywhere, "I'd rather be fighting the brigands."

Zabby could just see them in the distance; it was open countryside and they kept to the road, riding into the molten setting sun. She didn't know what she would do when she caught them; then, as her horse slackened his pace and settled into a canter, she realized that catching them shouldn't be her goal. She should follow them until they stopped — they would have to stop sometime — and then mark the place and find help. The roadway was empty now, but well traveled, and she was bound to come across a farmer or merchant who could at least carry a message, at best set upon the highwaymen with hoes and staves.

Her schemes became moot when the landscape rose and roughened and they entered a parkland. She lost sight of her quarry. Then she came to a crossroads. One roadway was broad and well maintained, the other narrow and rutted, but both bore the marks of recent hoofprints, and she had no idea which to follow. Perhaps they'd even split up. She listened, but if hoofbeats sounded, they were lost in the settling night noises.

She chose the road that continued westward and rode into the red-tinged darkness. *I can't go back to Charles — I can never face him again, unless I bring the queen back. If he ever knew . . .*

She slowed her horse to a walk. There was no point in hurrying in what might be the wrong direction. *I'll keep going west,* she thought, *and if I don't find the queen, at least I'll find the coast, and board a ship bound for Barbados. I cannot stay here.*

She rode for an hour or more until the night was so deep that she could no longer see the path. The horse would amble on for a time, then stop, hanging his head and dreaming of water and a warm stable, until Zabby dug in her heels and urged him on. Her head was completely clear now, she was sure of that, and she was mortified at the thoughts brought on by the shrine's fumes.

Her mind wandered to her father's home. That was where she belonged, managing his household, working by his side. She'd come to England to advance her store of knowledge and understanding, to expand her apprehension of the universe. Aye, she understood the world now. It was a base thing, as poisonous as Sulis's vapors. It had corrupted even her. Best to get away.

She wished she could be with Charles one last time, though, see that swarthy, handsome face, be the victim of his gentle teasing, brush against him once more when they bent over a lens.

She felt nothing but contempt for herself...but still, in the back of her mind, impish thoughts played devilish tricks. *If the queen is gone, perhaps Charles will come after you. Perhaps he will send his fleet to Barbados to fetch his new queen home.*

The more she tried to fight the thoughts, the more insidious they became. *They're only thoughts,* she told herself. *Let them be — thoughts are not dangerous in themselves.* But she remembered what Charles had once told her. Cromwell and a few others had an idea, and it spread like a disease until it chopped off a king's head. Ideas lead to action.

Sometime later she saw a dim light ahead, the first sign of companionship on the road.

Her horse nickered, still hoping for a stable, and Zabby hailed the two people approaching on foot.

A weary voice cried out, "Whoever you are, as you love your life and queen, help us!"

It was Beth, slow and footsore, supporting her dying queen.

Chapter 21

THE NEXT QUEEN

THEY DID NOT ADMIT she was dying, though—not all at once. The doctors at Bath, fearing a misdiagnosis might mean the gallows (as it might have, not many kings before) gave the queen a sedative and pronounced her safe enough to travel. If only they could get her home to her own physicians, she would be someone else's responsibility. To save her might bring great glory, but to fail would mean, at best, being demoted to horse-leech in some backwater village.

Two days later she was back in Whitehall and the deathwatch had officially begun. Courtiers bore the most confusing countenances, endeavoring to look solemn but all the while madly speculating who would be the next queen.

Beth had collapsed as soon as they had returned to Bath, and at Eliza's whispered suggestion remained in a swoon much longer than strictly necessary. Even Charles wouldn't interrogate an unconscious girl. Nor could Eliza provide him with much information. Accustomed to writing plots twice as convoluted, she easily guessed that lover and highwayman were one, and that Elphinstone tried to neatly kill two birds with one elf-shot. Exactly why he wished to kidnap the queen, and to what end, she was not sure, though she had a score of ideas.

But Eliza had no desire to betray Beth to the hangman, and stayed as mum as Charles's insistent wrath would allow. She told what she had seen—a group of masked men snatched up Beth and the queen—without adding what she assumed.

"Was it that damned Elphinstone?" Charles roared, to which Eliza quite calmly replied that he'd been masked, and one masked man looks much like another.

Alone together that first night, the three Elizabeths locked hands.

"We swore to stand by each other," Eliza said staunchly. "You don't have to tell us a thing, Beth-heart, and I vow I'll tell the king any tale you like. I know whatever happened wasn't of your doing."

"Oh, but it was! It was all my fault. He told me . . . he promised . . . and then . . ."

"Easy, sweeting. Many's the man deceived a maid. He loved you, is it, but he was really just after one thing? A common enough story, though he sought not a quim but a queen. He rooked the pawn to take the queen."

"No, he loved me — I know it!" Beth protested.

"Stick to that," Eliza said. "The king will forgive a pretty fool. A conspirator will swing. Whatever you knew, just keep those big eyes wet and say how you thought he loved you."

"I never meant the queen harm. You know that! She's been so good to me. When he did it, I couldn't believe ..."

"Hush," Eliza cautioned, and checked the hall outside their quarters before locking it. Then she nodded for Beth to continue.

When she finished, Zabby was stroking her philtrum pensively, a habit she'd picked up from Charles, who when thoughtful treated his mustache like a favorite pet.

"Did he have a grudge against the queen, do you know?" Zabby asked. "Does he hate Catholics, or did she wrong him in some way?"

"I don't know. I don't think so. What could she have done?"

"Then someone hired him. He did it for money, for you, but someone else wanted the queen dead." She thought she knew who but didn't want to say anything until she was sure.

"Oh, he wasn't going to kill her. He swore that to me."

"He swore he loved you."

"You see, so it must be true."

Eliza shook her head and sighed. What was to be done in the face of love? "He made use of you, Beth," she said patiently. "He never loved you."

"Then why did he let us go?"

There was a sharp rap at the door, and Prue, chambermaid to the maids of honor, came in. "Well, you three hoydens have certainly made a night of it, keeping the poor servants in a tizzy till the wee small hours. Don't expect your tea and cakes sharp at eight on the morrow, my ladies, as the likes of us won't be abed until sunrise. Riders here, guards there, soldiers molesting the kitchen wenches, looking for treason under their aprons. Lord above, you'd think the king was glad to have her back. You, Madam Zabby, scrub your nails and tidy your hair. You've a royal summons. The king's bedroom in a quarter hour. Another man would manage to spend the rest of the night with his wife after an ordeal like this . . . though if she's been raped perhaps he's lost his taste for her."

She sighed deeply. "A shame that footpad was too clumsy to make a proper go of it. We might have ourselves a fecund queen within six months. Well, perhaps a year for royal mourning, but m'dear, you could get him to sign the contract before her corpse was cold."

Zabby slapped her, and the wiry old woman took it without a flinch. Well-bred ladies were prone to slaps. She shrugged. "Oh, well. Smart money is on the other wench anyway. Perhaps I'll see if she needs tea or a foot rub."

"Barbara, you mean?" Zabby asked.

"That blown slut? The king'd sooner wed a sow. No, I mean that prissy minx Frances. She'll be the next queen if anything happens to this one. I wonder, will the king hang the highwaymen because they tried . . . or because they failed?" She left with a cackle.

Zabby smoothed the wrinkles from her clothes and left to answer the royal summons. When she was gone, Beth gasped.

"She didn't promise!"

"What?" Eliza asked.

"You swore you wouldn't tell. She didn't. Will she tell the king?"

"Never," Eliza said. "She may have lost her heart to that royal rake, but she's a loyal friend. Besides, what does she know? A given name? There are a hundred Harrys at court, a hundred thousand in England. But no, pet, she won't tell him a thing more than she has to. She's our friend."

Zabby thought so furiously that she scarcely noticed she was entering Charles's private chambers for the first time. They were in a borrowed estate, of course, but he'd had his Bath residence fitted up much like his bedroom at home. Eight ornate clocks ticked just out of synchrony, pendulums swinging, gears whispering. His bed was done up in royal purple, tufted with a hundred ermine pelts. She curtsied low as soon as she stepped across the threshold, but when she rose she saw he wasn't there yet.

She stood stiffly by the doorway for a time, but then when he still did not come, she began to explore the room. It was not the royal bedroom — that which held the marriage bed. That was where Catherine slept, where he often slept too, at least the latter part of the night. The queen lay in that other bedroom now, fevered, weak, waiting for the physicians to say if she would die. The royal chamber was practically a public room, and any courtier above a certain rank could enter freely at most hours of the day. Charles granted petitions from beneath the bedclothes, drafted proclamations in his bath, with three secretaries, a baron or two, and a host of ministers hovering over the steam.

But when he needed privacy — and for all that he was a gregarious man, Zabby sometimes thought his moments alone were the food that truly sustained him — he came to his own bedroom.

Zabby stroked the bed's deep plush and wished she were brave enough to lie down on it, just for a moment. It would be fodder for the fantasies she'd sworn off to no avail. To be on his bed, in his bed, with him in his bed . . . But what if he was to come in and catch her?

Or, her hopeful brain offered, *what if that's exactly why you're here?*

Impossible, she thought. The king always goes elsewhere for his liaisons. She knew that as well as any courtier. He went to the lady's rooms or, if there was a small obstacle such as a husband, to some bed or couch set aside specifically for that purpose. He never sullied the queen's bed with his extramarital passions, and he had never, to her knowledge, brought a woman to his private room.

She thought back to Prue's words. Nasty spite they might have been, but servants know everything, and if all the palace thought she had a chance (even if most put Frances ahead of her), why, then, it must be true. *Perhaps he has come to speak to me of the future,* she thought. *Have the doctors told him Catherine is not long for this world?* Her guilty rage at the thought had been enough to make her strike the gossiping servant, but if it was truly what the king wanted, why, how could she argue with her liege lord?

Better me than Barbara or Frances. Certainly neither of them had been in Charles's private bedroom.

And so she was half prepared for seduction when Charles came in, her breast pushing in a rapid rise and fall against her busk, the pale wisps at her temples trembling.

There was a portrait of Charles at Whitehall, stuck in a dim room because it wasn't very good, but still, who would risk ill fortune by destroying any image of a king? It showed him on a glistening, rearing sorrel with sweaty flanks and a foaming mouth, its ears laid back and eyes rolling. Whoever had ridden the poor beast to exhaustion, it was evidently not the king, for he perched on its back, fresh as a spring clover, with his armor impeccable and his helmet at a jaunty angle, holding a longsword improbably in one hand. It was a ridiculous picture, and perhaps because of it, Zabby had never envisioned Charles as a warlike king, though she knew he'd seen battle in his youth. He charmed, he debated, he occasionally demanded, but he did not fight.

The Charles who charged into the bedroom just then was King Henry at Bosworth Field. He was an enraged Celt in a war chariot charging the invading Romans, or, given his saturnine complexion, a Roman himself, armored in gold-plated iron with the Eagle behind him. His eyes flashed darkly, his lips were curled almost in a snarl, and he glared around the room as if looking for someone to kill with his bare hands.

His gaze settled on Zabby.

"You!" he shouted, and started for her, then stopped, breathing deeply to collect himself. When he spoke again he was more controlled, but there was rage just beneath.

"You must know," he said, coming near enough to kiss her if he'd cared to, before whirling away to pace like one of the leopards in his menagerie. "Nothing escapes those wide-open eyes of yours, Zabby. Who was it? No one will tell me a thing. Beth stays in her daze, Eliza quips like a comedienne. But you see things others do not see; you think things they'd never think. You were there—tell me, as you love your king, who was he, and why did he steal my queen?"

"Charles, I . . . I do not . . ."

He swept to her side and caught her hands. "You saved my life, Zabby. You keep my secret. I trust you more than any other woman in the world, save my own sister, but she is far away in France. Please. You know something. I can tell. Haven't we worked side by side in my elaboratory—*our* elaboratory—sharing every discovery?" He dropped one hand only to caress her cheek, letting his palm linger. Zabby could not retreat; the edge of the high bed pressed into her back.

She grabbed handfuls of her skirts to keep her own fingers from reaching for him.

"Your Majesty," she breathed, tilting her face.

With a roar he turned away again and resumed his pacing. "I am not a king! I am a servant! I am nothing!" he shouted. "If they think they can bully me, threaten me, steal my property for their own ends, force me to . . . Hell and damnation! I might as well be back in the Hague, or begging for a mutton chop in France. No king was ever used as I am. I want their blood, Zabby. Whoever has crossed me like this, they will pay with their pain, their lives, their very souls. I showed mercy once." He had let some of the lesser conspirators against his father keep their lives and estates. "Never again. Who was it? One who hates her, or me?"

"Neither, I think." She said it as a lure to bring him nearer, and it worked as well as any of the queen's own exquisite fishing flies.

He took her shoulders this time, and she thought, *If I can keep him here long enough he will touch my hips, my breast, my lips.* She was as dizzy and trembling as she'd been over the well of Sulis, poisoned by love, intoxicated by desire.

Everyone thinks I'm your lover, she wanted to say to him. *Why not make it true?*

With the queen your wife lying ill, perhaps dying, not two rooms away.

She closed her eyes and at last let go of her skirts. Up came her hands, touched Charles on the chest . . . and pushed him gently away.

I am his friend. I am a scientist beside him. I am his loyal subject. I will never be his lover.

I will never be queen.

"You must promise me something first," she said with a sigh.

His eyes narrowed, and for a moment he was the king again, not Charles — the man who could have her hanged for conspiracy simply for not revealing what she knew. Then his eyes softened.

"Little Beth. Your friend. Is she involved in this treason? I know there was some business with Elphinstone last spring. Was this the same man? I cannot believe that good Beth would conspire against me, or the queen, who loves her so."

"I swear to you, she knew nothing. You must promise me nothing will happen to her. She is as innocent as the morning star."

"The morning star, I believe, is named Lucifer."

"Charles!"

"Forgive me. Go on — what other demands do you have of your king? Ah, no, that's not fair. You are the one woman who never asks a thing of me. Pray, demand away, my sweet."

"Please, please don't let her know what I've said to you. Can you pretend you found out some other way?"

"Lie? To my ministers and my people?" He looked aghast, then laughed. "Zabby, a king does nothing *but* lie. Every smile when I see the rabble that killed my father is a lie. Every time I praise the Commons for granting me a pittance for defense of the kingdom, it is a lie. I see my cousin and fellow monarch Louis across the sea, ruling like a god, and I lie to myself and say the English way is better. Yes, Zabby, it is a small thing to lie for you."

And so she told him all she knew, save only Harry's name.

"Why did he let Catherine go?" Charles asked.

"When Beth knew what he was about, she refused to marry him. She loved him, Charles — oh, the little fool loved him! Yet when she knew what he had done, she would not fly with him. And he had done it for her! Treason, for her! To get money, to marry her! She says he did. I did not believe it, but he must have loved her, to risk all. If not he would have left her behind when he took the queen, or cast her aside after he had what he wanted. But when he couldn't have Beth, he let the queen go. He had success in his hand, and he threw it away, because she would not come with him. He was to take Beth to France and buy a farm and . . . Oh, Charles! To be loved like that!"

"I can only dream of it," he said softly.

Zabby almost laughed. "So many people love you," she said.

"Not like that," he said, staring at some inner vision. "Never like that."

There is one, she thought, so strongly he must feel it.

But he only drew her to the divan, where they sat together, thigh to thigh, and tried to make sense of it.

"Someone wants me to have a new queen," Charles said.

"Beth said he vowed he had never meant to kill the queen," Zabby said.

"What, then? Ransom her? Imprison her?"

"She said he told her Catherine would be sent to a distant island, to live comfortably among women."

"That makes no sense. Why steal a queen, yet ask for no money, and let her live?" Zabby frowned; then it suddenly dawned on her. Of course Barbara knew Charles would never marry her, but her son could still be a king.

"I think . . . I think perhaps someone wanted you to name one of your sons heir to the throne. One of your natural sons, I mean. If Catherine was dead, you'd marry again and get legitimate heirs, but if Catherine had simply disappeared, you might not marry. You'd wait, hoping for news, and one of your other sons might be the next king."

"And you say the highwayman met with Buckingham? That Buckingham then went to Barbara's apartments?" He glowered blackly.

Zabby had a sudden vision of the lovely, hated Barbara desperate on the gallows cart, the noose tightening, her exquisite face turning purple and grotesque. She despised Barbara, but mostly because she was Charles's lover. There were other sides of her too. She was the woman who helped the injured child on the wharf. She was the one who pitied the queen—not enough to give her back her husband, but a shred of sympathy was something.

Barbara was cunning, ruthless, ambitious...but was she capable of this terrible act?

"It could not have been Barbara," Zabby said with certainty. "She wants more, but I know her—she'd never be willing to risk what she already has. To kidnap the queen...If it worked, she might be mother to the next queen. If she failed..."

"She'd be dead," Charles said flatly.

Would he really do that? she wondered. Kill the woman who had given him so much pleasure for so long?

"You're right," he continued. "Either way, it could not be her. She knows I'd never wed her even if we were both free. And she wouldn't hazard what she has on such a chancy wager. But stay, what if another was advising her, pushing her? She'd never do it on her own, but if someone else laid all the plans, perhaps she'd join." He rubbed his finger along his mustache and frowned. "But who?"

"Buckingham." She was reluctant to suggest it. Buckingham

was the king's closest friend, and though the man had betrayed his sovereign before, he'd always wormed his way back into Charles's heart.

"But why? He has no sons to offer up to the throne."

"He and Barbara are both of the Villiers family. Perhaps that blood is close enough. Or maybe he didn't do it for Barbara's sake. There are other contenders, though. Some foreign princess, or . . . a court maiden."

"Ha! A court maiden. Is there such a thing?"

"There is one," she said. "Two," she added under her breath.

"Frances, you mean. Yes, I've heard the court gossip giving her the crown. I only hope Catherine has not."

Zabby waited for him to deny that he'd marry Frances if he could, but he said nothing more.

"I've seen Buckingham talking with her," Zabby went on. "All the ambassadors, too. Everyone believes that she will be in a position to influence you. And she seems so placid and biddable, each is sure they can make her their pawn if she is queen."

"Is that what they believe? The poor deluded fools. I've never met a woman more cruelly obstinate than that bewitching creature."

To her shame, Zabby felt tears begin to sting, and she cupped her temples with her hand to hide them.

"What a beast I am, dear!" Charles said, slipping an arm around her shoulders. "You must be dead tired. You went through nearly as much as poor Catherine, and look at me, keeping you up all hours speculating. You've been so helpful. I knew you would never fail me." He gave her a smile of such warmth that she knew it must be close to love. So close. Not quite close enough. "You've given me and my guards ample information to work with. I'm certain we'll track down the blackguards ere long. My best men are on it. When we have the culprits, we'll find out who is behind them. Tomorrow or the next day, if Catherine can manage, we'll away to Whitehall and put this all behind us."

He squeezed her shoulders, drawing her into those manly scents so unfamiliar to her, the radiating heat, the body soft and hard all at once.

"Oh, Charles!" she managed, and swayed into him, letting his chest absorb her tears.

Whether friend or lover or queen, I must be loyal to him above all else, she thought.

"There is one more thing I know," she murmured into his body.

"It can wait until the morrow, my love," he said, and though she knew he called her that absently, she clung to him.

"It cannot," she said, picturing, then banishing, Beth's sweet face. "I know his name. Harry Ransley."

She collapsed against him, and Charles swept her into his arms, laying her carefully in his violet bed. He kissed her forehead, her lashes.

"Thank you," he breathed into her ear. Then he left her there, alone, and went to wreak vengeance.

Harry was captured in a barn near Dover the next morning, and the rest of his band were taken on the docks, trying to find passage into France. The king made sure that none save his hand-picked guards knew that the notorious Elphinstone had been taken.

Soon enough, another select group was made aware of his capture. Men who made their living extracting secrets from prisoners by whatever means necessary, men with clever, precise fingers and whetted knives, men with bludgeons of lead shot cased in velvet, men whose lies and truths could slash the very soul, went to work on the conspirators.

Chapter 22

The Edge of the Precipice

As with any tasty bit of gossip, news of the queen's abduction spread through the court and the kitchens, thence like a plague to the populace. Like all such scandal, it was a joint of truth larded with savory speculation, but for once this was carefully guided by a team of courtiers charged with relaying misinformation.

The queen, it seems, had let it get about that she was jealous of all the women who had been charmed by the ne'er-do-well Elphinstone, and had jocularly demanded that she receive her fair share of the attention. She did not like it that the meanest of her ladies in waiting, her insignificant maids of honor, had had an exciting meeting with the famed highwayman. She complained loudly — there were people who had been instructed to swear they had heard her do so — and word had no doubt traveled to the footpad's lair. That bold and dashing scoundrel had taken this as a personal challenge, and put his mighty cunning to use to trap the poor queen alone and unprotected.

All the court laughed to think that the queen had been abducted by royal summons! It can't be a crime, the fops said, if Elphinstone was simply obeying the queen's orders. Why, he should get a knighthood out of it!

Beth fretted and paced, and her soft, gentle curves all wasted in sorrow as she mourned for her lost dream. In her inmost heart, hidden from all the world, she still thought her Harry would rescue her.

She was to marry the Earl of Thorne in a week.

Oh, Harry, why didn't I go with you? she thought. *You would have let the queen go anyway, I know it, if only I had tried harder to persuade you. Harry, my Harry, why didn't I go with you?*

And in a secret place, even deeper than her inmost heart, hidden as well as we can hide anything from ourselves, was a dark thought: *I should have let him keep the queen. At least we would have been together.*

Love will do that.

She was not allowed to mope. When they returned to the palace, her mother snatched her up like a raptor and tucked her under her wing. She still slept with the other girls, but all the day she spent with her mother, being prepared for her marriage.

"A dying queen has no need of you," she snapped when Beth protested that she had other duties. "Being maid of honor was a useful occupation, but now you have a better one."

Perhaps Beth was more fortunate than other girls. While most mothers taught their daughters to walk with their head erect, their limbs graceful, Lady Enfield told Beth in exquisite detail every variation of what might befall her on her wedding night and the nights to follow. Another mother would drill her child in the lute and the virginal, in obedience and modesty and industry. Beth learned when to give her husband oysters, when to slip saltpeter into his morning draught. She learned which arguments are worth winning, how to make defeat seem a victory. Her mother schooled her in the secret ways a woman can harness a man, break him, so that he believes he still runs free. She taught her how to lie, how to guard truth like a treasure and use it like a weapon. When Beth's attention wandered, as it did every few moments, her heart reaching out for her love, she received a smart rap on the legs with a cane.

In short, Lady Enfield taught her everything she wished she had known when, as a pretty young thing, she'd married Beth's father. The things that would have worked to keep almost any man tractable—any man save the Earl of Thorne.

Beth no longer fought her mother, no longer insisted she'd never marry Thorne. *Harry will save me,* she thought, *and if he doesn't, why, then, what in the world could possibly matter?* Plague or death, fire or flood. It would all be one without love.

She did not quite lose hope, but she'd almost achieved resignation. She spent long hours thinking of Harry wealthy and happy on a farm in Alsace, his sisters and mother relieved of their worries. In her most self-punishing times she envisioned him married to a black-eyed French girl and told herself that though she could never be happy again, at least she could be content knowing Harry was.

It was fortunate that Catherine's illness freed the maids of honor from their duties, for Eliza's own business kept her perpetually on her feet. Her father had taken rooms near the palace and visited her every day, dragging the unfortunate Ayelsworth along. To the young lord's surprise Eliza treated him with courtesy, or if she railed against him, she was so subtle that he could not quite be sure.

"My almanac tells me this will be an auspicious day for vows and agreements," her father said, thumbing through the well-worn volume. For a man so practical, so religious, he put an amazing amount of faith in that book of superstition, and rarely took an important step without consulting it. Because of his trusty Almanac, he'd never in his life bathed on a Friday, and thus never caught a cold.

Eliza smiled sweetly and said, "Oh, dearest Father, I could never take such a happy step during such a sad time. They say the queen is dying."

All the world admitted to it now, and in fact there seemed to be a contest among physicians to make the direst pronouncement. Once her death was assured, one said she would succumb to a putrefying fever, another to an eruption of bile, a third to a boiling of the blood. All they could agree on was that she was in great pain, and most certainly at death's very door.

"The signing of our marriage contract will be the start of the very happiest time of my life. Father, if we sign it as the queen is on her deathbed, I would always associate my greatest happiness with her great suffering. I am so eager to marry Lord Ayelsworth." She cast him a look that was probably meant to be yearning but struck him as distinctly carnivorous. "But how odd it would look to the rest of the world to be merry while everyone else is airing out their mourning garb."

He could see the reason in this, and consented to wait another two weeks, no more.

"In the meantime, dear Father, do try to enjoy all the things London has to offer. I'm sure some of them are far too crass for your tastes, but . . . say, the theater will be opening soon. I'm told the tragedies are quite improving. Every sort of vice is soundly punished. Shall I have them take a box for you?"

"I don't believe the theater is a proper place for a young lady on the eve of her nuptials," he said sternly.

She let her eyes widen slowly. "Heaven forefend! Why, I do believe they allow women on the stage!" She said this as though alluding to a housewife who allowed pigs in her buttery. "But you can tell me afterward, in the most polite terms, what message of virtue they meant to convey. For I think they mean well, those playwrights, even if they do cater a bit to popular vulgarity."

"Well, now . . ." he began.

"Oh, and if you don't care for them, only think how you'll be able to change them once you and the king are in nightly converse. You can see exactly how those playwrights go wrong and set them right, as soon as it is in your power." She gulped, fought back the memory of her father offering her virginity and fertility to this fop on a golden platter, and kissed his grizzled head. "I am so proud of you, Father. How this country will prosper once you take it firmly in hand!"

She'd practiced this speech, in male guise, in front of Killigrew, Nelly, and a dozen of the other actors until they applauded her hypocrisy. She (or rather Mr. Duncan) told them it was for her next play, and they thought it the most wonderful farce ever.

Her father ate it up and patted her hand.

"You'll be there?" she asked, a mite too earnestly. "Do you promise? Opening night? It is supposed to be the most incredible thing ever witnessed on the stage."

Later, Ayelsworth caught her alone. "Given up your pretty scribblings, my pet?" he asked. "When first we met I recall you had some notion of writing a play."

"Oh, that was but a poem, never a play. A foolish notion of childhood. Pray, never mention such things to my father." She squeezed out a painfully girlish laugh. "If he hears I'm such an infant, he won't let me marry for another five years."

So Ayelsworth wisely held his tongue.

Thus went Eliza's days. After spouting filial homage and stewing internally, she shed her skirts, donned her breeches, and slipped out into the night.

Her play had been polished to perfection, every actor drilled in each comedic nuance. Killigrew himself would recite the prologue. Each evening they rehearsed and drank and talked until near dawn.

"This play will be the making of you, Duncan," Killigrew said, slapping his friend on the back. "And the saving of me. You may not know, but I am a poor hand at money matters."

Eliza looked solemn. It was well known that if Killigrew had a sovereign in the morning he'd spend three at dinner, gamble away five more, and invest another ten in an impossible venture. Money flew from him like swallows in spring, and if it weren't for the support of the king, the King's Theater would have shut down long ago.

"After opening night, your name will be such that people will pay their shillings simply to read it on the notices. Duncan, my boy, you are my salvation. What will you have of me, eh? Your name in red splashed across the pit? The orange girls to carry you home? Ah, wait, you have an orange girl of your own now." For Nelly had joined their ranks, and got as much money for her saucy quips as for her firm round fruit. "Name it, Duncan — anything short of money and it will be yours."

"There's only one thing I want, my friend," she said in her deepest voice. "On opening night, after the curtain falls, take me onstage and let me tell the world who is the author of *Nunquam Satis*." Strapped tightly beneath her waistcoat, her bosom strained with anxious breath.

"That's all?" He sighed with relief. He was a bit drunk, and afraid he'd been too extravagant in his offer. "Certainly. You have my solemn oath on it."

And it was, after all, a prime day for vows.

"You must let me in to see her!" Zabby said, trying to shove her way past, but Penalva, one of the few Portuguese attendants left from the queen's homeland, understood English only when it was convenient — and at the moment it was most inconvenient. The dying queen was having her head shaved.

Zabby could see little past the woman's bulk, but the stench in the room was overpowering. Incense smoke hung in a churning cloud near the ceiling, a cloying odor of resins and spices. There was the smell of burning flesh, too, and Zabby thought they might be resorting to animal sacrifice to save their queen.

"I am her attendant, and attend her I will!" Zabby insisted, and dodged around fleshy arms.

As soon as she was through, she understood that the charred meat smell came from the red-hot glass cups that had been placed on Catherine's bare skin to draw out her ill humors. Other patches of skin were blistered and flushed from a paste made of beetle wings and ginger. In the corner of the room, tucked beneath a table, was a copper basin of blood. Far more, Zabby thought, than the poor queen could spare.

Catherine's eyes were open, but bleary and unfocused, and she mumbled something under her breath, more eloquent sigh than words. In a corner a priest chanted in Latin, and at her bedside an efficient-looking woman scraped away the last of the queen's beautiful black locks with a razor.

"What do you think you're doing?" Zabby asked, aghast, and was met with hisses from the Portuguese attendants.

"Hush," one said. "The angels are near. She is dying."

"If she's dying, it is because you are killing her. Where is the doctor?"

He sat in the corner paring his nails with the little blade he'd used to bleed her. He'd done quite literally all that was known to medical science. Now that it seemed to be failing, he blamed not his knowledge or yet his technique, but a higher power. In his complacence he seemed to say, *If God did not want this woman dead, I would have prevailed, but what can a physician do against the will of God?* He had bowed out of the battle gracefully, after, for form's sake, putting the queen through terrible torments.

"You should be giving her broth, keeping her warm, rubbing her limbs, perhaps — but what is this?" Her lip curled in disgust as a man in a gold-embroidered robe drew a live pigeon, pink-necked and struggling, from a basket and wrung its neck so hard its head tore off, spraying a mist of scarlet. He proceeded to bind the twitching carcass onto the sole of Catherine's bare foot, then reached for another bird, while at the other end a woman placed a cap of precious relics on Catherine's head.

Zabby gave a huff of disgust and went to find Charles, whom she'd not seen since the night in Bath when she'd revealed Beth's secret.

She had to ask a dozen pages and servants before she finally tracked him down on the tennis courts. She was shocked to discover that his opponent was Buckingham. Had Charles misunderstood her? It must be evident that Buckingham had something to do with the queen's kidnapping. If she perished, the fault would be his. Had she been wrong? Were things not as they appeared?

Perhaps Charles was lulling him into a false sense of security, the better to trap him later. If so, he was a master actor. He looked like he was thoroughly enjoying the game with his supposed dearest friend.

But the queen's survival was more important than figuring out Charles's scheme. Zabby had not been allowed to see Catherine for days and, now that she'd forced her way in, was appalled at her condition. Why, a healthy soldier couldn't survive that much bloodletting and blistering. Zabby had done what she could to make amends for her shameful desires by helping catch the queen's abductor. Now she set herself to a more difficult task — saving the queen from her own doctors.

Buckingham won by two points and leaped nimbly over the net to laugh and wrestle with his friend.

"Char . . . Your Majesty!" Zabby called from the sidelines, where she stood with the several dozen spectators, courtiers, and hopeful petitioners who, in ever-jostling rotation, followed the king wherever he went.

He rubbed his face vigorously with a cloth as he strolled up to her, still arm in arm with Buckingham. Zabby looked at the duke uncertainly, then came out with it.

"You must do something about the queen's treatment," she said sternly. "The doctors are fools who all want to show off their most outlandish cures to a royal audience, and her Portuguese attendants have the room sealed tight and full of smoke, chanting as loud as bargemen. She needs air, and quiet, and to keep her blood in her body."

Buckingham laughed. "Have you physicked your moppets and think you can cure the queen, pet?" He smiled, but there was malice behind it. "You're a loyal little maid of honor, I'm sure, and I've no doubt you'll have a position still, may the worst befall." He leaned in to Charles and said in the sort of whisper one uses on the stage, "And that position will be on her back in your bed, unless I miss my mark!"

Like everyone else at court, he believed Zabby was one of the king's many casual mistresses.

"I do beg Your Grace's pardon, but I know whereof I speak. They are killing the queen." She fixed Buckingham with a steely gaze, then looked pleadingly at Charles. "They seem to be trying so hard to kill her with their cures, I'd almost think it was by design . . . or by command."

Charles looked at her sharply, then without a word for Buckingham hurried toward the queen's apartments.

Zabby turned to follow him, but Buckingham caught her arm.

"What is your own design in this, miss?" he asked, as behind him a small page unfolded a footstool, climbed atop it, and affixed his master's golden mane of wig.

"None beyond the queen's well-being," she said.

"Perhaps the gamblers should pay more mind to you. Frances has Old Rowley trailing after her like a puppy, but you, miss, send him off like a cur at your command." He seemed to be talking almost to himself, calculating and speculating.

"If you'll excuse me," Zabby said.

"Is she really dying, or is it only a ploy for pity?"

She bit back what she wished to say. He was a duke, after all, and then too she hadn't the time to say all the things she wished to say.

"The queen is quite unwell," she said blandly, and again tried to leave.

"A hundred pounds if you tell me the moment she dies," he whispered.

This time she could not hide her disgust, but again held her tongue and walked away, while behind her Buckingham laughed.

Chapter 23

THE DEATHBED

ZABBY HURRIED to catch up with Charles, and was out of breath by the time she came in at his heels.

"Out!" he roared, and no one moved, each thinking he surely meant the other.

"Are you deaf or treasonous? Out! All of you!"

"Sire," said the presiding physician, "Her Majesty is in a most delicate state. To leave her now might have fatal consequences."

Charles's eyes grew large, and larger still, his face red, until the little doctor began to believe *he* might have a fatal consequence if he stayed. He scurried out the door.

The Portuguese ladies left with clucks and murmurs, prayers and signs, but the priest in the corner stayed until Charles relieved him of his censer and guided him bodily out the door.

Charles sighed, then choked on the fetid air.

"Is it too cold to have the window open?" he asked Zabby, and a tight little knot within her unbound itself. They were together again. The sickroom was their elaboratory, Catherine their experiment. He trusted her; he asked her advice. She was his partner once more. *Not the body,* she reminded herself, *but the mind. That's where the truly blessed union lies.*

"I shouldn't think so," she said, throwing open the shutters and sucking in a deep, relieved breath as the smoke dissipated. "Not for a while, at least. Air and light are what she needs, and to be left to rest."

"*Vis medicatrix naturae.*"

"Precisely! I told that to Chiffinch once, when he wanted to bleed the plague out of you."

"And he, perfidious man, quoted it back to me as his own a month later. Well, you've healed a king. Let us see if you can heal a queen. Hello, my love!" He'd finally noticed that Catherine was awake.

"What have you done?" she asked. "I am to have extreme unction now." Her cap of jewels and saints' knucklebones was askew. "Where is my priest? If I die unshriven..." Her words were heavy and slurred, and she could not focus on Charles, though she reached for his hand.

"But you are not going to die, my love," he said lightly. "I forbid it."

She squeezed his hand. "But how are the children, my darling?"

Charles exchanged a look of alarm with Zabby. "The... children?"

Catherine sighed and smiled. "Our little girl is so like you. She will be a beauty. But I am sorry about the boy. He is such an ugly baby."

Zabby nodded, and Charles, looking frightened, said after some hesitation, "I was a very homely child, they say, all red and black."

"Oh, if he grows to look like you I will be pleased." Her eyes closed, and for a time she seemed to sleep. She was in any event more peaceful than before, her head resting easily on the shorn locks of hair still scattered on her pillow, that slight smile of maternal pride hovering on her lips.

"She is raving," Charles whispered to Zabby across the room. "Her mind is gone. Is this, then, the end?"

"She has a high fever. You should have heard the things you said in your delirium. Give me a moment to examine her."

Zabby felt the queen's pulse, put her ear to her chest to listen to her breath, to her stomach to hear her intestinal sounds.

"Charles, I am no physician."

"You saved me."

"I helped keep you from dying. That's completely different. You had an illness I knew of, one that has no cure save to exhaust itself. If the patient endures longer than the disease, he lives; that is all. I do not know what is wrong with the queen. She said . . ." Zabby bit her lip, but again, she could not withhold any confidence from Charles. "She said she was with child, before we went to the shrine. She didn't want to tell you until she was sure, and then she began to have problems. Bleeding, pain." To her own surprise,

Zabby began to weep quietly. "Did the physician say whether she was still with child?"

"No. I never knew." His face hardened. "To steal the queen is treason, but to kill my unborn heir!" His fists clenched at his side, as if he, a monarch, would thrash his enemy like a common citizen. He started toward the door.

"Where are you going?"

"To order an execution. He's been questioned long enough."

"Wait!" she cried, and darted in front of him. "Have you found proof? Tell me! Is that why you were playing tennis with him, to keep him off his guard?"

"What?"

"Buckingham — he is to die? Did he do it for himself, or for Barbara?"

Charles took a breath as if to yell, but let it out in a long sigh. "I speak of that blackguard Elphinstone. Buckingham is not involved."

"But he must be, in some way. I heard him say quite clearly that the job came from him, and . . . Oh!" How could she have forgotten? In all her attempts to unravel the plot against the queen, that was the one morsel she'd neglected, the one unbelievable thing too impossible to even consider — so she hadn't. Now, glancing at the apparently sleeping queen, she said, "Buckingham told Harry the orders came directly from you."

She stared at him with her wide-open tawny eyes, full of hope and dread. Her own Charles would never be the sort of man to order his wife's kidnapping, possibly her murder. Nothing could make her believe it was true. But then, if he had done it so he could marry again . . . If he had done it for her . . .

A woman can forgive almost any crime done in her name.

"Would you believe such a thing of me?" he asked softly.

What could she say but no?

He smiled and touched her hair briefly. "Of course you wouldn't."

She noticed only later that he had never denied it, and it lingered like a worm in her mind, burrowing and writhing.

She turned her attention to Catherine, sweeping away her cut locks and bathing her face in mint water to cool her. Charles, distracted from his lethal mission, sat at his wife's bedside, looking alternately grieved and bored.

At length Catherine stirred again, and her eyes blearily found her two caretakers.

"You are here," she said to her husband. "I feared it was only a dream. I have so many fantastical dreams of late. There was a snake that came from a cave, and . . . but no matter. You are here after all. They told me you must not come, but I am glad you defied them." She gave a weak chuckle that disintegrated into a pained cough. "How silly I am. You are king! To think that there is anyone to defy, save God. But I am glad, for now I can go."

"Go? You mean die? No, nothing of the sort."

"There is only one thing I will regret in leaving this world," she said, her plaintive eyes regarding him. "My husband, my love, say it has not been a bad union. Say I have not disappointed you. I know I have caused you trouble, but oh, I have loved you so hard, and I've tried...tried...tried..."

Her voice trailed off and her eyes fogged for a moment, so that when she spoke again they could not tell if she was with them or in her own dream world.

"Now that you are with me I find I almost wish to remain. But no, it is too late for that. I know in dying I give you a greater gift than I could in life. They say I lost the child, that I may not be able to bear one even if I lived. They thought I did not hear them. Charles, my king and love, with me gone you can marry again. She will not love you as I love you. No one can...I do not think you know...But she will give you what I can't—an heir. A king needs sons. My womb will not provide, but still my body in its death will serve you."

Charles was weeping openly now. What he could not feel for his wife while she lived at his side he got an inkling of now as she all but sacrificed her life for him.

"Choose not a princess," she went on. "Why do you need a princess when your love will make her a queen? Marry a friend. Oh, Charles! It hurts me so!" She kneaded at her belly as if to drive the pain away.

"It hurts me so," Charles echoed.

"Will you hear my sins?"

"I will fetch the priest."

"No, you are my confessor. Forgive me. Once when I was angered I asked what you would do if I took a lover. Believe me, I never would, never could. We are made differently, men and women." She chuckled, then curled in pain. "When I came from the convent I scarcely knew that much about marital relations. My little maids of honor knew more than I, and they tried to guide me in the ways of men. But I did not understand until now."

"Forgive me," Charles said.

"There's nothing to forgive. I'm only glad to have had a little of your love, a touch or two, a brief joyous time as your wife."

"Oh, my Catherine, my darling, you must not die. Please." His tears fell on her breast. "Please, try to live. For my sake!"

Her eyes lit up. "Do you mean it?" she asked, weak, but with a sudden spark of vitality. "Oh, Charles, have I ever disobeyed you? If you say I must live, then I will!"

Charles, his husbandly duties (about which he was always punctilious) accomplished, wiped his tears, ordered a prompt execution, and sent a message to Lady Castlemaine to prepare for his night's recreation.

"You're a good girl, Zabby," Catherine said when the king had gone, condescendingly but lovingly patting her head.

Which is a far cry from *You'd have made a fine queen,* the sentiment she knew had been on the queen's lips not a moment before.

They say the king's touch has miraculous healing powers. So too, perhaps, his tears. From the moment his salt had landed on Catherine, she began to rally. She was weeks in bed, her mind continued to wander, and she became a little deaf, but by winter she was back in the presence chamber enduring spiteful looks from all who had lost money or power or the possibility of queenship from her refusal to die.

Not until Charles left did Zabby realize what he'd revealed—Beth's lover had been captured and would soon be executed.

The moment the queen was sleeping peacefully, Zabby slipped from her side, sent in one of her servants to attend her (with strict orders from the king not to allow any additional treatment except by his own approval), and went in search of information.

She was bewildered that Charles had kept the secret from her and, unless the court gossips had lost their passion, from the rest of the world, too. She thought he would have celebrated the capture of the man responsible for his queen's kidnapping, not to mention the scores of robberies he and his band had committed. It would have made Charles look a hero to the people, the avenger of his queen, and the savior of all travelers. She knew how he felt about the populace, a queer admixture of fear and anxiety to please. He hated them; he needed them.

"There you are!" came a brazen voice from down the hall.

Zabby sighed. Lady Castlemaine was the last person she wanted to deal with at the moment.

"Well, how does our dear queen?" Barbara tapped her red-heeled foot impatiently and her eyebrows arched high into her perfect forehead. She affected an air of scornful unconcern, but Zabby knew she must be fretting.

"The king tells her she must live," Zabby said.

"And that mewling wretch will do whatever her husband orders her," she said, but sighed with relief. The she lowered her voice. "It appears I am in your debt."

Zabby waited.

"It has reached me that there was some suspicion of a plot against the queen . . . by some party other than Elphinstone, I mean. You heard mention of treason, saw a certain someone go to my rooms afterward. You could have ruined me, yet you told Charles it could not have been my scheme. Why?" She looked genuinely troubled, and considerably older.

"Because I did not think you would do such a thing."

"What matter the truth of it? If I had such a chance to rid myself of my rival I'd take it, truth or no. Charles trusts you. If you had told him I was involved . . . well, I might have escaped burning, but I'd be exiled to Scotland at best, which is nearly as bad, and you'd reign supreme of all the harlots. You should have done me in while you had the chance."

What if she'd done as Barbara would have? With a little malice, oh, just a bit, and only the barest bending of truth, she could have doomed one of the three women who stood between her and Charles. And had she not alerted Charles to his wife's miserable treatment at the hands of her Portuguese ladies, doctors, and priests, the queen too would have perished, and then the field would be clear of all but Frances.

"You really are a little fool," Barbara said with something very like affection. "Well, this is the strangest rivalry I've ever known." She gave Zabby a wry smile. "Our Charles, if I may style him such, will be attending me tonight in my apartments. Perhaps you'd care to join us? No? Well, should you change your mind . . . Your face isn't near as fishy as once I thought."

She laughed and sailed off, but Zabby called softly after her, "Do you know they've captured Elphinstone?" She wasn't sure if she should mention it, but Charles hadn't said to keep it a secret, so perhaps it was now common knowledge. In any case, she had to find out, for Beth's sake.

"No!" She was back quick as a cat, eager for news. "Is he at Newgate? I'm a-dying to view the devilish fellow, though since he never had the sense to rob me, I ought to cut him."

"I don't know where he is. No one knows they've taken him. It has been kept quiet for some reason. Can you find out where he is, and what will happen? Charles said just now he's gone to order his execution, but there must be a trial, no?"

"And just why is it so important to you?" Barbara asked archly.

"It isn't . . . not to me."

"Ah, to your little mousy friend. She met Elphinstone before, did she not? Fancies herself in love with him? Poor wretch. Well, since you did me a favor, I'll do one for you and find out all about it. I would have anyway, because Elphinstone's a fascinating figure of a man. But if I can clear my debt of you with such a pittance!"

Zabby was left having no idea which of Barbara's words were false, which sincere, what was meant for kindness and what for scorn.

Barbara was true to her word, though, and before nightfall a note came for Zabby while she was in her room with Beth. She read it twice over quickly and then, as the missive instructed, tore it into tiny pieces and tossed it into the fire.

"Beth, dear, I have something to tell you. Harry — your Harry

—has been captured." She rushed to say it before she lost her nerve. "He's to be executed Friday."

She expected hysteria.

Beth blinked heavily, blinked again.

"So that's why he didn't come for me," she said. And then, "So soon?"

Zabby told her what Barbara's note had revealed: that Elphinstone had become such a popular figure, it was feared his execution would cause unrest. Someone might try to rescue him from Newgate Prison or the execution cart, so his arrest was secret, his trial swift, and his death was to be prompt.

Zabby thought her friend must be in shock. Surely tears would come soon; tears or screams or unconsciousness. But Beth said very calmly, "I do not think it would be possible to visit him in Newgate, do you? But surely I can attend his execution. Will you come with me? And Eliza too." She had the glassy, staring eyes of a madwoman, and she was almost smiling. "We'll go as boys, like before. I'd like to wear my buttercup lutestring silk, though it doesn't matter, really, does it?"

Beth suddenly reminded Zabby of St. Catherine on the wheel, smiling through her torture, so full of holy joy that the spiked wheel broke.

"Beth, I don't think you ought to go. Hold him in your heart, but don't go to see his suffering. He wouldn't like you to."

Beth gave her a quizzical little look.

"But if I don't see him again, how am I to marry him?"

Chapter 24

THE TYBURN JIG

THOUGH SHE FEARED for Beth's sanity, Zabby agreed to help her, and even pulled Eliza away from the last day's rehearsal to join them. Beth swore she'd go, with or without her comrades.

"We'd better accompany her," Eliza said in an aside. "In her state she's likely to toss herself into the Thames. She'd do best to forget that criminal love of hers and latch on to the earl. She needs a protector to save her from her own foolishness, and I for one won't be able to do it for long."

"Why, where will you be going?"

She gave Zabby a sly look. "Didn't you hear? My father has arranged a most suitable match." She gave such a screech of laughter that even Beth was dragged out of her faintly smiling somnambulism.

"And you're going to marry him?"

"Heavens, no!"

"Then what—"

But Beth urged them to hurry, and Zabby wouldn't get her answer until that night.

Zabby and Eliza both dressed in the formal black coat, weskit, and close-fitting breeches Charles and some of the older members of court had begun to favor, but Beth clad herself as gaily as she could and still be faintly masculine. Fortunately, foppery was still in its fullest flower among the young, and the rule was, if any creature appeared too feminine to be believed, it was in all probability a man. She could not wear her yellow lutestring, but she chose from among Eliza's disguises a suit of emerald and silver petticoat breeches that flowed in such profusion that, if not for the elegantly hosed calves exposed below, they might well have been a gown. Ribbons in a contrasting shade of pale green wove and fluttered at her breast and elbows, and her shirt, peeking through the pinking, was dyed sapphire.

She seemed calm, with just a little flutter in her breathing, and as proudly modest as a bride. She scrutinized herself in the glass, angling it to catch the dancing firelight, and pronounced herself ready. Then they snuck out into the chilly predawn gloom to meet Beth's groom at the Triple Tree.

They went first to the street outside the Newgate Press Yard, where it all began under the sun's first blessed rays. There was a double-barred gate—a grate, a space between housing a drowsing guard, and another set of bars—through which the girls could just see movement.

"Oh!" Beth cried, and Eliza squeezed her hand hard, digging her nails into the flesh to bring Beth to herself.

"We are men, and we don't know him. If Harry sees you weep he will lose heart. Be strong!"

The guard between the gates stirred himself. "You gentlemen are up betimes," he said, yawning and scratching.

"We were never yet to bed," Eliza said cheerily. "Why, is it morning? Pray, what is that glowing orb in the firmament? Could it be the sun I've heard the poets rave about? I don't believe I've ever seen such a thing. This must be daytime, gentlemen! A novelty! What are you about, good sir? What is this unattractive place?"

The guard looked at Eliza as if she were straight out of Bedlam; but then, gentlemen could afford to be peculiar. "This 'ere's Newgate. The prison," he added for clarification.

Eliza strutted forward to peer through the bars. "And who are they?"

"No one you need to know about."

"I like to know everything," she said, handing him a golden sovereign.

He leaned close to the gate and, spitting as he spoke, said, "Not a peep of it, but that there's the infamous Elphinstone and his band. 'E's to be hanged today. Mum's the word, though. If it got about, the ladies would all throw theirselves under the cart, and the men would all challenge 'im to a duel before we could 'ang 'im. 'Ere now, you'll not be wanting to dirty yer fine clothes, sir!" For Beth had her whole body pressed to the rusty bars, her hands slipping through, yearning to be with her love.

Something had caught Zabby's ear. "Hanged, did you say?"

"Ay, what else for the terror of the 'ighways — and the maiden-heads."

"I mean, nothing else? Only hanged? Not drawn and quartered? Not burned?"

"Yer a hard one, sir, if I do say! Hanging will do the job right enough, never you fear."

Zabby frowned, puzzled. Hanging was for everyday criminals, common thieves, and robbers. Surely Harry Ransley had been charged with treason. To kidnap the queen with intent of doing away with her, either by murder or secret imprisonment, was a high crime against the throne, and had direr consequences than mere death. A woman guilty of high treason was usually burned to death. A man was hung, drawn, and quartered, a gruesome process in which the culprit was strangled half to death, cut down just in time, only to have his abdomen sliced neatly open and his intestines slowly drawn out like so many yards of sausage before his still living (for a time, anyway) eyes. Then, when sufficiently dead, he was hacked into pieces and displayed about town, a head here, a leg there.

Many offenses were considered high treason. The old woman who shaved slivers from coins to melt down was treasonous, because she interfered with the national currency in a way that could, on a much larger scale, have catastrophic civil results. The woman who killed her neighbor was a simple murderess; the woman who slayed her husband or father committed treason, because she defied the natural order of authority, and by extension the Crown.

But rarely were such people actually burned or drawn and quartered. It was simply too messy, and though the public loved a good clean hanging, there would have been trouble if everyone technically charged with treason was immolated or mutilated. The English public had a strong stomach, but not quite that strong. Those terrible consequences were reserved for the worst of the worst.

No one could argue that to steal a queen was not a crime against the king, the highest of high treason.

What did Charles know? Why was he letting Harry off with a relatively dignified and quick hanging?

Or what, she suddenly thought, did he not want others to know?

A swarthy blacksmith came to strike off the fetters binding the prisoners' wrists and legs. They were then tied with rope, their arms bent before their breasts in prayerful pose and bound together, and to their bodies.

A small sound came from the pretty gentleman who was so fascinated by the proceedings. They had slipped a noose around one prisoner's neck.

"'E's a lucky one, 'im. Someone ordered 'im and 'is friends silken ropes."

"I hardly think comfort matters," Eliza said.

"Bless ye, sir, not comfort or fashion, but mercy. A silk rope lies close, ye see, and the knot slips that tight. A man might hang from a hempen rope a quarter hour before 'e perishes. A silk noose chokes 'im off quick as anything. Was a red-haired lady in the finest carriage you ever did see, pulled up late last night and handed 'em out. They say 'e 'ad 'em all, skivvy and quality alike. A fine lover's present, that."

Though the execution had not been announced, a crowd was already gathering. Apprentices, vendors, buskers, huswives, were drawn by the clang of the blacksmith's strike. They had lived and worked near Newgate long enough to know that sound meant a show. Those with the leisure to do so began to mill around the gate, and as a small crowd always draws a large crowd, the numbers quickly grew.

At eight the guards appeared, mounted with pistols and swords, and afoot with lances. Then the cart rumbled in, drawn by a pair of shaggy dray horses, already loaded with the three coffins that would be the criminals' couches on the way to Tyburn, their beds ever after.

The condemned climbed into the wagon, and now Zabby recognized the other two, the lean pistoleer and the solid barbarian skilled in pipe and deadly flail. The latter's teeth were cleaned of black grease now, and they gleamed white and even. Both of Harry's accomplices looked like gentlemen, or gentry at the least.

Beth stared at the lover she had scarcely touched, memorized him, burned him into her heart, as behind her the crowd began to murmur a name in rapturous awe. *Elphinstone!* Boys were sent running to spread the word, and by the time the cart rolled down Newgate Road with the city marshal at the head and the chaplain in a sedan, the crowd had burgeoned to a hundred. A thousand marched behind the cart on Holborn, two thousand at St. Giles. By the time the criminals were offered their penultimate drink at the Bowl Inn, the gathering had swelled to dangerous numbers. The three Elizabeths kept to the front as best they could, fighting the press together, and had an easier time than most, for their fine clothes commanded respect. Still, it was a long, slow trudge to the next tavern, the Mason's Arms, and on to Tyburn's triple gallows.

It was impossible for Beth to catch Harry's eye. She was lost in the crowd, and in any event, was at present the wrong gender to attract his attention. Plenty of other women were trying to do just that, though, throwing him kisses and hastily gathered nosegays of dried flowers.

Harry ignored them all—the morbidly flirtatious women hoping for a glance, a touch; the men, frankly admiring his luck (up until then); the curious cottagers longing to be a part of something famous, for the chance to say around a fire that night, *Yes, I saw him, and a fine brave sight he was, riding to his death without a care in the world, head high, curls bright on the knotted rope.* His companions were eager for their share of spirits at the two tavern stops, but Harry only shook his head and looked above and beyond the crowd. From time to time on the tortuous two-hour trek he spoke a low word to his friends, but apart from that he seemed hardly there at all.

If London had been warned of Elphinstone's imminent demise, it would have rallied a hundred thousand spectators, called forth chestnut and potato vendors, tapped casks of cider and strong ale. It would have summoned jugglers and balladeers. It would hawk pamphlets upon which were printed confessions that had never been made, final words that had yet to be spoken. As it was, word of mouth had drawn perhaps five thousand, half of which didn't quite believe this was the Elphinstone gang but refused to leave in case they were wrong.

The cart backed up underneath one of the gallows cross-bars and an assistant shimmied up, ready to catch the ropes and secure them.

"Last words! Last words!" the crowd roared.

The city marshal spurred his horse to the cartside and boomed, "By royal decree, the condemned are to have no last words."

The crowd hissed and spat and surged forward like an enraged cat. Already they had been robbed of so many pleasures in this ex-ecution — the festivities and food — now they were to be denied three final heroic or piteous or brazen speeches? Seats in the the-ater pit cost two shillings, but everyone was entitled to the free drama and pathos of a gallows epilogue.

The marshal called for silence and peace, but the crowd, that same animal that had killed a king, made its will and power known. The lancers acting as guards shifted nervously, the pistol men accompanying them reckoned up the mob's numbers and the time it would take to reload if it came to a fight. The guards would not defy the king's orders, but if there happened to be a delay and the prisoners happened to say a word or two in the interim, how were they to stop it? The marshal signaled to the executioner, and all fell quiet.

The highwayman who had played such a merry tune on his pipe half rose from his coffin, drawing breath to speak, but Harry stayed him with a hand. The man sat again, biting his lip. The prisoners would not speak. For a long moment there was silence. Then, from the tight press at the front, came a girl's sweet voice.

"Harry Ransley, I marry you!"

Everyone looked about, but they could not tell which girl had spoken. They did not regard the three noblemen at the front at all.

Harry, though, looked up in quick alarm and, as he had once before, saw through the mob, through her disguise, directly to Beth. He held her gaze only for an instant, long enough for a lifetime of love and apology to be translated straight to her heart. Then he looked off to the horizon of rooftops and said, loudly but apparently to no one, "And I marry you, my beloved Elizabeth."

There were two score Elizabeths in the crowd that day, and each carried the story away with her, some laughing to tell it, some weeping. A few never spoke of it at all, but kept it in their own hearts, a seed pearl of a precious secret, the day the bravest, most beautiful man on earth married them the moment before he died.

A couple could be married in their parish church after calling the banns with their whole community as witnesses, or, if they had a bit of money and didn't want to wait, by special license. But among the poor, it was common, and perfectly legal, to marry by mere declaration. A betrothal was spoken of in future tense: *I will marry you*. That could be broken. All that was really needed for a binding marriage was an espousal in the present tense: *I marry you*.

He did not look at her again. He did not have to. They had done all they could possibly do.

" 'Tis a new hangman," they heard someone beside them say. "One Jack Ketch. Hope he knows what he's about."

The three silken lines were stretched taut and tied off on the beam. Any moment now the driver would whip up the horses and the condemned would be dragged from their coffins to hang suspended until the life was choked out of them. But if a man was brave, if he kept his wits about him, if he did not hold on to hope for a last-second reprieve, he could hasten his end.

When the driver settled himself and the moment was near, the three men rose as one to hurl themselves from the back of the cart. If they jumped, it was likely their necks would snap instantly. If not, silk cord or no, their agony would be prolonged.

But there was a tangle; there was not room for all of them. Harry, the gentleman, stepped back so that his companions could have their easy deaths, and by the time the way was clear for him, by the time the silent air echoed with the twin snap of two necks breaking, it was too late and he was being dragged slowly off the cart, suspended in the air.

If the crowd hated him they would have let him hang, mocking his struggling and suffering as he turned purple and bloated and grotesque. But they loved Elphinstone, their hero, their legend, so once again they surged forward to grab hold of him, weigh him down, kill him as quickly as they could. Bad men must die, aye, but the best of the bad men must have a good end.

First upon him, wrapping himself around the criminal's legs like a drowning man, was a garishly dressed fop in emerald and silver, weeping as though his heart would break.

Chapter 25

THE NAKED TRUTH

*B*ETH HAD LOST HER MIND, Zabby was certain of it. That night was the premiere of *Nunquam Satis,* and Beth, instead of falling into despair or unconsciousness as they'd expected, quietly cleaned herself up and immediately dressed for the theater.

"Beth, love," Eliza said, "there is no need to show us your strength. Stay here. I . . . I will stay with you if you'd like." It would be the supreme sacrifice to give up attending the opening performance, for her plans for the rest of her life depended on it.

"No, I will go," Beth said, and fixed her hairpins and settled her petticoat exactly as if her true love had not been executed a bare two hours before. She smiled and took her friends' hands. "Don't worry. Don't you see? It doesn't matter anymore. Nothing matters now. We are well and truly married in the eyes of God, and that means we will be together for all eternity. What does this life matter to me now? It is a prison I will bear with good grace while I reside in it, looking forward only to my release. What are a few years against all eternity?" She gave an odd little laugh. "You haven't congratulated me yet on my marriage. Don't you think he looked well?"

"Will she kill herself, do you think?" Eliza asked Zabby later.

"I don't know. And to tell you truly, I don't know if I'd stop her."

"All the same, one or the other of us should stay with her until her marriage. Her second marriage. Lord, if her mother and the earl only knew! He's coming for her tomorrow, you know, with no idea he's getting a widow for a bride." Eliza's thoughts were firmly with her own problems, and she believed the best place for Beth was as the wife of a wealthy man who would pamper her and keep her from foolishness. "Do you think we should tell her that gentlemen who kidnap queens rarely make it to heaven?"

"No," Zabby said adamantly, not certain herself if that was true. "Knowing Beth, in her current state, it would only make her commit murder to join Harry in hell."

The queen, still recuperating, was not in attendance, but since maids of honor made such pretty ornaments, two of the three Elizabeths were still in the king's box. Beth sat very primly, completely unaware that her future husband, Thorne, watched her intently from a nearby seat.

His London home alone housed a hundred works of art, a thousand rare antiquities. His country estate boasted flowers from every corner of the globe, coaxed with glass and heat into spring bloom even in the declining season. And yet despite all this amassed beauty belonging to him and him alone, the only thing he'd thought of for the past six months was Elizabeth Foljambe. Out of all the more garish beauties of the court, with their paint and patches and protruding bosoms, he had instantly picked the one true, perfect jewel, the masterpiece. It did not matter that her mother was a syphilitic monster, any more than it mattered that a priceless sculpture had been hewn by a lunatic. It did not matter that she was poor. How many gems had been hidden in the hearth, coal-blackened to disguise their worth?

For the next three hours Thorne watched Beth watch the play.

For the next three hours Beth relived every happy moment with her Harry, forgetting, almost, that he was gone, thinking only of the time they would be together again. She concocted pretty little things to say to him, and wondered if there were flowers in heaven. If there were, Harry would surely have a nosegay of lily of the valley waiting for her.

For the next three hours, Zabby made her eyes ache by pretending to stare straight at the stage, all the while watching sidelong as Charles dallied under Barbara's skirts in a way he must believe subtle. Though it was a breech of protocol, Barbara sat in the queen's seat. There were those who said she was rapidly falling in Charles's favor, but to see her, she might just as well be queen. She was so radiantly lovely, with such animalistic energy, it did not seem that any queen or wife — or lowly maid of honor — could ever compete with her. But Zabby remembered what the Newgate guard had said about the red-haired woman in the splendid carriage who'd brought silken cords, and again she wondered, who, and what, was Barbara, really?

For the next three hours a scowling, starched, stiff man in a high-crowned hat said to the young lord who was his companion, "What was that? Why are they laughing? Was she referring to his privities? Whoever wrote this offal ought to have his ears nailed to the pillory. Tell me why that was amusing, eh? Eh?"

For the next three hours a handsome, sturdy young man with a tense, beardless face sat in the pit and mouthed every line of *Nunquam Satis,* interrupting himself to snarl whispered vitriol at the actors. "Hellfire, Beck, if you turn they can't see you roll your eyes, and then the next jest is lost! Hart, you pricklouse, from the belly! What's the use of me writing a clever line if it can't be heard over the harlots' banter?"

Near the end he slipped from his seat, trod on several toes, missed an offer to duel, and went backstage.

"Duncan, my man!" Killigrew embraced his friend. "You've saved the company! Did you see His Majesty laugh at all the right moments? He wore a smile the whole way through." This was perhaps because of where his hand was, or perhaps because he'd caught the eye of a piquantly lovely little red-haired orange girl making her saucy way through the pit. "It's a success, all thanks to you! Hark, do you hear the applause?" He shouted to a stagehand. "Close the curtain, quick, and send Doll out to give them another dance. Keep them cheering and then we'll have the flourish of raising the curtain in the end. Come here, Duncan, where you can see the audience. Isn't it glorious?"

He pulled Eliza into an alcove of fabric, a sort of makeshift room for quick costume changes attached to the main curtain. They peeked through a slit to see the audience on its feet, whooping as Doll pranced onstage in her tight pants and nearly sheer shirt for a reprise of the popular "breeches part." They cheered her and called for their other favorite actors to return as well. They guffawed and quoted their favorite clever lines to show that they'd had wit enough to understand them. They called for Killigrew, and then . . .

"Give us the playwright!" someone shouted, and it was echoed throughout the pit. The author's name was always left off his play for the first performance — if it was a crashing failure, his career wouldn't be ruined. Of course, there was the risky possibility that an unscrupulous competitor might claim authorship first, and no one would believe the real author later.

"Will you come out with me?" Killigrew asked.

Eliza's eyes were shining. "And as you promised, you'll tell the world my name? Let them know who has given them their pleasure today?"

"Of course! Conley, is it? Conley Duncan?" He took Eliza by the arm and started to pull her out, but she held her ground.

"No, that's not my real name. Will you tell them my real name?" She let her voice float up to her true feminine tones, but Killigrew didn't notice in the din.

"For certs. What is it?"

She told him, but he did not catch it above the clamor.

She tried again.

"Eliza Parsloe."

"Elijah? A good biblical name . . ."

"No!" she shouted. "Eliza. Elizabeth Parsloe."

Killigrew gasped, and shook his head. "A woman? I am ruined! Woe! Woe!" He had been a tragedian in his youth. "No, I don't believe it! I won't believe it! Oh-ho, you are a madman like all the others, and love your jest."

She could see he was desperate for it not to be so, and if it hadn't concerned her so nearly she might have backed away from the truth and laughed along with him, clapped her hat on her periwig, and strutted onstage, Conley Duncan to all the world.

"No one would believe a woman wrote a play like that. If you were a woman I'd be a laughingstock. The king would dismiss me. I'd lose everything. No, I don't believe it! Come on, to the stage, and stop this nonsense!"

He tried once more to drag her along, but she dug her fingers into his collar and latched firm. *I will make him believe me,* she thought fiercely. *He will know—they will all know—that I, a woman, wrote this most excellent play!*

With her free hand she tore at the buttons of her coat. "I will convince you of what I am!" she cried, as with a savage pull she ripped the ribbon that held her shirt closed at her throat, and liberated her unbound breasts.

Killigrew recoiled as if at a serpent, staggering backwards, and in so doing carried Eliza with him, out of the curtained alcove, out to where the entire cast of *Nunquam Satis* assembled for their final bows and flourishes. The curtain was speedily drawn back as Eliza shouted, "I, Eliza Parsloe, a woman, as you see, am the playwright you honor!"

In that instant, Jeremiah Parsloe decided it was not too late to find a modest second wife with wide hips and once again be fruitful and multiply.

Lord Ayelsworth, seeing the bounty of bosom that could be his, was just as eager to marry Eliza . . . until her father uttered the fatal words: "Not a penny!"

Zabby forgot, for a moment, all about plots and intrigue, tragedy and desire, and stared at her gallant friend in open-mouthed amazement. Suddenly she could see herself in Eliza — not half naked on the stage, perhaps, but covered in soot, stained with blood, indifferent to the world as she pursued her passion in the elaboratory. *That's the nature of a calling,* she realized. *It might not bring us happiness, but we have no other choice but to pursue it.*

Beth, taking it all in absently, wondered if, now that she was a married woman, she'd be allowed to have a friend as instantly notorious as Eliza. She soon shrugged it off — Harry didn't seem the sort of husband who would mind.

Killigrew, hot as a quartan ague and looking on the verge of an apoplectic fit, threw down his wig with a roar and stormed off to drink two bottles of Rhenish and read an old play about failed Roman senators who threw themselves on their swords.

But the audience went wild! In the pit, lords and 'prentices stood side by side on the quaking benches and set up a cry like barbarians going into battle. The ladies in the boxes laughed and shrilled, the whores in their vizard-masks hooted derision at their buxom competition. There were a few hisses, perhaps from those who had heard her declaration, but for the most part the audience saw a well-featured strapping girl with bare breasts, and who could ever expect more for their shillings?

Then Charles, to whom all the theater looked for an example, rose in his smooth, stately fashion. The crowd hushed, and Eliza, wide-eyed and trembling, on the verge of clutching her shirt together and running off the stage in tears, was paralyzed a moment longer. Would he frown and depart? Would he close the theater? There was an impossible moment of anticipation, gravid with possibility.

Charles met Eliza's eye, recognized her ruddy, handsome face ... and smiled. Then very deliberately he clapped his hands together ... once ... twice ... thrice.

Now there was nothing but applause. Killigrew wouldn't hear about it until the next morning, when he was too hung-over to fully appreciate it, but the king's three claps sealed the fate of *Nunquam Satis*. By midnight illicit printers were spewing out false copies of the play, and balladeers were already renaming their heroines Lady Nuncsat. The play ran for three weeks — a miracle in a time of short attention spans when a week was a good run. There was a great deal of initial confusion — was the author a woman who dressed like a man, or a man who thought he was a woman, or, oh, delicious speculation, a hermaphrodite?—which only fueled the popularity of both play and writer.

When he felt a little better, Killigrew hired Eliza to write three more plays immediately, and when enough time had passed to see the humor of it, he convinced her to become an actress as well. She would never manage the romantic leads, the tearing beauties, the lovely innocents, but she was a deft hand at the witty old women, the Puritanical hypocrites, the nursemaids and spinsters and relicts. And since she was so frequently the author, she made sure these undervalued characters had some of the cleverest lines.

Eliza knew none of this that night as she stood half naked before her father, fiancée, friends, and most of the royal court. When she saw her father storm out, she knew she'd lost her fortune, but she knew too she had enough to live as she wished. *I want to be free,* she thought, *and how much can it cost to be free?*

Despite her loss, despite her fears, she was radiantly happy. She was doing exactly what she wanted to do.

Without even bothering to cover her bosom, she found Nelly in the pit, gave her a broad wink, and made a courtier's elaborate bow, one hand on her heart, the other flung wide.

Had Catherine been entirely well, it is unlikely that Eliza would have been allowed to return to court. However fond she was of the braw plucky girl who'd taken her into the world of men and tried to save her from kidnappers, Catherine was still a product of her convent upbringing and would be hard pressed to find a suitable reason to keep a maid of honor who'd bared her breasts onstage. But she was not made aware of it until weeks later, and by then the story had changed so drastically, the queen did not know what to make of it. Some of the court—her Portuguese attendants, and those who lived for a tasty scandal—swore Eliza had been caught fornicating onstage while 'prentices in the pit tossed up for the next go at her. But those who had no particular grudge against either Eliza or sin only shrugged and said a woman wrote a good play, and as everyone had spent the first years of his life latched to a pair of teats, no one should pretend to be shocked by them now.

And so Catherine never formally dismissed her wayward maid, and though Eliza moved from Whitehall that night to take up permanent residence over the Cock and Pie Tavern, she was never barred from the palace.

The next day Eliza bounced up in a hackney and greeted the waiting Zabby with kisses. They had gathered to see Beth off to her wedding with Thorne.

"Did you see what Lady Castlemaine was wearing this morning?" Eliza asked, her face ruddy and radiant. "I saw her driving in the park. A man's tailored jacket and a trim little weskit, all in crimson, with a skirt, it's true, but she must have had her seamstresses up all night to be the first to adopt it. I warrant within a week all the fine ladies will be dressing half like men. Only think, I, a merchant's daughter, setting the mode! Beth, though . . . when her honey month is over she'll burst forth to set the trends herself. She's a face and figure to set the world alight. She'll do well enough with her earl, so long as she never speaks of what is past.

Some of us are meant for marriage, some for other things, and the only place for Beth is in a comfortable home with baskets of babes all about her."

"You don't believe she loved Harry?" Zabby asked.

"Oh, of course she did. And I'm not saying she'll come to love this Thorne in his place. Only, every person needs a profession. Not just for money, but for the soul, and the heart, and the brain, else she goes mad. I've found mine—the stage—and I warrant you found yours, too, amid lenses and potions and dead beasts in spirits. We're not fit to be wives. But most people aren't like you and me. They don't have a calling. They fall into whatever is handy. For a man, that's what his father did, farmer or soldier or pimp to the king. For a woman, pah, I think well of my sex, but if they're no worse than men, they're certainly no better. A woman tends to do what her mother does, and that's marry. Most folk do what's easiest."

"She'll be miserable with Thorne," Zabby said. "Misery's not so easy."

"Don't fear for Beth. She's the dearest thing in the world, but she's not made for anything beyond marriage, and there's no harm in that. It is her natural profession. She only made a false start in it, but thank the heavens her fright of a mother came through in the end. Have you seen Thorne? He's a handsome piece for such an old fellow, and rich as . . . well, as my father, I suppose. I vow Beth will end up happier than the pair of us, though troth, I can't imagine a happier creature than me. Look, here comes the blushing bride and the weeping mother. Her sores, I mean, for she looks as cross as ever. Yes, I'll hush now. Darling Beth, my congratulations! Lady Enfield." She curtsied to the diseased harridan.

"I've pulled it off," Lady Enfield crowed. "Despite her hoydenish companionship"—she glared at Eliza—"and the vile stink of the court, I kept my flower in the bud, squeezed tight shut."

"It is a splendid match," Eliza said, edging away from the hunched syphilitic horror but darting in to kiss Beth.

"Ten thousand a year settled on her for her use, and a thousand for my own self—have you ever heard the like?" For the first time in living memory, Lady Enfield smiled, a quick flash of crumbling teeth, a curl of ruined lips, gone almost as soon as it came. "He's a man, and foul, fouler than most, I dare say, but the name of Enfield is restored from this day forth, and my girl will bear children into riches and security. My job is done."

She took her daughter's hand. "Tell that husband of yours he needn't worry overmuch about his bargain. He'll find it cheaper than expected, for now I see you well and safely wed I'm free to leave this walking corpse that is my own body. I'll take my thousand for this year, as that's my due, but he'll not have to fret about paying it next year, for I'll be gone."

She laughed, without a trace of that quick smile, and Beth felt her throat catch. Just when she thought she was done with emotion, beyond the reach of either affection or grief, she felt again the terrible strength of her mother's love for her, vast and pitiless as the sea, and quite against her will found she loved her back. Hated her, resented her, pitied her, feared her, aye, but loved her too.

"Where are you to get married, Beth?" Zabby asked.

Lady Enfield answered for her. "The earl says in a little chapel not far from here, a place where his mother was wed. It's to be by special license, you know," she added proudly. "He arranged the whole thing. Ah, here he comes now."

His equipage, his leather, his horses, were black and gleaming, and even as they came to a halt, a boy swung down and began to polish the ebony wheels. The servants were thrashed for any imperfection, real or imagined, and Thorne's diligence kept them industrious. He descended from his carriage without so much as glancing to see if the steps had been lowered. If they had not, if by chance his foot met empty air, the entire carriage staff would have been severely whipped with the knout, a clever instrument the earl had adopted from a Russian friend. Twenty strokes of that terrible thing had been known to kill. He never settled for fewer than twenty-five.

He made a stiff bow to the assembled ladies, then without a word held his hand out to Beth, who shrank back.

"Go on, precious one, I'll be right behind you," Lady Enfield said with somewhat forced cheerfulness.

"No, my lady, you will not," Thorne said. "A marriage is a private affair between bride and groom. You've done your duty in the rearing of her. Now you turn her over to me. Completely. Good day, my lady."

"What are you about, sir? Not attend my own daughter's marriage? Infamous. I'll have you know . . ."

"Perhaps this will silence you." He handed her an overstuffed satchel that clinked with a particularly golden rattle. When she stared at him, mouth gaping below her gleaming hawk's beak, he simply dropped the bag at her feet, snatched Beth's hand, and guided her firmly toward the carriage.

"Mother..." Beth's plaintive voice sounded, in Lady Enfield's ears, exactly as it had in her childhood, when mother and baby were happy and the life ahead was full of promise.

Then she was gone, drawn away by the gleaming black horses.

Lady Enfield, shrunken, trembling, watched the child who had been the sole focus of her every energy, every thought, for the last sixteen years, fulfill the destiny she'd marked out for her.

"That's all a woman is," she said. "A womb that's full for a spell, then empty forever."

She watched until the black carriage turned the corner, then hobbled away, leaning heavily on her cane.

Chapter 26

The Elaboratory

ELIZA LEFT SOON AFTER, relieved to return to the merry, heartless world of the demimonde, where girls never married against their will. Zabby, not knowing what to do with herself, feeling empty without her friends, wandered through the palace until she found herself outside Charles's elaboratory. *Their* elaboratory, she corrected.

She was about to go in when a man she just barely recognized as the Italian ambassador addressed her from down the hall. He trotted to catch up with her.

"My lady," he said, "have you but a moment? I have these little trinkets, poor paltry things which have no home. Would you perhaps do me the honor of accepting them?" He held up a pair of pigeon-blood ruby ear-drops as large as grapes. "And then, but a moment, I would so love to discuss the Dutch question."

Zabby listened, half in a trance, as the ambassador pretended to solicit her opinion, all the while offering his (and presumably his country's) own and trying to discover what the king might think, and whether he could be swayed. It was on the tip of Zabby's tongue to say he ought to talk to Barbara or Frances if he wanted a royal mistress to do his bidding, but then it struck her, all in a flash. *I may not be a royal mistress, but all the world thinks I am. Why on earth don't I take advantage of that? Here is this little man actually asking me to take part in the affairs of the continent. Barbara would do it for jewels and tell the king whatever would be best for her. Frances would take the jewels and promptly forget what she was supposed to tell the king. But I...I can take the jewels, use them to set up my own elaboratory, and then use my power, the power they all think I have, to actually change the court, the country, the world! Why, with a word, supposedly from Charles, I could make this little man carry a new policy home to Italy.*

She recalled what her godmother had told her when she first came to court against her will. *The whole of civilization is made in these halls, child. Every bit of wit and beauty and learning passes like flies through a web, and those living here decide what sticks. A mind like yours, Zabby-heart, can shape society from here. Only get yourself listened to by the right ears, and soon the whole nation will be thinking as you think.*

She already was listened to by the right ears, by those syco-phants who through vicarious use of her body wanted to touch and please the king, her supposed lover; and by the king himself, her dear friend.

Why did I dream of being queen, she wondered as the Italian con-tinued to babble, *when I have twice poor Catherine's power at my fin-*

gertips, if only I choose to use it? I don't need to be Charles's lover to have everything I ever dreamed of!

The Italian walked away, satisfied, leaving her with a palm full of blood-colored stones and a hollow feeling in her heart.

It is nothing, she thought to herself. *The power, the influence — all nothing.*

That's not what I want.

I want him.

She wanted that powerful body she'd dragged from death's door so long ago. She'd dueled with Plague itself for the right to that man. When he'd lain weak as a blind spaniel pup, she'd cupped her body around his to keep him warm. She'd bathed every inch of him, held him in his delirium, and later, when his mind returned before his strength, laughed with him and philosophized, argued and bantered as if they were the only people left in the world, alone on the island of his bed. And later still, laboring side by side in the elaboratory, in a shared love of knowledge. Shared love. That must be close to love for each other.

She wanted the mind, the body, the man. She did not need the power, the honor. She did not even need the acknowledgment of the world. That was all just a salve for her intellect. She was not an enlightened human after all, but an animal. All she wanted was the frankness of lust, the stark honesty of sex, the bright, incendiary moment of skin on skin. She did not want to be the mistress of the king, but the lover of the man. He might have been a stable boy, but he happened to be the king. She decided then and there that she would have him, and hang the rest.

No ambitions clouded her mind now; there was no confusion in her intentions. She heard a clink of glass within the elaboratory, a crash and muted curse, and entered, intent on seduction.

There was death in the room. She could scent it as well as any hound. Not blood, not illness; simple death, the inexorable state. A sturdy oak table had been dragged to the center of the room, and on it lay something covered in a heavy swath of unbleached linen.

"Zabby, my dear, I was going to send a page to search you out. Has your pretty little friend gone to be wed yet? I heard it was to be today."

"She left just this past half hour."

"A shame. I'd hoped to send her my blessings, and a present, though the one she's bound to now is a richer man than I by far. It seems there's a hole in the privy purse, cut by Parliament. But it is you I'd hoped to talk with, sweetheart. Here, sit beside me." He took her to a crimson chaise he called the fainting couch, put there for the occasional lady spectator who thought she ought to be overcome by chemical fumes or live rabbit dissections.

"You are her friend, so I hope you can tell her, delicately, and, if I may suggest, not in writing, husbands being what they are."

Zabby sat beside him, hardly listening, wondering how to begin. There was his thigh, a bare inch from her own. Dare she touch it? Or perhaps his hand. The hand is a good way to start, chaste, yet so full of nerves that it thrills to the lightest touch.

"Will you tell her that, for her sake, his body and property were spared? Harry Ransley and his cohorts were allowed to request the judgment of God." It was a rarely used form of officially sanctioned suicide, in which a judgment was not passed and the public was left to draw its own conclusions. The suspect agreed to die, the state agreed to kill him, and nothing was said as to the reasons why. If the criminal was found guilty, his property was forfeited to the Crown. If he chose the judgment of God, his money and property passed as if he'd died in his sleep.

"You mean, they were never found guilty?"

"Nor did they admit guilt. They turned themselves over to a higher court, and the state's only role was to deliver them there. Harry—Elphinstone—came from a fine old family, one that supported my father in his troubles. I did not want to see them shamed."

"Charles, I was at his execution." This drew raised eyebrows. "He was only hung, not drawn, not gibbeted, not torn up and hung from the city walls. He kidnapped the queen—there was a plot against her. How could he not be charged with high treason?" For a moment, Zabby almost forgot about the proximity of his dark, warm skin, and she watched his long, sensuous mouth only for an answer.

"There was no plot," Charles said.

"But there was! I heard it that night in the park."

"You were mistaken." His voice was suddenly stiff.

"Charles." She took his hand now but didn't know if it was with lascivious intent. "This is me, Zabby. I know the truth...though evidently not all of it. Tell me. Please."

His hand was rigid in hers for a moment, then turned palm

up and clasped her own. "There are four people in this vast world who love me," he said with a deep sigh. "And three people I love."

"Oh, Charles, a hundred thousand people love you!"

He shook his head and looked out at the scene of those many years past, the one he saw daily as if he had been beneath the scaffold, not safe across the ocean. "The love of the people is the love of a whore, lasting only while I please them, while I pay them, while their lives are comfortable. What they feel, they feel for the king. For thirty years of my life, I was not a king. I was a pauper. Who loved me then? Can you guess, Zabby, who are the four who love me now?"

"Catherine, of course, and . . ." It would have burned her tongue to speak Barbara's name.

"My sister Minette is dearer to me than all the world. But we did not grow up together, and after rediscovering each other we soon parted, I to my kingdom, she to be the second lady of France. Perhaps that is why I love her so — we had not the leisure to quarrel. And Catherine loves me, yes." He gave a rueful smile. "But there is another, who was a boy beside me, raised almost as my brother, who saved my life in war and kept me from slitting my own throat in despair in my exile."

"Buckingham," Zabby said, beginning to understand.

"It is very lonely, being a king. You'd not think it, the way they clamor to hold my piss-pot. I'm never solitary, but I'm always alone. Yes, Buckingham is the only thing I have left from my childhood. When I look at his face I remember who I was, when I was happy, unafraid, when I knew, as only a child can know, that the whole world adored me and I was as safe in it as in my nurse's arms. Can you remember that feeling? Perhaps that's what the Philosopher's Stone brings, not eternal life but eternal childhood. Perhaps that is heaven."

"But he has not been a good friend to you."

"He has the very devil in him, I'll not deny that. Maybe it is the child still in him, unable to keep his fingers from the jam pot because he knows he is too well loved to be beaten for it. He has betrayed me before, or so it seemed, but when I heard the reasons I always excused it. I can't help it. He is my friend."

"But he stole your wife!"

"The plot was foiled, and no one must ever know that there was a plot. That is why Elphinstone was allowed, encouraged, to request the judgment of God." Charles did not mention that he had been tortured in subtle ways, threatened with unspeakable acts against his family, first to uncover the truth of the plot, and then to ensure that it never came to light. "If the people knew about it, I'd have no choice but to execute my dearest friend. That, or allow him to escape into exile, and to be without him . . . I know you don't understand it, but after all we've been through together, I can't part with him. He is wicked; he is Buckingham—it's saying the selfsame thing."

So much love for an unworthy friend, Zabby thought, *and none for me.*

"And there are plotters everywhere," he said, lowering his voice and pulling her closer. "Plotters who don't even know they have a plot in them." His mouth was near hers as he whispered his deepest fears to her. "Once they know that I am vulnerable, that my friends can betray me, my own queen can be taken, they will try to seize power. There are a thousand factions who would over-throw the kingdom. Yet I walk among them, in reach of a pistol or dagger every day, and none dares strike so long as I wear that impenetrable mantle of king. But let that royal cloak unravel even a thread, let them see I am weak, or mortal, or vulnerable, and from somewhere a waiting serpent will strike. Then there will be blood — mine on the butcher's block, or the blood of those hun-dred thousand you say love me in another civil war."

He stood, dropping her hand, and looked as if he was about to begin his habitual pacing. He could never be still for long. When he was ill and feverish, she'd pressed her body to his to calm his tremors. Now, seeing his anxious fears, she stood and pressed her body to his again, and did not know if she offered him her com-fort or her lust.

"You named three who love you. There is at least one more." She raised her face to his, but he did not bend to meet her and her lips brushed his cleft chin. She stood on tiptoe to trace the black stubble of his jaw with her mouth, and though she could feel his instant response to the pressure of her hips, as automatic as a sol-dier when he draws his sword at the trumpeting clarion, he stood still as a stock.

"Four who love you, and three you love. I know you do not love me." She let one hand wander up, one down. "But you desire me. Or if not me, then a woman, any woman. Please, Charles, let me be like the others." She kissed his throat and longed for his mouth. Still he did not embrace her.

"You don't have to love me as you love Barbara, or Frances. You don't have to love me at all. Only treat me like your other women. I don't care if you have them, too. I don't care if it is only once. Please!" She pulled him even closer, her thighs pressed eagerly to his. "You desire me, I can tell! Oh, Charles, kiss me!"

He took her shoulders, and she was sure he was about to force her back onto the couch and lie on top of her. But he only separated her from his warmth and shook his head.

Mortified, she cried, "Why? What's wrong with me? I know I'm not like the other women, not really, but I'm fashioned of the same parts and I promise you . . . I promise I'll . . ." Tears began to trickle and she lost the power of speech. She'd thrown herself at her king and he'd been repulsed by her. He'd bedded low-class actresses and kindly, sheep-faced Winifred Wells; hellcat Barbara who, rumor had it, threatened to dash his last bastard's brains out on the rocks if he wouldn't own him . . . yet he couldn't bring himself to spend a fraction of his passion on her. Was she that strange? That hideous? Was a learned woman such an unnatural thing that, after seeing her in his elaboratory, he no longer considered her the proper sex? He had so many women. Why not her?

His gentle voice only made her tears fall faster. "My sweet friend," he began, and did not know that word struck like a spear into her heart. "Whenever a woman looks at me, or whispers a word in my ear, when a man does me a kindness or pays me a compliment, when anyone inquires after my health or solicits my opinion or wonders if I liked the latest play, I ask myself one thing. And when a woman kisses me or fondles me or proclaims her undying devotion, I ask it again. It is the question by which I judge every human contact. *Would she, were I not the king? Would he, were I not the king?* Catherine passes the test, as does my dear sister, and in his own way, Buckingham, but no one else, not a man, woman, nor child in this world, save only one."

At last he kissed her, like the brush of a petal on her lips.

"Zabby, my love, can you doubt for a moment? I love Buckingham but I do not trust him. I trust Catherine but . . . but I do not love her. She is my wife and I will never put her aside, even to save the kingdom, but I do not love her. My sister is across the channel and might as well be across the ocean. Do you wonder who the third is? Who would I love but you? You, who raised me from the dead, preserved my secrets, toiled beside me in the quest for truth. You, with your clear-seeing eyes and clever mind."

"But don't you desire me? As you desire Barbara?"

"What, and make you one of many? I'd not give the others up," he told her frankly, "and you couldn't bear that. Besides, one desires what one cannot possess. That is the trick of whores the world over, you know, from the stews to Whitehall. They make you think there is always something more, some inaccessible tidbit always just out of reach, to keep you coming back. They tease and they conceal. You're too open to do that. I don't desire you, Zabby, because I already have you. I know you, and love you, and possess you to the core."

She trembled and reached for him again. "You do, Charles, oh, you do. But I want more."

"Foolish child," he said softly. "There isn't any more."

She made one last desperate attempt, despising herself even as she said it. "Am I really so ugly? I will blow out the lights..."

He took her face firmly in his hands and kissed her, a real kiss that made her weak and invincible all at once, a kiss that made her soul exult and sink, for the finest moment in her life, and for the certainty that it would soon end, and never happen again.

"You are a most beauteous creature," he said with a smile curling at the corner of his mouth so that, looking back on it, she could never tell if he was in jest. "And if I weren't so fond of you, I'd bed you in a trice."

Suddenly, Charles was his usual brisk self again. Several crises averted, he was ready to move on. Forward, always forward.

"As you know, the College of Physicians receives ten bodies a year from the unclaimed Tyburn corpses, of which two are passed to me. His family refused to claim him, and I didn't think he deserved a pauper's grave, though I couldn't exactly step in and order him buried at Westminster. So I claimed him for my elaboratory, and when he is forgotten I'll have his remains decently interred."

He pulled down the linen sheet and Zabby saw Harry, pale, still, with the strange marble solidity of death.

Though the taste of Charles was still on her tongue, she knew that this was all there was of love. Foolish passion, blind hope, misplaced trust, all ending in a cold slab of lifeless flesh. Had those two young lovers any idea it would come to this, that night they'd caressed in St. James's Park?

Or, Zabby wondered with a quick, hard swallow, had they known and not cared? *Is that the secret of love, knowing it can end, must end, very likely horribly, and yet persevering despite that certainty?* She knew there was some secret that she, with all her intellectual power, could not grasp. Was Beth, in her loveless marriage, better off than she herself was simply for having known love for that brief moment? Was Harry, with his bruised throat and hemorrhaged eyes, luckier because he'd understood the greatest of life's mysteries?

She stood at Charles's side and accepted the scalpel from his hand, hardly noticing when his fingers lingered on hers.

There's a secret in there, she thought, looking at Harry's chest where lay the silent heart that once beat for her friend.

With Charles at her side, she made the first incision to delve within and ferret it out.